DREAMING I

# DREAMING IRIS

John de Falbe

THE CUCKOO PRESS

First published in 2008
by The Cuckoo Press
10 Blacklands Terrace
London SW3 2SR

A CIP record for this book
is avaialble from the British Library

Typeset by CB editions
Cover designed by Shona Andrew
Printed in England by Biddles Ltd,
Kings Lynn, Norfolk

ISBN 10: 0–9542688–5–7
ISBN 13: 978–0–9542688–5–5

'If you but knew how terrible it is
to languish with the thirst of love'

Aleksandr Pushkin, *Eugene Onegin*,
translated by Vladimir Nabokov
(from Onegin's letter to Tatiana)

I BRING HOME a business associate for the weekend and it turns out he knows more about the place than I do myself!

It's not a calamity but I can't help feeling 'a little sour', as Teresa's father might say.

Just three months married and then this secret pops out. No wonder Teresa is on edge.

When I came back the other evening, midweek, the house was blasting with some outmoded rock music and I found her in her little dressing-room in the corner of the house. She had not heard me coming. She was sitting in the armchair staring at her toes, dark hair long and liquid about her shoulders. She saw me and smiled her gorgeous smile, then up she jumped, put her arms around my neck and said how glad she was to see me.

Don't get me wrong, it's not that I mistrust her affections. She was cool towards Lucas when he visited, surprisingly so considering they said they were old friends. Well, my Teresa usually takes a bit to get going with people – I like that about her, it shows that she takes them seriously. But afterwards she was reticent, when it seemed natural to me to talk about him.

You will wonder how it is possible that Lucas never registered the connection until moments after we turned off the motorway. I suppose the explanation lies in the nature of our working relationship. Although I hired him to work for me on this job, there's no more reason for him to know about my personal life than the next person in the Departure Lounge. Most of the time he lives in Moscow, so asking him to Sweynsend for the weekend when he was in London was a matter of basic hospitality. Of course he knew I had got married, but it was a quiet wedding. There was no question of him being invited. If he knew that I had bought a place in the country, I was never called upon to be more specific. I know it seems odd, but there it is. Like one of those crazy coincidences Peter Aaron goes on about. It's just the way it is. Life is full of surprises.

Then again, perhaps Lucas knew exactly who I was marrying and which house I had bought. That is a possibility I had not considered.

So there was something obscure in Teresa's attitude towards Lucas. Although she welcomed me as usual, I could not ignore the oddity of finding her sitting in this calm room with that racket. I expect it's okay in the right place, but you'd no more sit down and listen to it, without so much as a piece of crochet work to absorb the adrenalin, than you would to ZZ Top.

'What's the music?' I said.

'The Only Ones. "Another Girl Another Planet".'

When I looked blank, she added, 'Lucas always said it was the perfect pop song.'

'Lucas?'

The song is only two minutes long. Had she been playing it round and round, waiting for me to find her? Or had she in fact heard my return and set the scene up then?

And then it all came out, how once upon a time she had fallen head over heels for him and he wanted nothing to do with her. More followed, tied up with the death of poor young William Carew, the previous owner, whose family were here for generations. I thought I knew about that – her father had explained it to me as soon as I came here – but as Teresa's story unfolded I discovered I knew nothing. It was like seeing a carpet pulled aside and realising that I stood on the floor of a glass-bottomed boat, not the solid ground I had supposed. And if in Teresa's story there was an echo of an episode in my own past in the US, which I have struggled to turn away from because it is useless – well, that only made me feel more sympathetic towards her, while knowing too that such a futile love is never quite so vanished as you might assume or wish it to be.

We were still in Teresa's little room. The rim of the sun was dipping below the yew hedge at the far end of the lawn. The music had long ago stopped. Teresa was sitting across my lap with her right arm about my shoulder, and the golden light from outside burnished her hair. I thought back to when I first set eyes on her. It was after I bought the place. I was going to have a drink with her parents one Friday evening. As I passed the old School House where they still kept chickens, I heard an unfamiliar voice inside. I pushed the creaky door and there was this ravishing girl against the light, who looked up as if she had been caught in the act of something shameful. In fact she was talking to the chickens as she fed them, saying whatever it is that people say when they talk to chickens, and she was embarrassed at being overheard. I had the impression of long lashes and big eyes as she said, 'Oh dear, you caught me talking to the chickens. I'm Teresa Fairfax. You must be Mr Hood.' Her jet hair gleamed in the diffuse light from the filthy window behind. 'Jimmy. Don't apologise,' I said. 'I'm sure they need to be fed. I was on my way to have a drink with your parents. You gonna join us?'

And she did.

It turned out she was a solicitor in London. She was working on some fraud case that meant she had to travel a lot to Prague and Vienna. She'd just come home for the weekend. It was like having Juliet Binoche walk into your back yard. I knew this was an event that would continue to unfold.

'Why are you telling me all this, sweetheart?' I said.

She gestured with her free arm to take in our surroundings, this light room under the eaves of our house, Sweynsend Hall. 'What was the point of it all, if it is only to be forgotten?'

Teresa did not know of the room's existence in the old days. The only access to it is through a door in what is now our bedroom. 'I always thought it was the door to a cupboard,' she once said – I think it was when she was deciding how to redecorate it – 'until, exploring the house with William, it opened into the tiny lobby.' One wall of the lobby was the side of the bedroom chimney; opposite was a recessed cupboard containing Major Carew's tatty suits. Another door stood ahead. Tucked behind the chimney on the corner of the house was this sloping sliver of a room containing a leather trunk-armoire, a chest of drawers, a miniature wardrobe and a single mahogany bed. 'There was a hat box with the Major's top hat, an old Balliol tie, a photograph of his uncle who had rowed for Oxford sometime in the 1880s; another picture of his brother Arthur, aged ten or so, with a stiff collar and a tennis racket; and various others, George Dick John Henry, most of them cannon fodder. Jasper cufflinks and studs in a leather box with someone else's monogram on it, a copy of *Nollekens and His Times*, of de Quincey's *Confessions* unopened for fifty years, of Hardy's *Love Poems*, and a recent Penguin of Geoffrey Hill. It was a very male room. A book by a woman would have seemed out of place, a tulip among bulrushes. The place smelled of leather. It was the Major's private lair and no one else had disturbed it, not even his wife. It was too threadbare for her, too obvious even, a grown-up little boy's room.'

I bought the house empty, but each room was impregnated with its own particular smell. This one retained the leathery tang of an Edwardian man's dressing-room until Teresa occupied it. Now, with her belongings, it is a feminine room.

Three steps climb to a dark roof space, which was thick with dust when Teresa first went in there. There were a few split suitcases; washing bowls and jugs, chamber pots; a couple of packing cases full of letters, a portfolio. With William she had seen glimmers of light through cracks between the tiles. Straw was everywhere; it had been used to insulate the roof. It spooked her sister Elizabeth, but Teresa's greater familiarity with the chaos purged it of any menace. She knew that the bundles of letters were actually household accounts for the late nineteenth century, and that the death mask on top was made for the Major's uncle Robert, who was killed in the 1870s by a fall from a roof in Oxford when he was climbing into a college after lock-up. She knew that the portfolio held engravings collected by the Major's unmarried older half-sister Edith, because several of them depicted scenes on Greek islands around the 1890s (*The City of Ermoupolis, Syros, Looking Towards Ano Syros*). Edith was engaged at one time to a man who helped design the harbour at Piraeus. He died in mysterious circumstances somewhere near Corinth, but she remained devoted to his memory throughout her long life and hoarded any sentimental reminders. 'I sometimes wonder,' said Teresa, 'whether Edith's devotion was a fantasy necessary to her sense of herself, or whether it was an unselfish, unsought passion that arrived from nowhere to ruin her life.'

I wonder if there is a distinction – and if there is, whether it matters. You try so hard to forget things, because you must, and it feels like an honourable thing to do. Then years later something happens and the memories awake; or else nothing happens and you wake one morning remembering anyway, as you remembered yesterday and twice the week before that, and again twice the week before that, and you are weary of this pattern. You understand that if you have not forgotten by now then you will never forget and you could not forget: these memories are not trivial but your very heart and soul, burned into your being. Easier to chop off your leg than rid yourself of them. Somehow you have to accommodate them into your sense of who you are now, and who you will be, or you will become a stranger to yourself.

'The point,' I repeated. 'If only –'

'Jimmy, it's not just a question of reassuring you about what happened between me and Lucas, it's to do with the Carews and this house… Don't you ever feel overwhelmed by the futility of other people's lives, especially if they are more dramatic, and less futile, than your own?'

'Why are you upset?'

Instead of just telling me about Lucas, she wanted to embark on the whole story of the Carews. Apparently it was not possible to tell me about the one without first going into the other. And I cannot say I was not interested. You can't buy a place like this and profess indifference to what has gone before: continuity is its whole point. I say that even though I am the interloper, although I do not quite see it like that myself because the rupture had already occurred, the end had come for the Carews of Sweynsend. I have not examined my motives – perhaps I should?

but when I purchased the place four years ago it was with a view to maintaining it intact; restoring and modernising as necessary but essentially preserving what continuity I could. My belief is that the Carews, and now I, are part of the history of the place, not the other way round. After all, the house is older than the Carews and will presumably survive me and any descendants I may chance to have. Since first meeting Teresa, who grew up next door, and her parents, I have often heard stories about how things used to be. I have always asked questions, and understood the answers according to the limits of my knowledge: but my information has been disjointed, a collection of anecdotes and facts revealed as circumstance offered them. In the days following

Lucas's visit it emerged that Teresa wished to give a coherent picture, as it were a background to whatever it was she had to tell me about Lucas. I was due to work at home for the rest of the week, which may have weighed in her decision to relate these events to me now, anticipating that she might win my attention from the report I was supposed to be writing.

I myself was once in love – I mean in America, before I came to England and married Teresa. Unfortunately Iris never loved me. I always knew this, though she was kind. Rather than impose my miserable advances on her – well, never mind: here I am; I do not wish to write about myself other than to state that one of the hardest things to bear of all that fiasco was the sense not just of time and energy disappearing but, more to the point, a part of myself. Nobody knew about it, but it was intrinsic to me. Had I succeeded in winning her I would have been justified, I mean my longing for her would have become part of our story. As it was, I turned my back on it in order to have some kind of life. But it was like turning away from a part of myself. Knowing that nobody knew anything about it was a kind of death. So you see, I can understand that the overt tragedy in this business at Sweynsend is shadowed by another, subtler grief for all that has been and will be lost. I feel a sort of obligation to *myself* to write down what happened as much as to anyone else, because if I do not then it will disappear. You might say that would not matter, but I say it does, because allowing that to disappear would be to allow so much else to slip away – a kind of suicide by neglect. Those of us who cannot depend on God for meaning in our lives, and in the lives of those we love, must find it ourselves, or we might as well have never been. Without narrative and understanding, dust truly returns to dust. And so it is with what happened here at Sweynsend: the story, in all its sadness, must be told.

# Chapter One

TOM FAIRFAX, Teresa's father, was a dentist and a Catholic convert. After qualifying, he joined a practice in Rugby where he soon became a partner; he remained there until his retirement thirty-five years later. At first he lived in a tiny flat above an ironmonger's in Tullworth. Then he married, and when his wife soon afterwards became pregnant, the need to find somewhere larger became urgent. Luck brought them to Sweynsend.

Teresa never quite understood how her mother, a nineteen-year-old French girl, happened to be in Tullworth. She had joined a scheme whereby she would get English lessons as part payment for work on a production line. 'Learn English In Just Three Months! And Be Paid! All You Have To Do Is . . .' Of course it turned out to be a ruse to lure cheap labour. Credulous Marie Quercy came to meet her destiny as little more than a slave. The company provided cheap accommodation in a hostel but Marie was paid so badly that its cheapness was illusory and she found herself much worse off than if she had stayed at home in France. Nor was she learning any English to compensate.

Then she met Tom Fairfax and – so Teresa and Elizabeth imagined – they fell in love. For both broke utterly from their former lives and never looked beyond one another. The girls knew that their paternal grandfather had been captured at the Fall of Singapore and spent the following three years in a camp on the Burma Railway. On his return to England, finding nobody at home in

Ealing, he went first to his parents in Weybridge. The father, a retired brigadier, inspected his son with the watery eye of the dispossessed and said, 'Participating in the greatest disgrace to British arms in the history of the Empire – that would knock any fellow's pride, I expect.' With dour satisfaction, he added, 'Your wife has found consolation with a doctor chappie in Maidenhead.'

When Tom's father presented himself in Maidenhead, his stunned wife, who had believed him dead, agreed to return home. Everything might have come right had it not been for the pitiful and evident fact that Tom, their thirteen-year-old son, was reluctant to transfer his affections from the kind doctor back to his ruined father. It was the doctor who encouraged Tom to continue his studies, and the memory of him – he was killed by a van while crossing a road – that sustained his protégé through medical school. Tom's father, meanwhile, became a drinker and inflicted twenty years of misery on his wife before she died of cancer. He was dead two months later. On the face of it, Tom rejected his parents outright: he moved to Rugby when he was twenty-six and only saw them again a handful of times. But Teresa, who dimly recalls two or three tortuous visits which she believes were arranged by her mother, insists that the truth is more complicated. She says that her father suffers from an acute sense of having betrayed both his mother and his father, that it is his driving force. I do not know how she reaches this judgement since the opposite seems to be true and he never talks about such matters. I have a feeling that it has to do with the notion that she and her sister have of their parents' love for one another; that he could not allow his tainted parents close to his marriage for fear that the ambiguity of his feelings for them would in some way sully the love he bore his wife. The guilt he still feels for neglecting his parents, Teresa says, was always expressed as care for his own immediate family; but also, more deviously, in his care for the Carews and Sweynsend, as if his improbable devotion to them in some way cancelled out his failure as a son.

The girls believe that their parents chose their isolation. They never heard their mother express regret that she wasn't in France, and Tom always seemed to be content in his life as a provincial dentist. They did not choose this isolation because they were antisocial, or not primarily because of this. It was more of a retreat to a territory on which they could be equals: because Marie was foreign, they needed a private world where his ease and greater familiarity with their surroundings wouldn't tend to exclude her. And the obvious explanation for electing to live like this is that they fell – and remained – in love. Well, it can happen.

This is all very charming in retrospect, but in the autumn of 1962 they didn't know that their marriage would remain happy for thirty years and more, nor that they would find somewhere to live which suited them so well. They married two months after getting engaged, having met scarcely six weeks before that. She left her sweatshop, where at least there were other French girls, for a two-room flat that felt as if it was encased in permafrost, and a man whose language was strange to her – not, on the face of it, an advantageous exchange. In due course her parents overcame their dismay and grew very fond of him, but his parents never truly forgave him for converting himself from an Anglican bachelor into a married Catholic.

Tom's route to work in his crank-started Ford Pop took him through the little hamlet of Sweynsend, which at that date contained a church, a general-store-cum-post-office, a couple of farms and a handful of houses. There was never a pub. Sweynsend Hall was the largest of the houses. It was flanked by a long, red brick wall about twelve feet high that started at one of two immense brick gateposts and then at once was pierced by an arch with a small adjacent wicket gate, which was redundant because the main gates had long since fallen off or been removed. Thereafter, the wall formed the side of a barn and ran continuously along the road for about six hundred yards, opposite the churchyard. There were two other entrances: a gate from the lawn gave the house easy access to the church; another near the end of the wall, shortly before it turned away from the road, was the gardeners' entrance to the huge kitchen garden. At first glance from the road the house looked impressive, but it was dilapidated. As the eventual purchaser, I can vouch for this. It was a miracle it hadn't fallen down already. No working gutters or drainpipes, roof like a sieve, rotten windows all round, subsidence, cracks, dry rot . . . you name it.

Soon after I bought the place, Tom remarked to me that the Carews were 'not very flush with cash'. I treasure the understatement because it conveys not only the Carews' hopeless penury but also Tom's own acceptance of the situation as dignified and respectable. (The English class system, it seems, is sustained by forces from below as much as from above.) Had they been wealthy, or had the estate been maintained in a mildly conventional manner – had it been maintained at all – then Tom would never have stayed, or even come. In order to regard his own lifestyle as normal it was perhaps necessary for Tom to attribute some normality to the Carews' circumstances.

The Carews were flat broke. Any normal people would have sold up, quit, bought a condo in Florida or whatever English people do. Left it, I suppose. But the Carews were not interested in normality and never had any intention of leaving. By all accounts, Mrs Carew was a resourceful lady and did what she could to bring in a few pounds for the upkeep. One of her more straightforward ploys was market gardening: for some years she sold vegetables, fruit and flowers at a stall on the verge outside the gardeners' gate, where Tom sometimes used to stop on the way home to Tullworth. Mrs Carew wasn't often there in person but her presence was nonetheless felt. It was always 'Mrs Carew this,

Mrs Carew that', or 'Mrs Carew says'. Surprisingly, Mr Joy and his son, who looked after the stall and did the work in the garden in return for the free use of part of it, didn't appear to mind. The produce was good and they didn't regard the prices that Mrs Carew chose to set as any of their business.

From time to time, however, Tom encountered Mrs Carew herself. Being polite, he would have answered this determinedly nosey woman's questions patiently; being respectful, he wouldn't have thought her authority odd. Nor would he have appreciated how her interest in him was influenced by the fact that he was a presentable young man. So she knew that he was married and that he lived in a very small flat, and the news that his wife was pregnant was less than a day old before Mrs Carew knew it too, for he had bought all her roses. And, being nothing if not intelligent, she could see that they would want to move to somewhere larger. Mrs Carew knew that Marie was unlikely to find satisfactory work nearby precisely because she was French, and since she was herself half French – which few people knew – she was sympathetic. Help in the house being hard to find, and expensive, Mrs Fairfax might be a godsend and – the best sort of godsend – a cheap one. One thing the Carews didn't lack at Sweynsend was space. So one day when Tom drew up in his Ford Pop beside the stall to buy some more roses on his way home, Mr Joy said to him, 'Good evening to you too, Mr Fairfax. Mrs Carew said for me to tell you that s'posin you was to stop by, p'raps you'd be so kind as to pop into the 'all for a word.'

Tom might have looked at his watch. He would have wondered how long this was going to take, because Marie would be worried if he were more than a few minutes late. But it would have been foolhardy of him to ignore one of Mrs Carew's requests and drive on. Nor would he have wished to, for it had occurred to him that the solution to his problems might lie at Sweynsend despite its unpromising appearance. So he wrenched the car through a three-point turn, puttered back down the road and passed for the first time between the Hall's gateposts.

Leaving the car in the yard, he knocked on two or three doors hoping one would prove to be the back door. Later he discovered that he had been knocking on the door of a kitchen that hadn't been in use since the twenties, and its adjoining scullery and dairy.

Eliciting no response, he followed the drive round past a yew hedge to the front of the house. Attached to a Georgian façade were unusually restrained Victorian wings and, in the centre, a delicate white porch, whose half-glass door rattled as he pushed it open. He tugged the bell pull and straightened his tie.

With a squeak and shudder of stuck wood, the front door opened and Major Carew greeted him:

'Huh-huh! Thomas Fairfax, Mister Thomas Fairfax! I never thought I should welcome a Roundhead into my house!'

The first thing everyone says about the Major is that he possessed a beautiful voice, even in old age. He is said to have sung well, and his speaking voice modulated with his words almost as if he were singing. 'He spoke exquisite English too, with rhythm and cadences,' Tom told me one evening soon after I came here, probably when he described his first encounter with the Carews. I asked him what he meant by this and he smiled with that hint of withheld knowledge that might be mockery or self-mockery – you never really know with the English – but is suggestive, and ironic; it can be profoundly charming, or irritating. With Tom it is always the former, and as he explained, I wondered if his own speech was influenced by long exposure to the Major's. 'His voice was a gift that smoothed his passage through life, I suspect. It made him more attractive than his good looks and better company than his temperament alone allowed. He was clever and witty to a point, but his voice enhanced the effect of brain and wit. It obscured his selfishness from listeners and diverted them from his idleness. He was of average height and moved very languidly. He never rushed. He would saunter, heigh-hoing to nobody in particular; tap his fingers on a table top as he passed or, if he was outside, peer through chronically short-sighted, clear blue eyes at a plant.'

Although Teresa only remembers the Major's hair as being snow white, when her father greeted him for the first time it would have been black.

'No relation, I'm afraid,' said Tom Fairfax. 'Good evening, Major Carew.'

'You must not be afraid. I am comforted, Mister Fairfax. Since my wife told me you were taking the nursery I've been considering whether I shouldn't prime my matchlocks. Come in, let me give you a drink. You see,' he confided, indifferent to Tom's rising astonishment, 'my family acquired Sweynsend following the Restoration. I owe my inheritance to the King. And my wife, I might add, is descended from the Duke of Buckingham.'

Pausing only to indicate two ancient firearms resting on hooks inside the door, the Major entered the passage-room on the right of the hall. Already darkened by oak panelling, the room was thick with suspended swirls of blue smoke from the fireplace. Through the murk, Tom saw Mrs Carew seated with embroidery on her lap. She bestowed on him a smile like a prised-open vice, then addressed her husband: 'Do be quiet, Tip. How could Mr Fairfax be a Roundhead? He's a Catholic.'

'A Papist? Worse and worse!' He trembled with delight as he reached for the decanter. 'Sherry?'

'That would be lovely. Major . . .'

'Mr Fairfax,' Mrs Carew interrupted, 'we expect you and your wife would like to take the nursery.'

Despite Mrs Carew's breadth, her face still had a clear bone structure with a straight nose and unencumbered chin. 'She was oppressive when she looked at you,' Teresa said yesterday, sitting in my arms in her dressing-room. It seemed she felt it necessary to introduce the presiding figure to me anew, regardless of all that I had already heard. It struck me when she flicked some loose hair away from her forehead that the gesture was a nervous one, as if the act of speaking about Mrs Carew in this frank way might be held in evidence against her by the walls themselves. 'She challenged, testing to see how far you would let her push you. She had an inviolability that I've never come across in another human being. It may sound paradoxical but I think it was sustained, in part, by an impression of her own fragility, a sense of impending catastrophe, as if resistance to her will would cause her to shatter more immediately and violently, with greater consequence, than anyone else. I can't imagine anything frightening her, except loneliness.'

'Tip, he won't want the sweet,' Mrs Carew had said. 'Give him the dry.'

It was as if there had been an earlier meeting where all this had been agreed. Tom found it eerie. 'How very kind of you. Of course . . .'

'I suppose you'll want to have a look at it before agreeing. But before I take you up there, my husband has a proposal.'

'You make it sound as if I intend asking Mr Fairfax to sing, Delia. Can you sing, Mr Fairfax, by the way?'

'No.'

'Never mind. Now, it is simply this: you may have the flat for a modest rent, if it suits you, if in return you undertake some services for us.'

'What sort of services did you have in mind, Major?'

'A little Hoovering; some dusting, I imagine; nothing too onerous. I understand that your wife is expecting, and we shouldn't wish to impose. Then if you'd be so kind as to mow the lawns from time to time, I think we should rub along fairly smoothly. What is it you do yourself, Mr Fairfax?'

'I am a dentist.'

'So you said, I recall now. You're not a Roundhead after all, are you?'

'Don't be fatuous, Tip. He's a Catholic,' said Mrs Carew.

She heaved herself from the chair with the wooden action of a woman whose hips cause her pain that she has no intention of admitting for fear of handing an advantage to others. 'Now.'

It seemed that Tom was not to be allowed to drink his sherry. He followed her into the hall and up the wide staircase. The house was suffused with the scent of wood and smoke, a special blend which lingers still. High over the dogleg landing of the stairs is a wide, arched window, visible from the churchyard as a distinct focus of the house. Mrs Carew trod heavily along the corridor upstairs to the green baize door at the end. The other side was the nursery landing, an uneven, fraying slick of crimson lino between the first and second flights of the steep back stairs.

The far door opened to the nursery flat. It consisted of two rooms, one of which was so large and airy that the Fairfaxes' flat in Tullworth might have fitted into it twice over. Tall windows looked out to the yard on one side and the lawn on the other. A smaller room lay beyond, overlooking the lawn. There was no separate kitchen: a two-ring cooker and an aluminium sink were fixed in beside each other on one side of the main room. The bathroom and loo were reached from the landing.

Despite the untidiness and the damp and the cold (already evident in September), Tom agreed to take the nursery flat for a trial period of six months, subject to consultation with his wife. He was afraid it was a foolish thing to do because there was still no clear sense of what the household duties would entail. Certainly the Carews would want something from him, but they seemed ready to allow the space he wanted in return. It might turn out to be a drama of exhausting oddity, but he was intrigued.

In the following months Tom and Marie learned that the

Carews could also be kind. 'Here, have this,' Mrs Carew would say, producing a chair or a cabbage, a cupboard or a teapot. She didn't ask if these gifts were wanted any more than she knocked at ten o'clock in the evening before presenting them with a half-plucked duck. She might suddenly take things back if she decided she needed them herself, but seemingly without malice. Asking was not her style: she gave or took, bluntly.

As Marie got used to her landlady's surprising manner, she found it more reassuring than off-putting. It made her feel accepted as part of the place and she was glad to do what she could to help. She liked belonging in this capacious establishment, where no one objected to her planting herbs in the tubs in the yard and lavender in the neglected border.

Then one day in January the bedroom roof caved in. It wasn't just the plaster falling away from the ceiling: the rafters themselves had rotted and a section of roof came crashing into the room.

'I thought it would go one day,' the Major remarked.

Marie was out when it happened, but it was the middle of winter and she was heavily pregnant.

Mrs Carew manipulated a solution with characteristic twin shoves of bullying and generosity.

'They must go into the Manor,' she announced.

'What about Mrs Bromage?' said the Major.

'That old baggage will just have to budge up.'

So Mrs Bromage retreated into a corner of the Manor un-occupied for a generation, and the Fairfaxes moved into the house that would be their home for the rest of their lives.

# Chapter Two

S WEYNSEND MANOR is a single Jacobean house without additions or major alterations. Originally it was larger than the Hall, which was extended by the Victorians, and senior. At some point during the nineteenth century, however, it was divided in two and abandoned to a succession of tenants. I don't know why this happened. Some tale of woe may lurk behind it, but I've never discovered one. I think the explanation is simpler. Throughout the nineteenth century, the Sweynsend vicars were Carews. It suited them to use the Hall as their vicarage because they were enthusiastic in their calling and the Hall was adjacent to the church. They preferred to be identified with the church instead of dwelling in seigneurial detachment in the Manor. Nowadays, even from a secular point of view, the Hall would be regarded as more desirable than the Manor because of its garden, but that is the work of the Victorian parsons who must have seen possibilities for development at the Hall which the Manor lacked.

The approach to the Manor was shadowed by the same unkempt spinney that choked the entrance to the semi-derelict Kennels, a group of buildings around a yard that had been let for many years to a shady character called Stan, who kept horses and rusting pieces of farm machinery there. It had no grand gateposts such as the Victorians built for the Hall. A stranger would probably think that the unobtrusive drive was just a farm track, but it curved round for fifty yards behind some trees and tangled undergrowth and there, at the end, was the Manor, with roses climbing above the front door. Very pretty. I have recently spent a fortune doing it up – new roof, new windows, even the foundations on one side. All the exterior brickwork has been overhauled, and the interior has been stripped back and renewed. Although Tom patched it up as best he could, no substantial work had been done on it for over a hundred years. Teresa's childhood and youth were studded with fallen chimney-pots, slipped tiles, leaks and so forth, which the Carews never bothered about. Since the Fairfaxes paid a token rent which increased only once in thirty years, and then at Tom's suggestion, they felt that it was unfair to trouble their landlord. But the house was ready to collapse irredeemably without thorough care. It is no less than the truth to say that I rescued what was already widely regarded as a ruin.

It seems, in fact, that ruin is what the Carews once intended for the Manor. William told Teresa that there was a fire there long ago. Mrs Bromage called the Fire Brigade, but Mrs Carew was furious that she wasn't consulted first and parked her car across the driveway to prevent the fire engines from reaching the house. After the car was pushed aside it transpired that Mrs Bromage had been unduly alarmed. She had extinguished the blaze herself. When I mentioned this to Teresa's mother this morning, she said, 'Oh yes, Mrs Bromage used to go on about that.' Her lips were pinched in disapproval and her dark eyes avoided mine as she glared at an armful of daffodils that Teresa had left in the kitchen sink, ready for distribution into vases. Apparently Marie has a low opinion of Mrs Bromage, but discretion prevents her from saying so. A rock of loyalty in a fast-flowing stream, she has learned to be guarded about the dead and friendless. Teresa informs me that the Carews allowed Mrs Bromage to live there for almost nothing, until she died a few years later.

The terms of the Fairfaxes' tenure were never defined, but a pattern was established whereby they would look after the lawns and hedges of the Hall and be ready to help in the house as occasion required. The original idea of housework was given up as soon as the Fairfaxes moved into the Manor and Teresa was born. At first, Marie used to present herself at the Hall ready to work, with Teresa strapped to her back in a papoose, but this made the Carews uncomfortable: for though the agreement had been that she should work, they believed more generally that it was improper for a mother to be working at all, let alone a respectable lady. Believing Marie to be respectable if not altogether a lady (she was foreign, after all, and in questions of social classification – her own origins notwithstanding – Mrs Carew followed her husband's lead), they were unsettled when she threatened to stick to the bargain. This made Tom glad to do other work in the garden. As children, Teresa and Elizabeth were allowed to accompany him on the strict understanding that they behaved themselves.

A short path led through the trees from the Manor, emerging between the old Victorian School House and a collapsed cow byre on the edge of the Hall's yard. The way was always dark, dank and overhung except around the bonfire patch. Nettles grew with ferocious persistence despite Tom's efforts. Rats were sometimes seen among the decayed bricks of the byre.

The School House was inhabited by Jed's chickens. Jed must be about eighty-five now but I don't imagine he has changed much in the last thirty years: head like a conker, spiky teeth, stalwart in his dislikes. Born in the Home Farm across the fields, he has lived in Sweynsend all his life. He is married to Mabel, who is still the postmistress; they have a daughter living in Birmingham. Jed was a sort of honorary gamekeeper at the Hall and used to wander about the fields and covers nurturing pheasants for the Major to shoot. He also kept sheep and chickens. After the frequent sleepless nights of her childhood, as Teresa watched the world materialise through the dark from her bedroom window, she would see Jed setting out across the dim fields on his early stroll with his gun snapped open over his crooked arm. During the next half-hour she would hear two or three shots, then he would return through the mist with a rabbit or two dangling from his knotted fist, his steps firm and steady over the swelling land. 'I suppose there must have been a time when he wasn't retired, but I've no idea what he did then,' Teresa says. I imagine him to have been a lucky officer's batman, serving faithfully in Egypt, Burma or Malaya, pathetically homesick.

We were ambling in the afternoon sunshine alongside the ha-ha. The ordered view it once bisected, from the front door to the ridge-and-furrow fields beyond, was spoiled in the Major's day by the new road driven through the Sweynsend estate. I am aware that the collapse of the ha-ha's retaining wall is an image pregnant with doom, but I would not have bought Sweynsend if I were ready to accept the necessity of such a fate: the ditch has been dug out and the wall rebuilt. I might not have done this – it would have been much more sensible, given the truncated view, to have the bank bulldozed into the ditch – had not Teresa happened to tell me during the winter I moved in that the spring spectacle of daffodils on the bank rising to the ha-ha was one of the most beautiful she knew. When spring came round I remembered this. The ha-ha is necessary for the daffodils to achieve their concentrated force, so it had to stay if Teresa was not to lose her bank of daffs. Now you can walk along the top, behind the monkeypuzzle and the ilex trees, to a secluded summerhouse from which a little bridge spans the ha-ha to the flat ground beyond, where Teresa told me that the Major played lawn tennis with his brothers before the First World War. William had once shown her some old photographs, she said, with boys in white trousers, and vast-skirted ladies watching from beyond the touchlines. I thought a hard court would be more use but Teresa insisted that it should be grass, so that is what we have constructed there, and we overlooked it as I sat listening in the summerhouse. She stood in the doorway surveying the shades of those long-ago players, so that my view of our tennis court, laid over its predecessor, was shaped as much by the contours of her body as by her words. She was wearing a long skirt, in a gauzy fabric that revealed her legs against the sunlight; they seemed very long. Her voice had a narrative urgency that always animates her conjuring of memories.

If the girls were going into the Hall's garden they would either walk across the cobbles to the shed beneath the nursery wing, where the mower was kept, then out the opposite door to the croquet lawn; or they would go round by the drive, perhaps collecting the wooden barrow from behind the yew hedge which screens the boot room, to the open area of gravel in front of the house which is divided by the daffodils and the ha-ha from the meadow with Jed's sheep and the huge, hollow ash tree solemnly sighing. Here Teresa would experience a skitter of fear because it felt like a private, adult domain. The clustered shrubs past the end of the house and the tall monkeypuzzle tree were more enticing: the grass unfolds into the garden itself, round to the croquet lawn at the back of the house and the red brick wall adjoining the road. Mrs Carew would be cross if she found Elizabeth or Teresa alone on the lawn because she was convinced that children would damage the turf that the Major required to be immaculate for his croquet. They went instead among the hedges and shrubs that lead to the kitchen garden which their father maintained: the box-lined pathways and screens of yew, the little areas of lawn dividing the peony beds and all the paths in the kitchen garden itself. They were allowed to play there, and Tom even made a turf-edged sandpit beneath the ilex tree.

I may seem to be running on but you must understand that all this is important. Not just for the sentimental reason that Sweynsend was the Fairfaxes' home and so they loved it – the Hall, as well as the Manor. No, the point is that the Carews welcomed the Fairfaxes to Sweynsend and let them make their home there. The arrangement worked because they were useful to one another. And as the lavender that began in the yard wound its way further each year in a fragrant, shimmering fringe about the outbuildings, and the purple campanula bloomed on the roadside, and the copse in front of the Manor glowed with blue-bells, the Carews appreciated that their surprising tenants loved the place.

Everyone else who ever had anything to do with Sweynsend Hall and the Carews associated the place with pain and trouble.


Ever since the Fairfaxes came to Sweynsend, most of the people living in the village have worked in nearby light industries. Choosing to live there because it seems charmingly rural, they attempt to transform it into a freak outcrop of suburbia. There is the church, Blake Farm, and a scattering of other farm cottages, but mock-Tudor dwellings with grandiose doorknockers and bulls-eye windows have appeared like cellophane-wrapped bou-quets of dahlias in a mediaeval rose garden. Yet the village is truly old. The sharp angle in the street suggests the boundary of an ancient demesne, and the grazing half of the Hall's big field is scored as if a giant had pulled a taloned hand back and forth across the landscape. These strips must long pre-date enclosure. The village's name is said to derive from a Viking leader called Sweyn who came here. The church too reveals that the village has been a Christian community for a thousand years, although its comically pockmarked exterior confuses church historians as much as residents. The clue is over the road, in the Hall, which has taken the history of Sweynsend into itself and lets it out in discrete strands like a harassed, cunning spider. Thus it was the Major who caused the once-uniform cladding on the church to be stripped away in places to expose the earlier brickwork in the suspect name of historical veracity, of which he – for the glori-fication of his ancestry – was the undisputed tyrant in Sweynsend.

Just as the Carews came to dominate the church in Sweynsend, so the Hall itself dominates the village. Secure behind its red brick wall, it makes an imperious claim on your attention, as if anything that happens in the village can only happen under its aegis: if the Hall isn't concerned, then the thing doesn't happen. Unless you count the Post Office, there is no meeting-point apart from the church, and within living memory the Post Office has been managed by Mabel and can therefore scarcely claim inde-pendence, while the church is cheek-by-jowl with the Hall. The name Carew features inside the church more often than Christ and, says Teresa, 'with the Major and his wife sat like Pomp and Majesty in their pew each Sunday, year in year out, a girl might be forgiven for attributing sinister heresies to the place.'

Only Blake Farm provided an alternative. The Simmonds children were close to Teresa and Elizabeth in age and they saw them often, although the differences that later became obvious meant that the bonds they formed were the product of familiar-ity rather than true friendship. Hayley was between Elizabeth and Teresa in age, so Marie and Mrs Simmonds packed the girls off to play with one another. But Hayley was shy and the Fairfax girls were impatient. They must have been a torment to her; she is a sad dope even now. But she had brothers. Not that they were juvenile tearaways either, but they were at least objects of curios-ity. As a boy, Michael only wanted to play with machines. Sissy girls were no use to him and, since he was clever, by the time he was old enough to be interested in girls he wasn't much at home. His brother John was cheerful and obliging but also rather dull, for which I suppose we should be thankful since he would other-wise have moved away and we would now miss his benign pres-ence in the village. Teresa has known him all her life and there is a comforting, fraternal solidity to him. If it seems to me that the only associations people ever had within the village were shaped by the Hall, the Fairfaxes' relationship with the Simmondses appears as an exception.

The lives of those who lived in Sweynsend tended to be directed outside. The girls went to school in Tullworth until they were eleven, when they were sent to a convent school the other side of Rugby; Marie drove them there and back every day. It's a nice irony that Tom first stopped in Sweynsend in order to buy something because all shopping (*pace* Mabel) took place outside the village, as did any entertainment or social event that wasn't at their home or at the Hall. Even Teresa's best childhood friend, Melanie Moore, usually came to the Fairfaxes, where there was more space and freedom to play. Her mother was so house-proud that the girls couldn't do anything without her simultaneously trying to erase all evidence of their activity. She hovered at doorways with cloths and detergent. Teresa remembers her plumping up cushions and forcing unwanted sticking-plasters on her. Perhaps Mrs Moore was unhappy or disliked my Teresa. In any case, the family moved to Birmingham when Teresa was fourteen. Most of Sweynsend's inhabitants valued the place (as they do now) because they could use it as a dormitory, without the usual obligations and encroachments of village life. And those few who attended church regarded the Fairfaxes as beyond the pale because they were Catholics.

The position was confused further by the ambivalence of their relationship with the Carews.

Take, for example, 'An Afternoon at the Hall', a fundraising occasion for the benefit of the church roof. Perhaps because this singular event did not fit with the routine disinterest between the Hall and the village, people didn't know quite how to behave, and Teresa's twelve-year-old sensitivity was alert.

She and Elizabeth had spent the previous week helping their mother prepare an enormous quantity of food for Mrs Carew.

Teresa has scant interest in food and has therefore forgotten what it was but Elizabeth would remember, I expect, if I asked her – which I will not. Teresa remembers tramping back and forth through the trees to the Hall's back door and the pantry with bowls covered by tea-towels and plate after plate of sandwiches; and she remembers the groundless certainty that it was all paid for by her parents. Mrs Carew would say, 'Marie!' (always rolling the *r* in the back of her throat), 'I want cheese straws, and sandwiches for seventy, and ten cakes!' And her mother would prepare all these, knowing there was no likelihood of the Carews reimbursing her. Meanwhile her father would have been informed by the Major in a subordinate clause of the forthcoming event. Obtaining the details from Marie, he set about smartening up the garden and organising seating outside, with a back-up indoors in case of rain; and, on this occasion, rather more.

Teresa's parents knew that the aim was to raise money for the church roof. The Carews didn't tell them how this was going to be done and, since it was not the Fairfaxes' business, they didn't ask: until, thinking it odd to hear no mention at all of the afternoon's main concern and not wishing the Carews to appear ridiculous, Marie enquired of Mrs Carew 'if Tom should be a little bit busy about it because I think he's a little bit anxious' – the French, if you ask me, are as adept as the English at circumlocution. Mrs Carew (herself half French, don't forget) replied that she assumed the Major, by which she meant Tom on the Major's behalf, had it all under control. When Marie ventured to doubt this, she was told that something must be done at once – meaning that the Major had obviously overlooked this detail and so Tom had better hurry up and get something together.

It was already ten o'clock on the Saturday morning. The girls were released from kitchen duty and sent off to their father. After quick consultation, Elizabeth went to look for eggs in the old Kennels where they kept chickens, so that they could muster an egg-and-spoon race, and Teresa set up the Carews' croquet hoops in a cluster in front of a thick box hedge. Lacking coconuts, she picked cabbages, which she split across the stalks and rammed onto the hoops. Meanwhile, Tom persuaded the Major to lay out some of his books on the dining-room table and sideboards, a small exhibition for which a fee could be charged. This seemed the height of eccentricity to the Major. He said that people were welcome to look at his books for free provided they didn't have mutton fat on their fingers.

'And what about putting some of those gewgaws and what-nots you've showed me on display in the small dining-room, like the tiny silver vase that fits into a lapel for a button-hole? Instead of "guess the weight of the cake" we can have "guess the purpose of . . ."'

'And what will the prizes be? Will I forfeit the object if some cretin guesses right?'

'It doesn't matter what the prizes are.'

'We'll give them a cabbage or something.'

'So long as you make them pay for their guess.'

'My dear Tom, you should have been a Captain of Industry!'

'Of course, Major, if you have objects you don't mind parting with . . .'

Few of Sweynsend's residents had ever been the other side of the Hall's red brick wall, let alone inside the house. When they began to arrive after midday, it was clear from the roving eyes how curious they were. It was a fine June afternoon and it seemed that nobody had passed up the opportunity to come and sit on the lawn at Sweynsend Hall and join in the fun. They ran egg-and-spoon races until the eggs were all smashed, and they wore through sacks in sack races. Not only did they win all the cabbages on Teresa's improvised shies, but they also cleared out most of the kitchen garden in a sequence of games hastily impro-vised by her father. They circulated round and round the Major's

*ABC for Young Patriots* and *Marmaduke Multiplier*, and they won all manner of spindles and mincers, buttonhooks and thingummyjigs – the Major got dreadfully overexcited and Mrs Carew had to prevent him from including pieces of silver. Marie's food, of course, was all eaten. By the final reckoning nearly three hundred pounds were raised, and the vicar thanked the Carews from his pulpit the next day.

What is hard to understand is that the Fairfaxes not only organised and financed the occasion but, I believe, did so gladly. If nobody else in the village appreciated how short of cash the Carews were, it was because they struggled to appear well-off. Their idea of themselves and their station in life demanded a display of affluence that had no correlation to their meagre means: and so the house fell down around their ears and they probably ate onion soup and potatoes for dinner. The loss of most of their vegetables that afternoon would have been a blow. Most of their guests would have been richer in cash; some could have easily afforded a donation equal to the amount that was raised. The Fairfaxes knew how hard-up the Carews were and still they were not asked for a proper rent, so they were pleased that their landlords got credit for generosity. Similarly, it would have been futile to resent the lack of credit given to themselves. People saw them that afternoon because they were organising games, producing food, collecting money and telling them where to find the lavatory, but they were neither guests nor hosts. Everyone knew that they weren't the Carews' servants, but they did not perceive them as the Carews' friends either. The only label which clearly applied to them, and which at the same time seemed to justify their anomalous position, was that they were Catholics. Strictly speaking, they had no business at the church gathering: it wouldn't have done at all to give them credit. Instead, the visitors were able to feel a little superior to the Fairfaxes – although it was disconcerting to see how the Major enjoyed talking to Tom, and that his family were at ease with the Carews in a way that was unique in the village. Not that the Fairfaxes did not get on with the people in the village: they lived there very happily. But it is a fact that, because they were Catholics, and because of their relationship with the Carews, people were unsure how to deal with them and they remained on the margins of village life. Which suited them quite well.

Nobody experiences childhood as strange, for when only one thing is known then it is normal. It's only when you can measure your experience against other people's that you begin to feel how your own might have been unusual. Each family has different parents and circumstances. The concept of a norm often collapses on inspection and the phrase 'unusual childhood' ceases to have meaning. When I was a boy my dad, who was British, never took me to baseball games, but he sometimes tried to teach me cricket in our yard. And we used to go on holiday to Canada because his sister lived in Ottawa. But weird as these practices seemed to my friends, they do not add up to an unusual childhood. All our childhoods are composed of ten thousand such peculiarities. It is not an individual taste or event that makes you unusual, but a pattern that for some reason inhibits you from engaging with the world. Elizabeth and Teresa stayed snug in their family discipline, ignorant of the images and aspirations of popular culture: their upbringing was sheltered to a degree that must, even then, have been truly unusual. It is in the nature of such an upbringing, if it is happy, that it stays sheltered for a long time. Theirs was happy – such things do occur, it seems – but I do not propose to describe the Fairfaxes any further. Instead, I shall turn to the Carews, of whom the same cannot be said. Were it not for them, and events at the Hall, I don't know how those girls would ever have emerged from their chrysalis life.

# Chapter Three

THE CAREWS had four children, all defiant believers in patri-archy and primogeniture except for Joanna. Since she was the eldest her dissent might be regarded as circumstantial, though I gather she is by nature contrary. She lives in Australia with her husband and six reputedly troublesome children. She is a logi-cian, I understand, specialising in a branch known as Fuzzy Logic. Hal, Jem and Hugh – the sons – used to appear at the Hall from time to time. They were all manifestly a combination of their par-ents – forceful and clever, equipped with bewitching charm and dilettante curiosity. These traits were differently balanced in them but they held one notable feature in common which had no clear origin, and that was a talent for making money.

Hal, the eldest, was a financier of some kind, but his business life was a diversion from what he cared for. Expecting his parents to move out to the Manor in favour of his family at Sweynsend Hall, he spent considerable sums over the years on its mainte-nance. It was he who had the roof repaired on the nursery. He kept a protective eye on the property to ensure that it would come to him intact, but as it became apparent that his parents had not the least intention of moving, he despaired of ever living there himself while he was young enough to enjoy it and at last determined to take no further responsibility for the place. Instead, he bought a much more elegant, Georgian mansion in Yorkshire.

Mrs Carew used to tell Teresa and Elizabeth how handsome Jem was. The photographs of him as a child, with his responsive saucer eyes, show that he was very pretty. He seemed fragile and pressurised as an adult, as if a harsh word or a loud noise would make him explode like a dropped light bulb, yet this impression was misleading because he had joined the army after leaving school and served with distinction in Malaya and Kenya. He demobbed when he married and then became an art dealer, specialising in Islamic art which he sold to oil-rich clients in the Gulf. He liked vintage cars, wore a Mughal turban pin in his tie, and his house in Kent was said to be filled with exotic ornaments including a collection of eighteenth-century French clockwork songbirds.

The third brother was Hugh, who made his money in commercial property. Tall and gangly, with a high, domed bald head and thick spectacles, he rarely spoke and never raised his voice. He wore a long imitation-astrakhan coat, and was rumoured to live in a castle with circular rooms on the Yorkshire coast which was expected to be undermined by erosion within a century.

The Fairfax girls knew the Major and Mrs Carew's grandchildren by hearsay, but they rarely encountered them. There was William, of course, and Sam, his younger brother – these were Hal's children. Jem's children were Henry, Josephine and Susie. Hugh had two girls, Julia and Poppy, whom Teresa knew better because they were nearer in age. Teresa has never met any of Joanna's children except for two ignorant hulks in blazers who appeared at the Major's funeral; she has forgotten their names.

Aside from her daughter's children, Mrs Carew spoke of her grandchildren often and always with approval. Sam was so glamorous, William always won scholarships, Josephine was a brilliant musician, Henry had won seven rosettes at a gymkhana . . . They were all brilliant at something, it seemed, unlike the dull Fairfax girls: Teresa and Elizabeth couldn't understand it when later they were so critical of their proud grandmother.

She died when Teresa was thirteen, and it was at her funeral that Teresa first began to suspect that her experience of the Carews and Sweynsend Hall was out of joint.

About a year before this event, Mrs Carew had had a hip replacement. 'She was in hospital for nearly five months,' Teresa told me yesterday. 'This didn't seem strange to me because I knew nothing about such things. My mother once referred to complications, but she and my father were very discreet. So far as Elizabeth and I knew, the length of her stay in hospital was related to her size. She was a big, wide woman. You only had to look at her to see that a hip replacement must be a serious affair.

'When eventually she returned home, she was gaunt. It was shocking to see someone so changed. But it couldn't be kept from us that Mrs Carew was senile, and the mental change was even more shocking than the physical. She wasn't loud, erratic or unscrupulous – she had been all of these in the past to a degree we never guessed at, and was still considered sane. Instead she was utterly docile, but she had plainly lost her mind. She would sit quietly in a room while the Major chatted with my father, and then she would ask him for permission to do something. No more, 'Blast! Fetch me my address book, Tip! I haven't got Sir Tarquin's number here . . .' When she saw us now she simpered, in a parody of a little girl with a crush on an older girl, or she patted us fondly with her shrunken hand in a way she'd never done before. She confused us with her grandchildren, her sisters, and the friends of her own childhood, or she imagined we were about to marry her grandchildren. 'Are you a virgin?' she would say with a giggle; then, 'Sweet sixteen and never been kissed!' She would take out her make-up compact and daub her face until the Major said, 'Delia, dear, that's enough now,' when she would snap the compact shut and return it guiltily to her handbag. It was embarrassing and upsetting – because of the change more than the antics themselves. Her new manner was so alien to the character everyone knew and feared that you longed for her to start bossing people around again. It was bewildering to see someone who had exercised so much power lose her dignity so completely.'

We had walked back inside from the garden as Teresa was speaking, into the passage-room where the behaviour she was describing would have occurred. Mrs Carew used to sit in a low chair to the right of the fireplace, in front of one of the tall sash windows where hung beautiful but threadbare curtains embroidered with fruit by the Major's grandmother. Teresa was searching out a tape, which she now clicked on. A few gentle, deliberate guitar notes introduced a female singer's voice. I heard, 'Looking counterclockwise . . .' She knew I would not know it, and I did not need to ask whether this too was a song she connected with Lucas. 'After a few months,' she added, 'the Major found her dead on the bathroom floor. Apparently she died of a stroke.'

Teresa sat down in the place where Mrs Carew used to sit. Nobody had wished Mrs Carew a long life in this condition, she explained, but she was unprepared for the mood prevailing at the funeral. 'There was an aura of light-headedness among her family. Not relief because her suffering was over, but a kind of exhilarated tension. I suppose they all felt sad, in their way, but as Hal read the lesson I could see his eyes glint as if the words for the burial of the dead were printed on a faded map of El Dorado.'

A wake was held at the Hall afterwards, with refreshments organised by the Fairfaxes (for which Hal was careful to reimburse them). It was the first such occasion Teresa had been to. As she offered round plates laden with sausages and sandwiches, she was surprised to hear jokes and lively conversation. Despite their loss, the family seemed to have suddenly come alive. And if Elizabeth remembers no such thing then I don't therefore doubt it, for she was younger than Teresa and is anyway less sensitive to the dynamics of what happens around her. Not that Teresa couldn't make up such a thing, but why would she?

It reminds me of the story that Iris's husband wrote, or is said to have written, about the creep Benjamin Sachs. He could have made it up, but why would he? He made up other things – he is a novelist, after all – but even taking into account that his story about Sachs was intended to exculpate himself from passive collusion, he could have made up a much less unlikely story (so far as I understand it). It all became public soon after I bought Sweynsend. Although I pretty much cut myself off from my previous life, I still have a couple of friends in New York who let me know what's going on. I think it was Alec Kronenberg, my Yale buddy, who told me how Sachs, who had apparently vanished, was identified as the victim of his own explosion in Wisconsin or somewhere; and then, some months later, Aaron was taken into custody because it turned out he had known all along that Sachs was the so-called Phantom of Liberty. It must have been hard for Iris, having his name dragged through the press because of that; it must put a strain on a marriage. I gather they are coming over to the UK for a while. Well, I am a sucker for unlikely stories. Sweynsend is full of them, and no one better at telling them than Teresa. Perhaps that's partly why I married her: through her stories, her company, she helped me to a new sense of myself, one in which I could see some future.

# Chapter Four

THE FAIRFAXES continued to live in the Manor for a negligible rent. They were grateful for this, and had no wish to desert the Major. For it was now obvious to his family that the Major could not do without the Fairfaxes, but if any of them had hoped that the old man might be persuaded to move somewhere more manageable, they were mistaken. He intended to occupy the Hall alone until he died, without anyone squeezing him into a renovated nursery flat or, still worse, an old people's home.

Meanwhile he was proud to say that he had never cooked a meal for himself, while brooms and Hoovers had never featured in his domestic routines. When it was suggested that he should employ a housekeeper, he responded with crisp good cheer that he was sure Mrs Fairfax could manage.

Perhaps he really didn't get the point. More likely, he was being devious. He could affect naïveté so disarmingly that, where his wife had blackmailed and bullied, he could get what he wanted with minimum effort. 'Oh, no, he never asked me if I would keep house for him,' Marie once told me, with an evasive smile indicating that she did not expect me to understand why she complied with his wishes. 'He left that to Hal,' she said. He was interested in his books, his garden, and his ancestors' letters. He used five rooms in the house. Otherwise, provided he was dry and fed — as the family realised with gathering dismay — the Major couldn't have cared less about looking after the place.

Since he liked to maintain the impression that Marie was a kind neighbour rather than a housekeeper, as if her services were part of the nature of things and above discussion, her routine required stealth.

She used to go in by the back door after breakfast every day except Sunday. The ostensible point of this was to ask the Major if he wanted anything, 'because I am just popping to ze shops.' 'How kind you are, Marie,' he would say (he pronounced her name Maree, without any pretence of a French accent), 'I do need some toothpaste, since you ask.' The daily question gave her the chance to look in without embarrassing him, and to tidy up the kitchen. Then, avoiding him carefully, she would spend some time with the Hoover and a duster. She always knew where he was because he would accompany his steady clatter across the wooden floors with a succession of singsong 'huh-huh' sounds in descending major thirds. When he went upstairs for fifteen minutes after breakfast, she skimmed round the passage-room, removing his coffee-cup from the previous evening, seeing that his pipe was in its place and inspecting his supply of tobacco. When he came down, she went to do the upstairs chores.

Major Carew's needs were simple. For lunch he liked a slice of pork pie, a tomato, a slice of bread, a glass of wine. A couple of radishes were sufficient to give him a pleasant surprise. With his afternoon tea he took a slice of cake (caraway seed or fruit; never chocolate), and for breakfast he ate toast and marmalade. It would have been just as easy to satisfy him for supper, but Marie felt he ought to eat one proper meal each day and so she used to cook supper for him either at home or in his own kitchen, preparing it in such a way that she could leave it in his oven and trust him to take it out himself at eight o'clock and decant it onto a waiting plate. The pudding would be in the fridge, usually a fruit crumble, which he knew how to reheat; it kept him going for about a week.

Marie always said that these routines were for the Major's benefit, and no doubt this was true: if he wanted anything, or if he wanted to tell her that Hal and family, or Cousin Dick and Lady Cookleborough, were due for dinner tomorrow, then he knew exactly when and where to find her. It is not hard to believe that he would take advantage of someone foolish enough to provide such services without complaint. What is harder to comprehend is why Marie should put up with it. But Teresa says that her mother valued these routines for herself too. She admired the Major's continuing zest for life: it goes a long way towards redeeming the old and infirm from what might appear to be bad manners. As Teresa says, fuss and attention make her mother uncomfortable. She liked being necessary to him. She trusted him to appreciate her, and I dare say he did. She took it as a mark of respect that he didn't find it necessary for anything to be said.

Once a year the Fairfaxes went to France, when other arrangements had to be made for the Major. As Elizabeth and Teresa changed schools and then went to university, their parents would leave Sweynsend to visit them. The Major went visiting several times a year too. The routine was not inflexible but it formed a grid to the lives of those who lived at Sweynsend, which would support any number of variants.

I have described the routine as Marie's, as if no one else had anything to do with it. It was certainly managed by Marie, but Teresa, Elizabeth and their father also had roles to play. If the Major mentioned to Marie that he wanted to have a word with Tom about something then, in the evening, Tom would come over with Elizabeth or Teresa; or, if the supper was very simple, alone. Sometimes the Major would ask particularly after one of the girls, signalling that whichever he had spoken of would be most welcome that evening. I sometimes wonder how conscious the Major was of this system: he can't have failed to observe a connection between his enquiries and the girls' appearances. Beneath his insouciance, did he value it (as Marie believes), or did he take it for granted? Either way, he operated it with the skill of a spymaster – which, it turned out, is what he was.

Standing in for their mother in the morning – 'the *levée*', they called it – was the hardest for the girls, because careful timing was needed, and a subtlety that comes of knowing somebody's habits extremely well. Their approach had to be tangential – a friend dropping in just as the Major finished his breakfast, to ask if he wanted anything; a little surprise – not altogether unexpected, to be sure, but neither bossy nor insinuating. He radiated a sort of devil-may-care self-sufficiency which nobody, it seems, could help but endorse, in spite of his manifold incompetences. He knew someone was making his bed or loitering in the kitchen while he ate his breakfast, but he paid no attention. After eating, he would open his letters with a tarnished steel paperknife which was kept on the turntable. It was unnerving to watch him do this because his hands shook so that the blade stabbed this way and that as he mangled the envelope. Then he would light a cigarette and put on his reading glasses which had a lens blanked out because he was almost blind in one eye. He held the paper about two inches in front of the other lens and his head would move to and fro as he picked out each word through the coils of smoke. Hanging about in the kitchen or passage, whichever Fairfax female was on duty would hear before long the first in a series of 'huh-huhs', culminating in the scrape of his chair, and this was the moment to show herself. It was of the utmost importance not to disturb the Major until then. I don't know why they believed this – I never heard of any rebuke – but believe it they did. Marie impressed upon her daughters that on no account should they bother him before he was ready. However, pure silence would have unsettled him because he expected someone to be there, so they had to do familiar-sounding things while being careful to keep the noise to a minimum. Marie could clean the fridge or sort jars of pickle in the pantry without thinking about the Major at all, but she was highly attuned to his movements and rhythms, so that as soon as she heard his first 'huh-huh' she would switch into a sequence of precise responses. On the infrequent occasions when the girls replaced their mother in the mornings, they tried to do as she would, knowing how the old man was accustomed to her.

Elizabeth found this waiting especially awkward. 'It made me so nervous!' she told me on one of her rare visits from Manchester (yes, she has escaped, if living in the rich suburb of Wilmslow can be called an escape from anywhere – except, possibly, Hell). She has dyed blond hair that looks like it sounds (dead) and wears scent so noxious that I have to open the window of any room she is in, and preferably also the door. I long to tell her to go and have a bath. Her conviction that she is more glamorous than her sister, who hardly wears make-up at all, and does what she wants instead of what the magazines tell women they ought to want, is comic. How do two sisters raised, so to speak, in the same pod, get to be so different? 'I'd drop something with a crash,' she said, 'on that awful stone floor. "Huh!" he'd go next door, as if someone had pushed him off his chair. So in I'd go. But instead of finding him sprawled on the floor he was sitting there all shifty-looking.' Elizabeth would have interrupted him while he was reading a letter. Being courteous to a lady even though he was ninety, he would feel obliged to remove his glasses and stand up before speaking. Or else she would be late, and he would wander round distractedly, tapping the furniture until she appeared. On such a morning Elizabeth would arrive back at the Manor in a state of guilty excitement, ready to giggle.

The trickiest aspect of the *levée* was making the Major's bed. It was never in great disarray, but it was a tough old horse-hair mattress with a complicated system of sheets and blankets and counterpanes. For Teresa, the pay-off for doing it was the opportunity to snoop.

On one wall of the bedroom hung two oils of horses, so badly painted that they seemed like pictures from the top of toy farm kits. A photograph of Mrs Carew in her twenties in a silver frame stood on the table beside the bed. 'It always surprised me to see how beautiful she was,' says Teresa. 'But not harmless, never innocent.' Otherwise, there were a number of miniatures and photographs of people unknown to her. Judging by their clothes and the foxing of the paper, they must have died more than fifty years previously. She discovered that the wardrobe and chest-of-drawers were still full of Mrs Carew's clothes, including a Fortuny gown, and she knew – or thought she knew – about the cupboard in the corner where the Major kept his ancient clothes, because the door was sometimes ajar. But she never knew there was a door in the back of it; she never found this little hidey-hole, the dressing-room, her sanctuary.

The evening visits tended to be mellower. Apart from getting the Major's supper, there was no work to be done. Whereas in the mornings he didn't want company for its own sake, he liked to chat and tell a story or two in the evening. If Marie was on her own then she would be unlikely to sit down with him, but, if someone else were there, then one would prepare supper while the other sat across the fireplace from him with a glass of sherry. Whoever was doing the food would try to spend as little time in the kitchen as possible. If Tom were there he poured out the sherry, and, as he handed a glass to the Major, the Major would introduce a topic.

'Do you know what chapbooks are, Teresa?'

She shook her head.

The Major wagged a hooked finger in the air. 'Tom, be so kind as to pass me those little fellows on the table there, would you?'

Tom scanned the table on which stood framed photographs in elaborate silver frames of each of the Major's children on their wedding-day; an empty glass vase; a cracked cribbage board; a cluster of books and papers, on top of which lay two tiny, old booklets which Tom handed to the Major. Putting on his reading glasses, the Major closely examined each one in turn, leaning back in his chair to gain the maximum benefit of the standard lamp behind. 'Huh-huh! Huhhuh!' he chanted as he removed his spectacles, and passed the chapbooks to Teresa. 'Josephine found them in the rat loft when she was looking for Penny Reds.'

Josephine was then about twenty and unlikely to be scrabbling about in the filth in search of damaged Penny Reds, so it had to be assumed that they were found ten years ago and put away in a drawer for safekeeping. Since his wife's death, the Major seemed to spend much of his time rediscovering things that had been put away in this manner, and his conversation often proceeded from whatever he had found.

Leafing through, Teresa saw sequences of very simple coloured pictures. In one, a boy chased a dog; in the other, a dog grabbed a chicken from a kitchen table and then was chased by the cook. The edges and covers were scuffed but the colours inside were good, considering the state in which they were found. For the rat loft was an empty room, in the same wing as the nursery but separate from it, accessible only by a staircase from the lobby where the mower was kept. It must once have been a groom's room, but for a long time it had served as a repository for old newspapers and supposedly worthless letters. Papers weren't stacked there in bundles or boxes but strewn all over the place, as if someone had brought them all upstairs in order deliberately to scatter them, without any expectation of future retrieval. It was a strange display of semi-preservation, requiring more effort than burning them or keeping them safe in boxes. It now forms part of a well-appointed flat which I let to a warehousing specialist, a Muslim from the new Industrial Park a few miles away.

'Hawkers would have brought chapbooks to the back door for the servants' children,' said the Major. 'They are the eighteenth- and nineteenth-century equivalent of comics. Unsuitable, of course, for a gentleman's offspring, though people will let their children read anything these days. Yes, Teresa, I know we disagree on this matter, but the young must learn to excuse prejudices in the old just as the old are obliged to in the young . . . Anyway, because they were cheap and considered to be disposable, they are now quite scarce, I believe.'

Another occasion Teresa has described to me is the Major's presentation of *The Black Book; or Corruption Unmasked*.

'My grandson William was here at the weekend, lamenting the corruption he reads about so avidly in the newspapers. I told him that corruption and outrage are not new. Between you and me, Teresa, I think he was a little shocked. Have a look on the fourth shelf up for *The Black Book*. It's in the middle stack, two volumes about four from the left.'

Catching her father's eye, Teresa went to fetch the book. Those leather-bound volumes belonged so much to the room's atmo- sphere that the idea of them having a life of their own was almost disrespectful. When she couldn't find it, the Major came to look himself. Unable to read the letters clearly, he brought his face up close to the row of spines, at the same time moving his fingers over them, feeling the leather's texture and the degree of wear, searching for recognisable features. When he came to the place where he expected to find *The Black Book*, there was a gap. 'Oh bother!' he said, 'What's that one to the left? Is it John Clare? And Launcelot Andrewes on the other side? I thought so. Bother. Whatever did William do with it?'

'I think this must be what you're looking for, Major,' said Tom. 'Here, on the table.'

'Ah. Yes, yes. Thank you, Tom. Now Teresa, have a look at that.' He shuffled back to his chair. 'It's a catalogue of corruption in government and society compiled by the Chartists, published in 1820 or thereabouts. It'll make your hair stand on end, I shouldn't wonder.'

The sombre-looking book in her hands was volume two, which was an appendix to volume one. It consisted largely of lists. 'Instances of Ecclesiastical Pluralism in West Yorkshire' was the heading above several pages detailing the outrages of one gang. A certain George Evesham, the Major pointed out, was accused of holding seven local livings, from which he derived an income of £17,000 per year.

'If we could only persuade some go-ahead publisher to reprint *that!*' the Major declared, in the tone he reserved for criticising the level of education in the country or lambasting the Church of England as a den of illiterate communist nincompoops.

The Church of England was an institution close to the Major's heart, and in his last years he had particular reason to be grateful to it because it provided him with matter for innumerable arguments and satirical diatribes. Without it, what would he have complained about? Probably his kind neighbours. And his powers of contempt and ridicule were considerable. The 1662 Prayer Book and Authorised Version were held by him to be sarosanct. 'Cranmer's Thirty-Nine Articles haven't dated one jot,' he would say with a twinkle. 'The government ought to learn them by heart, together with the Ten Commandments, before taking office.' It was immaterial that some two thousand priests had resigned when the English Prayer Book was introduced to replace the Latin. The Major deemed it a good thing that a seventeenth-century congregation should understand the language; he didn't think they should have been expected to learn Latin. He waved away any inconsistency in his argument and if challenged would insist, 'People *ought* to understand the Queen's English.

The grunts that nowadays pass for language will have us stomping round campfires in animal skins again, brandishing clubs.'

Teresa never ventured to answer him herself. In her church they had Latin Mass, which she could not understand any more than the Major would have (for he was not a classicist). Moreover, she sympathised with his prejudice even if she disputed his logic. And who was she to argue with the him? He was ninety, and she was a Catholic. It was a subject she tried to avoid.

# Chapter Five

I ALWAYS ASK myself, how did they think it would end?
One has the impression of everybody behaving as if life
would continue at Sweysend in this manner for ever, the Major
going on as he always had, supported by the framework that he
chose to regard as invisible. But it was an existence rooted in
contradiction for he was only able to regard the framework as
invisible because he could afford to; and he could only afford to
because he had the good fortune to be in reasonable health while
knowing that his days must be finite. He rightly presumed that
people would prefer to go along with things as they were, if they
could, until his death, rather than force painful changes that
would necessarily be short-lived. The illusion that he was in
control suited everybody. Their denial was only possible because
they understood it to be a denial – and yet it was real enough
because, incredibly, the question of how it would end does not
appear, after all, to have been addressed.

I asked Teresa about this while we were having supper yesterday.
It was a beautiful, warm evening. We sat without candles, and the
sash windows were open wide so that we could smell the garden
outside. Teresa told me that she remembered talking about it with
Elizabeth, but that the subject was off-limits with her parents.

'How do you mean, "off-limits"?' I asked. 'What did they do if
you raised it? Send you to your room? Tell you to stand in the
corner?'

'You have to remember that they were very protective towards the Major and Mrs Carew,' she said. 'They knew that people would have liked them to gossip about things at the Hall, but they never did. I'm sure they talked about things between themselves, but they did not include us. Had they done so, it would have given the wrong message: it would have made it seem all right to talk about the Carews' private affairs in public.'

'Even to you?'

'Especially to us.'

'And did the two of you not talk about it?'

'Of course we did. And sometimes other people asked us about it. Knowing nothing made it easier to talk about, in a way. We could speculate innocently.'

'My dear Teresa, were you ever innocent?'

She rested her dark, astute eyes on me for a moment; her soup spoon halted on its way to her lips.

'Oh,' she said, 'I was always innocent in deed. You wouldn't believe how innocent. But not in thought, no. Never in thought.'

I had anticipated her sudden gravity and the self-mocking chuckle that followed, and I laughed.

'And you, Jimmy,' she said, teasing me in turn, 'are you innocent?'

'Of what? What is the charge?'

'Then you are not innocent,' she said.

'Such an accusation, so early in a marriage . . . Is that –'

'What, cricket?'

'I don't know about cricket, but is it kind?'

'Kind or not – wouldn't it be dreary to be married to someone so very innocent?'

'I expect it would. So what form did your "innocent speculation" take?'

And she told me about a visit she paid to Mabel at the post office one afternoon:

47

In the field to her left as she walked, separating the Manor from the rest of the village, the grass was already knee high. Only the Major could neglect a valuable stretch of land with such assurance. New houses sprang up around the village each year, but this paddock in the middle survived, unkempt but intact. Teresa never heard anyone talk about it, but it occurred to her that people must offer to buy pieces of it from time to time, and be refused. On the far side, beyond the sagging fence, a short tarmac road with trimmed verges ran up to four new suburban villas looking across the paddock towards the Manor. It was probably their inhabitants, if anyone, who, eager to preserve their outlook, chased away intruders and prevented people from dumping rubbish.

A few steps further along the pavement, Teresa came to Mabel's gate. There was a faded notice with curled edges in the window, saying 'Post Office and General Store'. Nothing else revealed that this was not an ordinary dwelling, but Mabel's wasn't a bustling business. She presented herself more as a public benefactor than a shopkeeper eager for profit. It was her home too, and she liked to have it looking like a home, with a wicket gate and a neat garden path bordered by marigolds, Michaelmas daisies and stone cats. Residents did not need placards announcing 'Mabel's Village Store' or advertisements for ice cream to know that she was there. And there was no longer any passing trade in Sweynsend, nor any prospect of it since the new road was built.

'Morning, Mabel.'

'Yer oughtn't to be out wirout a scarf. Y'll catch yer death!'

'It's spring, Mabel!'

'Spring's as maybe.'

'I saw Jed crossing the fields earlier on. The sun's more likely to miss a morning than Jed.'

''E likes 'is walk, Jed does.'

The shop consisted of one room lined with scarred shelves, on which stood tattered regiments of tins and defeated packets of food. At certain points the ranks parted for the benefit of grotesque plastic dolls, like mascots. Pink combs and Disney keyrings on cardboard backing hung like banners from parapets. The only things Teresa had ever bought there were stamps, milk and tinned tomatoes.

'So what can I do for you this morning, Teresa?' she asked.

'Half a dozen first-class stamps please.'

Mabel lifted her dog-eared book onto the counter, which naturally fell open at the page for second-class stamps. Without thinking, she began to tear off a strip.

'Oh, could I have first-class please?'

Mabel's bent fingers stopped. She looked at the stamps.

'Daft as a dandelion, I am.'

She turned the page and grunted, as if reprimanding the two quarter-sheets of first-class stamps she saw there for not previously coming to her fingers.

Reaching into her bag for her purse, Teresa saw two envelopes she had put there earlier. 'And I've a couple of letters to post for the Major,' she said, and put them on the counter.

'"Hal Carew Esquire",' Mabel read aloud. 'The Major's 'and-writing isn't what it was now, is it?' she said with a sly smile.

'No, I suppose not. But he is ninety. It's not surprising.'

'Now did I say it was surprising?' she answered as Teresa gave her some money. She sorted out the change in silence. 'That's two pounds – and three is five. I wonder what they'll do with the Hall when 'e goes to meet 'is Maker.'

Teresa returned the change to her purse. 'I don't know, Mabel.'

'They'll sell, I shouldn't wonder.'

'Oh, I don't think so,' Teresa replied, finding herself drawn in against her will and better judgement.

'Hal's got his place up north though, ain't 'e? They've all got places of their own. What would they want with Sweynsend Hall?'

'I'm sure they won't sell. Anyway, the Major will outlive us all.'

'He's ninety. You said it yourself, love. Mark my words, they'll sell to one of them developers, or we'll get an American. Or an A-rab.'

'I'm sure there's no need to worry,' Teresa said jauntily.

'Well someone's got to, else you lot'll be out on yer ear!'

'Thanks for the stamps. See you, Mabel.'

'And tell the Major I've something more to say to 'im before we meet up there,' she said, jabbing her thumb towards the ceiling. 'Or down there,' and she looked grimly at the floor.

'If you tell him what I think you're thinking, you'll certainly end up down there,' Teresa said. 'Thanks for the stamps.'

'Right you are.'

We had long ago finished dinner but were still facing one another across the table, sipping our wine. Twilight was closing on the summer evening outside. We were almost in darkness. I stood up to light candles. 'The Major's death threatened us,' Teresa continued, 'like a . . .'

'Like a what?'

'Like an assassin's raised arm glimpsed in a mirror.' She raised her right arm melodramatically, then dropped it. 'We never discussed it at home. There wasn't any point. Mabel's probes reminded me that everyone else in the village must have been talking about it for years. They probably thought we knew the answer. Perhaps they even imagined that the Carews' property in Sweynsend would be left to us. Not knowing the Carews as well as we did, they may have thought our avoidance of the issue was a sham, a deliberate evasion… Until they had answers they would reserve the right to remain suspicious. But we knew nothing and, had we asked the Carews what they planned for the place after the Major's death, they would have thought us – quite rightly – impertinent. Only with Elizabeth did I ever talk about it, and then we knew so little that our speculation never got anywhere.

'Later that same evening, after my parents had gone to bed, I went into Elizabeth's room and told her about my visit to Mabel. Her curtains weren't closed. Moonlight silvered the field I had walked past during the afternoon. When I brought my face close to the glass, I could see the lights of the houses on the other side.

'Elizabeth was leaning back against her stashed pillows with her knees drawn up, wearing a white towelling dressing-gown. She was reading a magazine and listening to music through headphones. She was winding and unwinding a loose strand of her blond hair around the middle finger of her right hand as if she were playing with a cosy little animal. I approached softly and pulled at the marshmallow disc of one of her earphones. "Boo!"'

Elizabeth shrieked. Then she hunkered up, pushing the headphones down round her neck. As the magazine tumbled to the floor, Teresa sat down on her bed.

Elizabeth had lace-fringed pillows, a frilly valance on her bed and a candy-pink duvet with a pattern of indeterminate wildflowers. Although no more experienced than Teresa in affairs of the heart, Elizabeth's flagrant femininity contrived to make her appear expert. With her delicate little nose she was thought as a child to be prettier than her sister. She has a ready, uncomplicated smile while Teresa is one of those beautiful women who are plagued by builders calling, 'Cheer up, love! It may never happen!', thereby making her cross when she had merely been thoughtful. Believing her younger sister to be more attractive, Teresa has probably always been heavy-handed with her.

Removing her headphones altogether, Elizabeth swung her legs straight out over the other side of the bed and in two paces she was at the window. She opened the casement two notches and then, at the full extent of her reach, raising her heels from the floor, she plucked first one and then the other curtain and swept them together with a clatter of mahogany rings.

'I saw Mabel today,' Teresa said. 'She asked what was going to happen when the Major dies.'

Elizabeth was about to climb back into bed but now she checked herself. With a sigh that hinted at the world's unfairness to her, she picked up her hairbrush. 'Sometimes I think if a man offered to brush my hair twice a day, I'd marry him, just like that. However ugly.'

She dropped her head so that her hair fell in a cascade and began to brush in firm, slow arcs.

'She was saying that Hal and the others won't want to live here and so it'll be sold,' Teresa said. '"To an American or an A-rab," she said.'

Still bent over at the waist, Elizabeth held her hair aside for a moment and looked at Teresa as if she had just told her that Mabel's mother was alive and well and running a chain of night-clubs. Then she frowned. 'Maybe she's right,' she said. Letting her hair drop again, she resumed her brushing.

'I don't believe it.'

Elizabeth straightened up. Yanking the hairs from the bristles of her brush, she released them over the wastepaper basket where they floated down like unstrung gossamer. When she had finished she got back into bed and said, 'I can't imagine any of the Carews coming here. Anyway, none of their wives would want to live here.'

'Then it will be sold, unless it goes to one of the grandchildren. Or gets put into trust for them, or something.'

Elizabeth drew up her knees and fiddled with her toes. 'I just can't imagine William coming to live here. I mean, why would he? It would be weird.'

'Anything apart from the Major would be weird.'

'They'll sell it. They'll have to,' Elizabeth repeated. 'Unless they're rich enough just to let it sit here and fall down.'

'I can't believe that. You don't just sell somewhere like Sweynsend unless you really need the money.'

Elizabeth flicked out the cassette in her machine and reached across to select another from a stack on her bedside table.

Teresa inspected the fingernails of her left hand. 'So you see,' she said to me, 'I did talk about what was going to happen to Sweynsend with Elizabeth. We even fantasised about Dad buying it. The trouble was that Elizabeth never understood that, even if a miracle happened and Dad did buy it, it wouldn't be the same because we weren't Carews.'

'And me?'

'That's different. You're out of the loop.'

In December of that year, the Major tripped over an electric blow-heater and cracked two ribs. All of a sudden he was shrunken. Two vivid eyes peered from his broken-backed wing chair like a cat resisting capture: a man defined by his capacity for thought, determined that his mind should not be dulled by drugs or senility.

Every winter was cold at Sweynsend, but that one was especially cruel. The Major wore fingerless woollen mittens all the time and a thick, padded anorak on top of his frayed jersey, even when he was sitting beside the fire. Such precautions were worn with the indifference of a skin, as if the cold itself were of no consequence to him. Mental energy sustained him. His resilience was astounding. Teresa says she once forgot to put on a couple of extra layers before sitting with him and she shivered for an hour, unable to concentrate on what he was saying. Although his face had been a constant grey-blue since his fall he still did not acknowledge the temperature, but he must have felt it because occasionally he resorted to that fatal contraption.

A few days later, the Major noticed that the pistols were missing from their hooks inside the front door, which upset him. Not that he imagined himself shooting intruders with them, for he knew that guns which hadn't been fired since the Thirty Years War were unlikely to be efficient weapons. The only thing up their breeches was dust, unless mice had got stuck there. What disturbed him was that he couldn't identify exactly when the robbery had occurred. Someone had walked into his unlocked house and taken his guns: it might have been six months ago, or it might have been the previous day. Nothing else appeared to have gone, but he couldn't be any more sure of this than that the culprit wasn't someone he knew and trusted. Until now, he had felt himself to be master of his own domain. Although he didn't care about the actual loss of his pistols, their anonymous removal admitted a mocking, disruptive presence into his home.

The Fairfaxes' telephone scarcely stopped ringing over the next three months. Every evening one of the Carew brothers or their wives would call. The nature of their anxiety was puzzling. In part, their concern for the Major was pure: they suddenly realised that he was an old, fragile, mortal man, and they wanted to care for him – which, in the circumstances, meant pestering the Fairfaxes to care for him. The Fairfaxes didn't mind this, although there were times when the Carews were insensitive to their suppertime and peace. It was natural for the Major's relatives to worry; they were right to worry. But the Fairfaxes sensed that they were afraid of the old man's death as much for themselves as for him. Instead of allowing the sad but inevitable event to follow its own course, providing the Major with whatever comforts they could, they seemed determined to disallow it altogether. They were panicked by the very idea, and the chief aim of speaking to the Fairfaxes appeared to be to extract reassurances that he wasn't going to die after all. The conversation of these highly intelligent men was interlaced with questions like 'There's no cause for immediate alarm, is there?' 'He's not going to die on us, is he?'

But of course he did die.

It happened one evening early in March. Both Elizabeth and Teresa were away.

It seems that Tom, perturbed by unusual confusion in the Major's behaviour, had twice stayed with him throughout his supper and then continued to hover in the background, listening for sounds of distress or a fall, until he was sure he was safe in bed. So Marie wasn't unduly alarmed when he didn't join her for supper at home. She put his food on a low heat in the oven and ate hers alone in front of the TV.

According to precedent, Tom would have let the Major shuffle off alone to the sitting-room after his supper, with one translucent hand touching the wall and the other twined around a walking stick. It looked a painful manoeuvre, but it was vital to him that he maintain this vestigial independence. On this occasion, however, he didn't feel up to the pretence and suffered Tom to take his arm. When the Major was settled in his chair, Tom returned to the kitchen to make coffee for him. He made a cup for himself too, for the Major's dried-flower fragility upset him like the packed bags and overcoat of a beloved friend, and he wished to remain alert with him as long as he was able.

The Major was trying to fill his pipe when Tom rejoined him, but his hands were shaking too much to get the tobacco into the bowl. Shreds were sprinkled over his lap and the edges of the chair. He was very agitated. Ashamed of his debility more than the mess itself, he was trying to stuff ever larger pinches of tobacco into the increasingly convulsed bowl of his pipe. The lack of his customary noises and imprecations confirmed his desperation. Tom gently held the stem of the pipe so that the Major's target, at least, was stationary. Slowly, without either of them referring to what was happening beneath their eyes, the matter was accomplished. Then, like a struggling bird, the Major's fingers sought out Tom's wrist and tried to pat it in gratitude both for his help and for his silence.

Tom struck a match and held it over the bowl of the pipe. The Major sucked feebly and the flame dipped. After one or two more attempts he breathed a word, and there was a faint pitch to it, and the suggestion of an aspirant, a ghostly 'huh-huh!' meaning, perhaps, 'Oh well, I just haven't the vim in me to light it. Never mind, it's comforting just to hold it, in the circumstances.'

They exchanged a few words about the coming of spring. It had been a fine day. During the afternoon the Major had ventured out as far as the rose that climbed over the window of his study, and he had noticed a bud. After mentioning this the Major fell silent and Tom, seeing that chat was exhausting him, did not persist. A few moments later the Major said he thought he would go to bed. 'I know it's early, but I find I'm unaccountably tired. Would you be so kind as to lend me your arm, Tom?'

Tom helped the Major up from his chair. 'Don't worry about the fire and the lights. I'll deal with them,' he said.

'I'm very grateful, Tom.' He was gripping Tom's forearm with both hands. Before reaching for his stick, he added: 'And to Marie. For all you've done for me.'

Then he took up his stick. With Tom still supporting him on his left, he went out of his sitting-room with its smoke-blackened mirror and crossed the hall to the stairs, where his grandfather as a boy, dressed in knickerbockers and leaning against the flank of a pony, surveyed him from a picture frame high up on the wall.

The Major said good night to Tom. 'I'll be quite all right now, thank you.' Transferring his left hand from Tom to the banister, he began the slow, tortuous climb. Downstairs in the shadows Tom could hear each footfall on the broad wooden steps: each one safely achieved was a relief. 'Huh!' the Major gasped, sensing the top as he reached the halfway dogleg beneath the high, arched window. A slanting shaft of moonlight above made his grandfather's blond locks glisten.

Tom was about to move away when he heard the Major stumble.

As the Major crumpled and his stick clattered downstairs, Tom bounded up towards him. The Major's upper body was on the landing. With one hand he was still grasping for the newel post: he must have been concentrating so hard on stepping upwards that he didn't realise he had reached the top and the sturdy cushion of wood he expected to meet his aching foot was not there. Instead, he felt his foot plunge into a void and was pulled down through a riot of bumps and noises, a jumble of half-glimpsed memories – the brass candle snuffer he'd used as a child still there on the night table on the landing, unnoticed for years until now, as he fell – and meaningless angles, suddenly fading.

He was still breathing. Tom lifted him up and took him into his cold bedroom. The Major didn't seem to be aware of Tom's presence. When he found himself transported to his bed he opened his eyes for an instant in surprise; of recognition, perhaps, that the anticipated haven should turn out to be this, his bed; or that this formlessness was death. Ten minutes later his breath ceased altogether.

When at last Tom returned home, Marie knew immediately what had happened because he was weeping, a phenomenon she had apparently never seen before.

Although owing to his great age the Major's death cannot really have been a surprise, he was loved by his family and they were shocked by his passing. As he was lowered into the grave beside his wife, he was accompanied by susurrous sobs from his grandchildren that would surely have gratified him. Yet Teresa's memory of it is embittered by two small details.

The Carew brothers arranged for the undertakers to lay the Major in his coffin in the dining-room. Their idea was that he should be taken out of the French doors, across the lawn, and through the gate in the wall opposite the church. This gate had not been used at Mrs Carew's funeral because she was brought by the undertakers. In fact nobody could actually remember it ever being open, though it was known to have been used at the Major's christening for he used to say that he wished to be carried out through the same door that he was carried in.

And he was. But only just.

The gate was half hidden behind ivy and overgrown shrubs, like a neglected tombstone. The steps approaching it were broken and buried in a thick mulch of wind-blown leaves. By the weekend before it was clear that the Carews hadn't thought to check that it still opened, or to tidy around it, so Tom and Teresa took the matter into their own hands. They clipped back the intrusive foliage, repaired the treacherous steps and brought some shovels full of gravel round from the front of the house to scatter at the gate's threshold. When at last they opened the gate, they found that the top half was rotten. Tom had to fix a wooden brace across the uprights to prevent it collapsing the next day. Finally they gave it a fresh coat of white paint. They were glad to do this puny service for the Major but Teresa couldn't help noticing – and despising herself for doing so – that none of the Carews ever commented on it.

After the funeral there was a wake at the Hall. Whereas eight years previously, for the Major's wife, it was the Fairfaxes who had organised it, now the Carews did it themselves. Or rather, they hired a firm of caterers to do it. The Fairfaxes had been asked over to the Hall on the morning before the funeral to help get the house in order. They were relieved not to have to arrange everything themselves but still anxious to do what they could to make the arrival of two hundred people in the house as comfortable as possible.

An hour before the service was due to begin, Teresa happened to pass by the door of the passage-room, where the Major spent most of his time during the last years of his life. Hal and Hugh had moved the furniture to one side, exposing the hearth where the fire had spat onto it. Ash and charcoal had been ground into the carpet. Years of crumbs and wisps of tobacco were encrusted round his chair. Now one of the Australian grandsons was shoving a Hoover back and forth. 'I thought Whatsername, Marie, was supposed to keep this place clean,' he grumbled, at once business-like, prim and effortlessly offensive.

'I strode into the room with clenched fists, ready for battle,' Teresa told me. 'But the man's back was turned. Instead, standing beside William, slighter than him, was a stranger. He was watching me. Dust and grainy smoke swam in a shaft of sunlight between us, but his eyes were as blue as Hockney's swimming-pools.'

'Lucas?' I said.

Teresa nodded.

It is possible to maintain a belief in one's innocence after certain encounters which are only understood later to have been defining moments of the heart, perhaps because they were implausibly brief, or we were young. Then we understand that, afterwards, our innocence was never quite the same as we had believed. In the candlelight I saw that Teresa's eyes were watchful. I tried to read them for innocence, but could not. I do not know whether this was a consequence of faltering light, when reactions, if not already dulled by alcohol, are shadow-bound; or whether my power to read her is being undermined by reflection; or whether the innocence is not there after all, and the failure lies in my inability to acknowledge its absence.

The Carews were all gone by early evening. As Hal was saying goodbye to Tom, he casually asked if he wouldn't mind keeping an eye on the Hall.

The Fairfaxes had expected some sort of announcement regarding Sweynsend's future. The complete absence of any information seemed extraordinary, even insulting. And then, at last, it dawned on them that the Carews didn't know what was going to happen either.

# Chapter Six

Teresa's family teased her when she began working as a solicitor in Tullworth, just as they did when she chose to study law.

'God protect the innocent,' said Marie, though Tom said that he wouldn't mind having her on his side in a dispute.

She travelled between home and her office by bicycle. Leaving Tullworth in the evening by the main road to the southwest, she crossed the traffic lights and then rode up the gentle hill, past a lay-by where a group of sallow gypsies and their rusting vans could sometimes be seen. After a couple of miles of level cycling she turned off to the right, along the old road that runs through Sweynsend. Around the time she was born, a bypass was built which lay gun-barrel straight across the Carews' fields and was rejoined by the loop through the village.

On her left was the tufty wedge of land beyond the Hall's garden wall, trapped between the two roads, where Jed sometimes put a few of his sheep. Then came the great red wall, familiar and comforting with its warty weeds. On her right as she cycled was a series of bungalows built in the seventies, and then the church. Six weeks after the Major's death, passing the entrance to the Hall, she wondered, as usual, when something was going to happen. Hal had called by twice since the funeral to pick up some things, and on the last occasion he mentioned that Sweynsend had been left to William. He had said it lightly as he was getting into his car, as if it were something the Fairfaxes might have known. When he saw that his news surprised them, his face buckled in a jolly, lopsided leer that reminded Teresa of his mother.

Teresa had known William slightly since childhood. He belonged to a remote world of private schools and wealth. Although aware of his visits to the Hall over the years, she seldom saw him or exchanged a greeting. He was of medium height, with untidy, coarse brown hair that had been very blond when he was a child. He was decent-looking but his face was too slack to be handsome. 'He used to remind me of our old kitchen table,' Teresa told me, 'which was given to us by Mrs Carew. It was a very ordinary 1930s deal table, quite adequate in itself but incapable of rousing the daily pleasure you might hope for if you'd been able to choose one for yourself. But if William got excited, his loose features surrendered to a bewildering range of expressions, leaving the unnerving impression that he lacked some elementary control over himself. It was nice to think of having him as our neighbour, though. And I must admit, Jimmy, that the glimpse of his friend at the Major's funeral made the situation more exciting to me than it should have.'

We were driving back from London when she said this. She had come down for the night because she wanted to look at some wallpaper samples for the drawing-room. I had already been there for three days, following two in New York where I presented to my coffee-shop clients the results of the Moscow survey I commissioned from Lucas. They have been clients of mine since before I sold my agency in '86, and they increasingly use me now as a consultant, rather than the company who bought me out for my client list.

Instead of staying down the next night, we had dinner near our flat, in our favourite restaurant at the top of Draycott Avenue, and then got into the car and drove up to Leicestershire in the darkness. It's a good time for talking.

'Should have?' I said.

'Well, it was only a glimpse…'

'Sometimes that's all it takes.' I took my hand off the steering-wheel and placed it, uxoriously, on her thigh.

Teresa laughed and squeezed my hand. 'Jimmy,' she said, 'you are sweet.'

But I am not. I am a fraud.

Hal's aside to the Fairfaxes raised more questions than it answered. They still didn't know where they fitted into the Carews' plans for Sweynsend. They didn't even know whether William was going to live at the Hall. Teresa's parents were anxious because they loved the leaky Manor – it was their home – but they began to suspect that this was being deliberately turned to account. As Tom said, there was nothing to stop them living somewhere else. They didn't have to carry on indefinitely as care-takers of this decaying estate. Without them, on the other hand, the Carew edifices in Sweynsend would fall down altogether.

Teresa leaned her bicycle against the side of the house and went indoors, rubbing her cold hands in anticipation of the kitchen's warmth. Partially covering the hall's dark and nubbled boards was an old Bokhara rug, frayed along the edge where it lay beneath a row of coat hooks. She was about to hang up her coat when she heard a strange male voice. Trailing her coat behind her, she pushed open the kitchen door.

William Carew sat at the table. He was holding out a mug that Marie was filling from the teapot. Instead of standing up at Teresa's entrance, he tipped his chair back and grinned like an innocent with an inherently guilty conscience, waiting for someone to speak. So completely did he fail to behave as Teresa expected that he seemed not bad-mannered but gauche. His shoulders were round for someone still under thirty, and his hair needed washing.

'Ah, here is Teresa,' said Marie.

William stretched his hand across the table. 'William Carew.' He was wearing a tweed jacket with a tie, and brown corduroys.

'Hello,' Teresa said.

'I came over to say, to sort of present myself if you . . .' He stared intently at one of his thumbnails, but his script wasn't there and he looked up again at Teresa. 'Your poor mother, I've been boring her for far too long. She's been plying me with tea.'

'Not at all, William.' Turning to Teresa, Marie explained with approval, 'Now that William has come to live here, he thought he would come and meet us properly.'

Teresa had expected it to be strange having him next door, but she never imagined he'd act as if they had never met.

William examined his tea. He seemed to be checking whether or not a skin had formed on the surface. 'The thing is,' he resumed, 'the thing is, you all know much more than me about the place. I was hoping to sort of enlist your support. Sort of unscramble things a bit.'

Teresa waited for him to continue, suspended between the relief of a safe landing and sudden terror of disaster. Nothing had been vouchsafed to the Fairfaxes about the Carews' plans, and now suddenly William was in their – in *his* – kitchen, asking for help before saying anything about his intentions. Teresa didn't know what he had said to her mother, but it was reassuring to see that he didn't seem to have worried her.

'I want to repair things a bit. You know, get a hold of the place.'

Marie narrowed her eyes at Teresa, forbidding her to laugh at this ludicrous statement.

'Thing is,' he continued, 'thing is . . . No . . . I'm j-jumping the gun. I was telling your mother, but of course you don't know. Well, you know that my grandfather left Sweynsend to me. I don't know why, I mean I never imagined this would happen so I hadn't thought about it . . . But now I'm here, and the idea is that my father and uncles leave me to my own devices, which is fine by me, but the problem is I know nothing about the place. I mean, I hardly knew of the existence of this house and the Kennels!'

Imitating William's speech, Teresa made him sound vague and uncertain, not pompous. 'His eyes were wide,' she said to me, 'either in astonishment at his own ignorance, or at the length of his speech. He also wanted us to sympathise with him for inheriting all this without knowing anything about it. It was nice to feel needed, I suppose, and it enabled a relationship that might have been prevented by pride, or snobbery. After all, how should an ignorant young landlord and an informed sitting tenant – family – behave towards each other? Not that he wasn't vulnerable, as we discovered later with such abysmal clarity.'

Teresa's unflinching eyes would have unnerved William further. 'Where did you think we lived?' she asked.

'Well I knew you – you lived here, in the Manor, but I'd never seen it except through the trees.'

'You haven't met Stan then.'

William shook his head.

Stan had been renting the whole complex – the largest purpose-built Kennels in the county, comprising not only kennels for a pack of hounds but also stables, barns, living quarters and a smithy – since the Hunt was disbanded in the nineteen-fifties. He had been paying nine pounds per week then, and that was still what he paid; not a penny had been spent on the upkeep of the buildings. A succession of dogs and cadaverous nags had been incarcerated there by him over the years, and the yard was a necropolis of agricultural machinery. Nobody knew exactly what he did for a living.

The problem now was stark. Unless Stan could be evicted the place would collapse altogether, but evicting him would be unpleasant and difficult.

The front door banged. 'Hello! Anyone at home?' Tom called from the hall.

'In the kitchen!' Marie replied. 'William is here!'

I imagine Tom shrugging off his raincoat, one hand already reaching for a coathanger. He is not the kind of man to hang his coat directly from a hook. His hair was grey and, though thin, it was properly cut. 'William?' he said, twitching the collar of his jacket.

'William Carew.'

'Ah! Has he come to evict us?'

Tom paused on the threshold, meeting William's consternation with a cheerful smile. 'That's a relief,' he said. 'Then let's have a drink.'

Tom kept his wine in the disused porch that led to the Kennels. It was on the other side of the kitchen, and to reach it he had to squeeze past William's chair. William tipped forward, half-standing as he tried to get out of Tom's way. 'Don't move, old chap,' said Tom. 'Old age hasn't given me a belly yet,' and he winked at Marie who had been teasing him recently for putting on weight. In fact he was very slim, which she was proud of. 'Teresa dear, can you get some glasses? Marie, if you wouldn't mind passing the corkscrew . . .?' He opened the door and, stooping, reached into the darkness for a bottle. 'Elizabeth not back yet?'

'She rang to say she's staying another day,' said Marie. 'She says she will be back tomorrow.'

'Elizabeth went to London yesterday for a job interview,' Tom said to William as he returned to the table. 'She finished at Warwick University last year. Anyway. Welcome,' and he poured out the wine.

William responded with a faint bow, which Tom registered in an instant of stillness.

Marie suggested that they go through to the drawing-room.

'Yes, quite right, Marie, whatever are we doing standing about in the kitchen?'

After his openness with Marie and Teresa, William was nervous of Tom. He held his glass near his lips and his eyes darted over the rim as if in search of a post in the conversation to which he could tether himself.

'Before you came in, interrupting us so loudly,' Teresa said to her father, 'William was saying that he's going to live at the Hall.'

William nodded. 'Yes, I'm going to sort of see how things go . . .'

Tom raised his eyebrows as he sat down, pointing William towards the sofa.

It was a deep sofa and William lowered himself into it like a novice in a cardinal's company, careful not to spill his drink.

'And of course I hope you'll stay here . . .' said William, facing Tom but still tugging at a cushion behind him.

Tom inclined his head but said nothing.

'On the same terms as before,' William blurted into the silence. Now Tom smiled. 'How kind.'

William blushed. 'And I was hoping,' he continued, 'that you would show me the ropes here a bit. As I was explaining to your wife and Teresa, I'm a bit g-green about the place.'

'Which place? It sounds uncomfortable,' said Teresa.

Tom ignored her. 'Naturally, we'll do whatever we can.'

Teresa was amazed by her father. 'Instead of helping William,' she said to me, 'he steered him slyly into a cul-de sac and then waited for him to deliver himself up. I have no idea whether William originally intended allowing us to stay on the same terms as we had with his grandfather but, once he had made the offer, he couldn't revoke it. I was embarrassed by Dad's gangster manner. Where did he learn it? Still, I have to say I was impressed by how quickly he resolved the important question.'

'Dad, you sound so solemn!' Teresa said.

'Well, it's a serious matter. I want William to believe that we will do what we can,' he replied, side-stepping her remark.

Marie reiterated her husband's readiness to help, whereupon

William mentioned the boiler and the electrics before embarking on a more general invitation to the Fairfaxes to go over to the Hall and help him get to know its peculiarities. Then – Teresa missed the connection – he was talking about his grandparents. He said that the Major was a wonderful singer: after leaving Oxford in 1921, he had travelled around busking with a couple of friends. They pushed their luggage and guitars in an old pram, he said. It all sounded very doubtful to Teresa but she didn't challenge him.

When eventually William stood up to leave, he asked the Fairfaxes to supper the following evening. There was a predictable protest by Teresa's parents as they assured him that they didn't want to impose. When he repeated his invitation they agreed that it would be a great pleasure, but Marie still offered to cook. He insisted that he would cook himself. 'After all, you always made supper for my grandfather,' he said.

Tom saw him out of the front door, then closed it firmly behind him. 'Well,' he said, returning to the drawing-room, 'what on earth is he going to do here?'


We were beyond the intersection with the M25 by now and the road was dark beyond the beams of my headlights and those of the cars we overtook. I love driving on motorways at night, watching the red pinpricks of tail lights gradually approach; for a moment you are suspended in the other car's feeble orbit and then you plunge on into the darkness alone. It is mesmerising. It makes me feel tiny, but free and purposeful.

'Hearing you describe your father's response to William's arrival makes me wonder what he was like about me,' I said. 'I remember going to see him when I was thinking of buying, and we had a proper talk after I completed, but I don't remember him playing any of the little games you describe.'

'Why would he? With you, the situation was totally different. He could not expect to influence you, still less intimidate you, which is arguably what he did with William. The situation was clear.'

'Not so clear at the outset. He could have been a very difficult sitting tenant. I could have had to pay him off. That was why I went to see him before I made an offer, to see which way the wind blew. As it was, we found our interests coincided. If I'd thought he was going to be trouble, either I wouldn't have bought the place or I would have done so expecting to write him a big cheque.'

'Well, there you go.'

'What I don't understand about William,' I said, 'is why he didn't just ask you to dinner in the first place. Why did he force himself through all those flaming hoops, then surrendering his head on a plate to your dad? How naïve can you be!'

'Yes, but to be fair – imagine a scene in which the new owner of the Hall saunters over, raps on our door and says, "Hi, I've just moved in next door and I'd like to invite you all to dinner tomorrow." You might do this, Jimmy, but I can't fit William into the leading role. It's too arrogant for him. He was terrified of appearing lordly, which could be irritating because he was inept at asking people to do things. In running his estate he tended to squander other people's time in desperate attempts to avoid confronting them directly with what he proposed. He clung to some puerile misconceptions about equality.'

It transpired that William was a very good cook, however, and in the following months he cooked for the Fairfaxes many times. He enjoyed the fuss of it, and he enjoyed pleasing people. In this respect he was more subtle than perhaps he realised, for both Marie and Elizabeth appreciated good food and it had apparently never occurred to either of them that a man might cook as well as a woman. They were enchanted by his culinary competence and they clapped in delight as if he were a performing poodle.

Teresa developed the habit of going to join William and her sister who, having no job, was often at the Hall during the day. Still in her work clothes, Teresa entered by the back door and went up the scullery steps in case they were in the kitchen. If she did not find them there she would clop down the stone-flagged passage to the hall and go into the airy dining-room. If the French windows were open she would see Elizabeth and William sprawled on a faded woollen rug, a bottle of white wine in a cooler beside them. She would kick off her shoes, still unfamiliar with the idea of being barefoot and loose-haired in Sweynsend's sequestered garden. Sometimes they would stroll to the far end to collect some vegetables for supper. More often they chatted on the lawn, enjoying the warm evenings of early summer. But her memory of that season does not include other friends: she had broken up with a boyfriend quite recently and was glad of the leisure provided by William at Sweynsend. She had a feeling too, like an apprehension of a change in the weather, that something was going to happen, for which she wanted to be ready.

One day Teresa asked William who his friend was at his grandfather's funeral.

'Lucas? He's a friend from school.'

'What was he doing at your grandfather's funeral?' Elizabeth asked.

'Why this interest in Lucas all of a sudden?'

'It wasn't me who asked, it was Teresa.'

William turned to Teresa. 'No reason. I just remembered seeing him there,' she said.

'You'll meet him soon enough, I should think. He always seems to make girls wobbly-kneed, I can't quite see why. He leads them a dance, and they let him. We used to play in a band together.'

'So what was he doing at the Major's funeral?' said Elizabeth.

'Not a great opportunity for pulling birds, I wouldn't have thought.'

William was drinking: he spluttered and coughed; wiped his mouth with the back of his hand, then Elizabeth reached out to take his glass from him and he said, 'He came home with me a couple of times, I mean to Yorkshire, and on the way we stopped off here for a night. He took a shine to my grandfather.'

'That doesn't exactly explain why he came to the funeral,' said Elizabeth, as if she were personally owed a more satisfactory explanation.

William cleared his throat. 'He's very . . . j-jumpy.' He cleared his throat again. 'He goes zooming in different directions. I was with him in London. I mentioned that my grandfather had just died and he asked if he could come to the funeral. I don't really know why. He's like that.'

Elizabeth filled up his glass and returned it to him. Her free hand came to rest on a magazine, which she began leafing through.

'Thanks,' said William. 'It's as if he does things just for the sake of seeing what they're like. Only you can't be sure because I think he did like my grandfather, and came to the funeral not as a voyeur but to pay his respects, so to speak.'

'Ginger and maple-syrup ice cream!' Elizabeth cried.

'How do you know him?' Teresa asked.

'Hey, what is this? Do you work for MI5, Teresa, like my grandfather? I told you, anyway: we were at school together. We played in a band.'

'Your grandfather worked for MI5?'

'Yes.'

'I never knew that!' Teresa said.

'So, what about your band?' said Elizabeth.

William blushed. 'What about it?'

'Were you the singer?'

'Lucas was the singer. I played guitar. And wrote songs.'

'How sweet,' Elizabeth cooed.

'I don't know about "sweet". But it was incredibly good fun. There's nothing quite like playing loud rock'n'roll.'

'I bet you were sweet,' Elizabeth repeated, and looked down again at her magazine. 'There's a recipe here for ginger-and-maple ice cream.'

'So your grandfather was in MI5,' said Teresa.

'Yes. Where do you think he got all his books? He spent twenty years meeting people in secondhand bookshops in places like Holt, or Newcastle-on-Tyne.'

At this moment Tom and Marie appeared beyond the low box hedge surrounding the octagonal terrace outside the drawing-room. Tom waved and stepped among the broken, overgrown tiles to pull out a few weeds.

'Dad,' Teresa called, 'did you know that the Major was a spy?'

Tom looked towards William. 'I don't think he was actually a spy himself,' he said.

'Well, in MI5 then,' Teresa said. 'Same difference.'

'I doubt it.'

Marie sat stiffly in an ancient wicker deckchair, as if she couldn't accustom herself to relaxing at the Hall.


William insisted that his grandmother had loathed little boys.

He and his brother Sam used to hide in the dense yew tree. They climbed up among the topmost branches, out of range of their grandmother's stream of orders: do this, get me that, tell so and so; I want. Among the bristling foliage, their lynx eyes watched the house and lawn. Their mother knew they went there, but Mrs Carew never discovered their sanctuary.

In that great house where there were so many bedrooms, the children slept in the night-nursery. It had ivory-coloured wall-paper with a pretty pattern of wild roses. It should have been a welcoming room but Teresa saw William shudder when she went in there with him one day. There were two little beds, still with their dank sheets and blankets although nobody had slept in them for years. In the deep, wedge-shaped recess where the fireplace is, stood a cot. The fire had not been lit for decades and there was no artificial replacement. The room was freezing and you could smell the damp. William approached the window and turned back the shutters to reveal a colony of putrid mould and mushrooms. 'The only good thing about sleeping here,' he said, 'was that my mother spent longer saying goodnight.' The stained wallpaper was hanging loose in one or two places, as in so many other rooms in the house, and a rash of abscess-like bulges fanned across the ceiling from one degenerate corner.

When Teresa was about six, the Carews put in a new kitchen. It was paid for by the sale of a tiny Rembrandt etching which had been overlooked for sale previously because it hung forgotten behind a door that always stood open. Mrs Carew was an extremely good cook, 'or that's what everyone says,' William told Teresa, and she agreed that her family also believed this to be true. The cupboards and drawers were made of thickly varnished pine with clumpy mouldings. The sinks were dark brown and the floor was a nasty oatmeal-coloured vinyl. Perhaps the ugly assembly was fashionable when it was installed, though I doubt it. It was the only room to have been decorated within the last century, but it looked more tatty and rancid, more dated, than all the other rooms. In fact it had been redecorated twice, because the kitchen had been moved from the old kitchen in the twenties. But thanks to the Aga it was the only warm room in the house, except for the adjacent gun-room.

We have turned things round again now, removing the wall that separated the gun-room from the kitchen and replacing it with a wide arch, so that the two rooms are knocked together but the integrity of each is preserved – at least that's the idea.

Back then, the gun-room's focus was a round table surrounded by rush-seated chairs. A small collection of Coronation china was displayed on fretworked shelves between the two windows. The oldest piece was a jug commemorating Queen Victoria's accession, the most recent a mug celebrating the Prince of Wales's marriage. Despite its name, the gun-room was no longer home to any guns: it had been used as a dining-room since the kitchen was moved up beside it, the third one in the house but the most convenient. William found a nest of leatherbound volumes in the cupboard beneath the old gun cabinet. They were church accounts from the seventeenth century.

The room also housed the large safe, whose contents William and Elizabeth were inspecting when Teresa joined them on the day that Mrs Carew's cooking cropped up in their conversation. The heavy doors were open wide and a number of impractical silver utensils were sitting on the table, including a Georgian teapot and three pairs of sugar-tongs.

'But when I think of her cooking,' said William, 'I just remember her couscous.'

'Her what?'

'Couscous.'

Apparently when he was six, William had stayed at Sweynsend with his brother for a whole week, homesick and frightened, while his parents were on holiday. Mrs Carew could be presumed to manage food reliably for the children, but she decided one day to produce couscous. 'I had never had it before and it was full of spices. I hated it,' said William. 'It was typical of her to intimidate us with unfamiliar things. But you ate what she told you to eat. You j-just did. So I sat there crying over my couscous and when I had finished she said, "There now, you liked that after all, didn't you?" and she stared and you just had to say yes, because otherwise it would have been criticising her, and so she said, "W-well then. Have some more," knowing that

73

I loathed it, twisting the knife because I didn't have the courage to stand up to her, aged six. And of course I had to eat it all up too.'

'Oh, you poor thing!' cried Elizabeth. 'It makes me want to cry just thinking about it! Oh shit!' She was holding a silver sugar dredger and tipped it without thinking so that a sparse white cascade fell to the floor.

'What about your brother?' Teresa asked as Elizabeth laid aside the dredger and left the room.

'That's what made it so awful. He liked it! And then my grandmother used that to make mischief!'

Elizabeth returned and began sweeping the sugar into a dustpan.

'"Isn't William being silly!"' William continued. '"You'd expect a boy of nearly seven to be more grown-up, wouldn't you?" Of course, Sam – who is younger – says yes, because you don't say no to her, and then she says, "William, Sam thinks you're a little boy, he's not going to have anything to do with you this afternoon. Isn't that right, Sam?" Sam looks hopelessly at me. "What?" she says, "I can't hear you." "Yes," he says.'

Elizabeth thrust the dustpan onto the table beside the dredger. The trickle of sugar, now mixed with dust, was dashed to the floor again: she didn't appear to notice. She sank into a chair as if William's anguish at the memory of his grandmother's intimidation was too much for her sensitive person to contemplate standing up. 'What about your grandfather?' she asked.

'Oh, he j-just sat there and said nothing.'

As the girls got to know William better, more emerged about his grandparents. In the glare of his memories, their characters appeared very different from those the girls had known. Especially Mrs Carew, who still dominated William's view of the Major although he had outlived her by eight years. Elizabeth spent more time with him and consequently heard more of these tales, which sometimes she would relate to her family. Teresa wondered if all the stories were true, or if William was dramatising for entertainment's sake.

Old Mr Joy, who did the kitchen garden during the fifties and sixties, had had to stop when his sciatica became too bad. He lived in a labourer's cottage down near the osier beds where Mrs Carew would visit him with gifts of fruit or vegetables every few days. According to Elizabeth, she remarked once that his kitchen chairs were very nice. Mr Joy said thankyou, they were just ordinary farmhouse chairs. Yes, said Mrs Carew, they were quite ordinary, a bit the worse for wear and tear, but still quite nice. 'I'll give you five pounds each for them.' Mr Joy replied that he wasn't thinking of selling, but Mrs Carew told him, 'Think, you could get some new ones and have a little left over.' Why, he'd be doing himself a favour. So the deal was done, because you didn't say no to Mrs Carew, and two weeks later Mrs Carew sold them all to Hal for forty pounds each. When he discovered the chairs' provenance he was furious, but his mother remained unabashed. He offered them back to Mr Joy with apologies for his mother, but Mr Joy didn't want them now because he was disgusted and anyway he had bought new chairs. So instead Hal asked him if he too would accept forty pounds each for them, and he did. Meanwhile Mrs Carew kept her money and congratulated herself on having made a fool of both Mr Joy and her son.

'She was a monster!' Elizabeth concluded.

Her family were listening to her tale at the end of supper one day, remnants of apples and cheese on the table before them. It was just the four of them at home for a change: William had been in London for a couple of days and was due back that evening.

'Is that William's opinion, or yours?' said Tom, who had listened to his daughter impassively.

Elizabeth paid no attention. 'Did you know that she was a drug addict too?' she continued, confident that everyone was enjoying the story as much as herself.

'It isn't very edifying to hear you say all these things about Mrs Carew, after all she did for us,' said Tom. 'She wasn't the stablest of people, but for any of us to dwell on her cruelties without mentioning her kindness is a betrayal. It's false, and you know it. She was very fond of Mr Joy, in her own way.'

'Don't you understand that she was in pain, Elizabeth?' said Marie. 'You are cruel yourself! All those years she was taking morphine, she was in pain! She was a sick woman. It is not surprising she sometimes did strange things. Why does William tell you all this, anyway?'

'And what does he do, by the way,' said Tom, 'when he's not telling you how awful his grandparents were?'

'He writes.'

'Writes? And is that going to put the place back together?'

'Oh, for God's sake!' cried Elizabeth, and strutted from the room in righteous fury.

The front door was heard to close.


A few days previously, Teresa had gone as usual to join her sister and William after work. Entering by the front door, she saw that one of the study windows was wide open. Elizabeth was sitting on the broad sill with her back against the frame, one leg braced by the ball of her left foot against the opposite side of the frame as she listened. She heard William say, 'It's all good material.'

'What for?' said Elizabeth.

'Writing poetry. You have to be on the *qui vive* all the time, then act fast when inspiration strikes!'

'You write poetry?' said Elizabeth with a reverence that seemed ridiculous to Teresa, who was sure that her sister didn't know what William meant by 'on the *qui vive*' anyway. While the picture he gave of himself as a bard grabbing a pen to record his spontaneous eruption of poetry might encourage himself, it also seemed intended to impress Elizabeth. The remark seemed so silly. She wanted to call out that anyone could write poetry.

The study is a narrow room lined with bookshelves. Its two windows are set in the wide façade of the house and there is a correspondingly generous fireplace, above which hung a foxed Hogarth print in a cheap black frame. A scroll-top desk stood near the door. Between the fireplace and the window was a small sofa, and the other end was cluttered with boxes and old wooden filing cabinets. It must have been years since the room was properly cleaned because the Major always said it wasn't necessary. No one had been in it except for him, he said, so it wouldn't need cleaning. Marie used to flick a duster round, or run the Hoover across the floor when he wasn't looking, but a layer of dust had accumulated and cobwebs trailed from the top shelves. On a sunny evening, however, with the window wide open, it was still a pretty room. Its peacefulness and the sense it had of being a private domain reminded Teresa of the Major.

William was standing in front of the dusty fireplace with a drink in one hand, as if he were about to deliver a speech to Elizabeth. Her right leg swung free inside the room, making an arc of her long pink cotton skirt. Balanced on her raised left knee, in the cleft of two fingers, a half-empty wine glass winked against the sunlight.

'Teresa!' said William, seeing her first, 'Have some *cassis*!' As he turned towards her, his drink slopped a little over the edge of his glass. He switched it to his other hand and licked his fingers. 'We've been going through papers,' he said.

He left the room, and Elizabeth shifted round so that she was sitting upright on the window seat. She smiled at Teresa without quite meeting her eyes. 'It's really extraordinary, the stuff in here,' she said.

Bundles of curl-edged letters bound with string peeped from a broken cardboard box on the sofa. Other boxes at the far end of the room had obviously been plundered. On the floor near Elizabeth's feet was a pile of fragile folio books which she must have removed from the window seat in order to sit there.

'Oh!' Elizabeth sighed. 'We've been finding all sorts of things. Poor William! It's so hard for him to know where to begin.'

'Begin what?'

'You know – sorting.'

'I thought that was what the Major spent all his time doing,' said Teresa, for during his last years he had given the impression that he was ordering everything conscientiously for the motley aggregate of family interest that he called posterity.

'Oh, there are ribbons round some of the bundles, and labels, but then what?'

William returned with Teresa's drink. She thanked him and asked what they had found.

'There's a stash of old school reports, my father's and so on. Gardening diaries, that sort of thing. But also,' he said, with triumph in his eyes, 'there's the notifications from the War Office of his brothers' deaths during the First War.'

'Well, I suppose they had to be somewhere,' Teresa answered.

'Teresa, you're so cold!' Elizabeth cried, setting down her glass. 'I mean, it's amazing! Look!'

I was startled when Teresa reported that her sister had described her as cold. But it makes sense, on reflection, and points up a striking difference between the two of them. Teresa does not mind people showing no emotion, indeed she often appreciates it. A case in point, I think, would be my relatively businesslike and practical approach to Sweynsend. But she does not confuse lack of emotional display with lack of emotional capacity and is repelled by false displays of emotion. They make her freeze up. Since Elizabeth is prone to gush, as it were to piggyback on other people's emotions, it is not surprising that Teresa should strike her sometimes as cold. Dimly perceiving a lack of emotional depth in herself and suspecting that this amounts to a social failing, Elizabeth compensates by making excessive, indiscriminate use of the language and gestures of emotion; while Teresa, aware of emotional depths in herself and therefore respectful of them, even afraid, is careful in her emotional expression and unnerved by those who are not.

In a tumble of ankles and skirt, Elizabeth slid from her seat and crossed to the sofa, where she crouched over a little rosewood box. When she opened the lid, only a tray with pencils was visible. Picking one out, she pressed its end to a tiny button at the back, which released a catch so that the tray could be lifted out. Beneath was a little cache of papers. She plucked out the top two and presented them to Teresa before resuming her seat to await a suitable response. She crossed her legs, smoothing her skirt over her knees daintily, as if it were a crinoline instead of cheap Indian cotton.

The discoloured papers were edged in black, weighty with duty. Teresa cast her eye over the top one: 'War Office . . . Lieutenant Carew . . . Forward position . . . Courage in the face of the enemy . . . fell . . .' But she was prevented from reading either of them properly because William was already spouting about their importance to him. These were authentic War Office notices, he said. As such, they were remarkable documents, but never mind that, they explained so much about his family: here was the root of the decline, the first explosion . . . It was incredible to find these, he repeated, incredible. He seemed to overlook that millions of such letters were written and that most, like these, would have been preserved.

'You see?' said Elizabeth with condescension.

It was not that Teresa did not find the documents interesting, but she was irritated by the sense that a particular response was expected of her only to suit their mood. 'What else have you found?' she asked.

'A letter from Robert Graves!' said William.

With a flourish, he produced a modern brown envelope from a folder that he pulled from behind the stack of boxes. 'Letter from Robert Graves', it said on the outside, in the Major's spindly handwriting. Before Teresa had a chance to look inside, William snatched his trophy back and said, 'There's another one from Edward Bawden. My grandfather had asked him to illustrate an alphabet he wrote. And look at this!' he continued, before she had a chance to ask who Edward Bawden was, or whether he ever did the illustrations. 'Look at this!'

He leaned across the boxes and flipped open a panel in the corner, revealing a series of unexpected hidey-holes. Teresa was surprised: only four inches wide, the door was a continuous piece of wood bisecting the junction between the four upper shelves; it looked like a fixed panel. 'Look at the labels,' he said, pointing to the faded script on each little shelf inside. 'Hackney. Sweynsend. Shottisley. And at the top, Jamaica!'

Teresa had no more idea why Shottisley, the neighbouring village, was on this label than she understood what Hackney or Jamaica had to do with the Carews. Knowing this, Elizabeth explained with alacrity: 'The Shottisley estate was sold off after the First World War and the Hackney estate sometime in the last century. William doesn't know what "Jamaica" means but he says it must mean that they owned a plantation once.'

'Sugar and slaves. Good Christian men, my forebears,' said William, stuffing his free hand into his trouser pocket.

'What's on the shelves?' Teresa asked.

'Oh, nothing. Rubbish. A bottle of glue, circa 1937, a few rotten elastic bands. But the labels are still there! It's incredible!'

Teresa did not think the Major was the sort of person who changed labels. The plain truth was that he didn't use the cupboard at all. His father and grandfather were probably the same. Why should they be surprised at the lack of change?

'If there's nothing there,' she said, 'how can you be sure about the plantation in Jamaica?'

'Well, obviously!' said Elizabeth, her voice lifting in exasperation. 'If "Shottisley" and "Hackney" both refer to estates that were sold off, then so must "Jamaica".' She touched one corner of her mouth with her little finger, as if she felt a speck of spittle there.

'I suppose it might,' Teresa conceded, 'but then again it might not.'

'But it must do!' cried William. 'And I had no idea! Just imagine, my ancestors were slave-owners! It's perfectly frightful!'

Teresa had no opinion about the Carew ancestors, but she found that she minded hearing the Major, whom she respected and even loved in her own way, being the object of insinuations that he would surely have regarded as ridiculous. It distressed her that his own grandson should trivialise him so wantonly. 'Maybe that's what they thought too – which is why they sold off the estate,' she said.

Her suggestion silenced them, as if the happy hours they had spent inflaming each other with fantasies of Carew slave-owners preaching good will towards men were now puffed away; as if, while protesting their disgust, they relished a voyeuristic *frisson* of obscenity.

After a pause, William relented. 'I suppose it's possible.'

'Well, you've certainly found a lot of stuff,' Teresa said, attempting to sound more enthusiastic, though she wasn't sure that the word 'found' was justified, since nothing was hidden.

'But the problem is, what to do with it all?' said William.

'Put it in a cupboard,' Teresa said brightly.

William placed his glass on the mantelpiece. Opening out his hands, he said, like a priest to an oafish recusant, 'You're determined not to see the point. There's masses, Teresa.'

'Well then, two cupboards. You're not short of space.'

He threw up his hands.

'Jesus, Teresa!' said Elizabeth, standing up suddenly. 'You won't take it seriously, will you? You think it's so simple, but you don't understand. I mean, where do you start?'

Teresa shrugged.

'Shit!' Elizabeth cried, and walked out of the room.

Teresa turned to William. 'Was it something I said?'

'Don't worry. I just think you underestimate it, that's all.'

'What's that to Elizabeth?'

'Maybe she thinks you're patronising her.'

'Well what's it got to do with her?'


Although Teresa had seen Elizabeth quit the room in a rage before, she was no less dismayed to see her do so again. But on the second occasion, that evening when Elizabeth broke the news of William's poetry to her parents, Teresa wondered if she hadn't been wrong to point out to William that his family's papers were none of Elizabeth's business. Her interest in William's inheritance was conspicuous and without embarrassment.

When Tom asked what William did all day, he voiced a misgiving of Teresa's. Despite William's parade of good intentions when he came to live at Sweynsend, three months had passed and he had done nothing – or nothing that anybody could see, apart from mowing the lawns. No builder had been mentioned, no surveyor or land agent, no architect . . . Yet the Fairfaxes were wary of pronouncing him negligent because they had no knowledge of his financial resources. They supposed that his father was rich because William apparently had sufficient private income to make conventional work unnecessary, but they did not know if he had capital available for putting his intentions into practice. It was a delicate subject, and in the end it was no business of theirs how he chose to spend his money or his time.

Repeatedly, however, when she went across to the Hall, Teresa found the two of them scavenging through drawers and cupboards or mooching around in a room, and she couldn't understand what was going on. They looked for all the world like a pair of genteel thieves in search of valuables. It even occurred to her that William was searching through the house for objects to sell so that he could raise money for the place.

One day, following the sound of voices upstairs, she found them in the little dressing room beyond the bedroom. They had just investigated the boxes of papers in the adjacent attic. William was fussing over them like an old man marooned in the present and nervous of mortality; not for any (vain) hope of their monetary value but for their historical links with himself. His thrill at finding his grandfather's uncle Robert's death mask was macabre. In the same box was a pair of hunting whips with malacca handles, which he hung on the hooks in the hall that used to be occupied by the Major's pistols. And when Teresa heard him tell Elizabeth that all this junk was good material for his poetry, she realised that his fascination with his family's influence conferred, in his own eyes, some vague authenticity on himself as a poet. The poetry itself was a detail: it was the image of a poet that so enchanted him, a mind romantically in thrall to its heritage. And, deliberately or not – Teresa did not know – he was inveigling Elizabeth with this image.

It is hard to believe that Elizabeth and Teresa ever shared more than the circumstantial closeness of having grown up together without other siblings, but Teresa insists that they were once each other's greatest friend and confidante. Their lives are so different now and they appear to have so little in common that it requires an imaginative stretch to account for an earlier, more substantial relationship. Perhaps it was innocence that preserved each of them in the eyes of the other. Not just summer-frock-and-skipping-rope-innocence, although no doubt that had once been there too. By this stage, after all, Teresa was twenty-four and Elizabeth was twenty-two, they had both been to university and they certainly didn't think of themselves as innocents. Hadn't they both lost their virginity long ago? Not that this presaged an enduring affair for either of them. In Teresa's case, she tells me it was 'merely the first in a sequence of miserable encounters with an arrogant shit whom I failed to despise soon enough'. When she did despise him, she despised herself too for having succumbed, but this did not alter the sense she now had of being a person with experience. And hadn't they both smoked hash and drunk too much cheap wine as students? They thought their eyes were open to the world, they thought they could jostle their way in life quite skilfully.

In spite of living in the shadow of the Carews, they had never encountered real trouble. I said earlier that their lives were sheltered, as if they were protected from accident. It is true that they weren't exposed to trouble, but that in itself was accidental. Nothing challenged their image of themselves or of each other, and so they were close. William used to describe young girls as 'fillies', which infuriated Teresa because it was so condescending. But it occurs to me that she was also disconcerted by the word's metaphorical accuracy: for they *were* blithe fillies in green pastures thinking that because they proceeded without mishap they were adepts. They had never met the storms or swamps or bandits or parasites without which no traveller can call himself experienced.

Teresa was finding that she did not know her sister as well as she had thought. She knew that Elizabeth hadn't got a clue about poetry, and she knew that Elizabeth knew this too, which made it all the more puzzling that she should now voice opinions about it. Ordinarily she would have had little patience with a man of

William's pretensions, let alone his physical plainness. She tended towards routinely handsome, straightforward men, preferably sportsmen. But the situation was no longer ordinary. Perhaps William was the first complicated man she had met, the first man in whom unusual behaviour and tastes appeared not, in fact, as pretension, but as integral to his personality. In part, this may have been possible because he had the means and setting in which to make real – or indulge – aspects of himself which in another person would forever remain latent. Thus she was able to see moods and enthusiasms run their course in him and recur; and, in the romantic view of himself that he encouraged, she came to see not confused poses but consistent character.

One beautiful, soft evening in July they decided to walk across the fields to the woods, which were known as the Covers because they were planted for rearing pheasants. The grass was sweet-scented and warm; the leaves were poised in the still air as if about to take wing from the gnarled and swooping boughs of the ash tree. Leaving the front door wide open, they walked to the small gate at the far end of the ha-ha and entered the paddock. Three sheep scrambled from the lee of the ancient tree's blasted trunk and bustled off like indignant aunts.

'Scram!' said William, waving a silver-tipped cane of his grandfather's at them. He had just come back from Tullworth on his new motorbike, of which he was very proud, and he was still wearing his leathers. He cut a preposterous figure to Teresa as he creaked, bow-legged, across the field, padded and ribbed like the Michelin man.

They walked round the low-hanging branches of a copper beech and William jabbed at a molehill. Then they came to the first gate, whose rotting wood was braced by the brambles growing over it. William climbed over first, saying that he would check to see if it was safe. As he dropped to the other side, his stick nearly tripped him, but he disguised it with a little hop. Then he turned and held out his hand for Elizabeth, forgetting that the Fairfax girls had been used to these gates all their lives. To Teresa's surprise, instead of ignoring William, Elizabeth squealed when the gate quivered under her weight, tottered feebly, and then extended her hand in a parody of femininity as she gratefully accepted his support.

'Oh!' she gasped, as her feet touched the ground.

When she was out of the way, Teresa climbed over before William had a chance to force the same display on her. They waited while a couple of lorries hurtled along the straight road as if ripping a chasm in the earth's crust. Then they scuttled across between two approaching cars to the opposite verge.

'Awful road,' said William.

Teresa said that it was better than having the lorries through the village.

'Still.'

'I think it's horrid,' said Elizabeth.

Paying no attention to her sister, Teresa asked, 'Aren't you pretty well screened from it, though?' And she indicated the high bank covered with shrubs, and the beautiful cut-and-laid hedge which ran all along this stretch of road.

'I suppose so. My grandfather made himself a pain in the arse over it. They thought he was being obstreperous. Now he just looks ahead of his time.'

'I'm sure he was being obstreperous too,' Teresa said.

The next gate was even more rickety. About two feet beyond was a barbed-wire fence: the gate was redundant since it only gave on to a dangerous road, and it had simply been fenced off by the farmer who rented the land. Again, William got over first and then Elizabeth followed with the same peculiar flutter. Now William was in a quandary, for there wasn't enough room for Teresa to come over the gate too until one of them was the other side of the fence. She urged him not to wait for her and he duly started to manoeuvre himself through the fence. It wasn't a difficult fence – there were only two slack strands of wire – but he was very concerned not to scratch his gleaming leather carapace. When at last he had steered himself through, Teresa climbed over the gate herself. Then she put one foot on the lower strand of wire and lifted the upper one so that Elizabeth could get through easily; William did the same, so there was a gaping hole for her to pass through. Nevertheless, Elizabeth scratched the back of her hand, and she yelped. She stayed crouched between the wires, transfixed by the dash of blood.

'Good –' William gulped. 'Good heavens! Are you all right?'

'Course she is,' Teresa said. 'Come on.' And she shook the wires to remind her sister that she wanted to go through herself.

'But I've cut myself!' Elizabeth cried.

'Is it bad? Should you go back?' said William.

Elizabeth continued to stare at her hand.

'It's only a tiny little scratch,' Teresa said. She knew that Elizabeth was fascinated by any symptoms of illness in herself, but it seemed the height of silliness for William to encourage the fuss.

'There's blood, Teresa, I scratched it on the rusty wire! Help me!'

Teresa laughed; William glared at her. 'We must go back,' he said to Elizabeth, 'so that you can clean it.'

She gave him a pained look and said he was very kind, 'which is more than I can say for some people around here.' She allowed him to help her over the gate as if her arm was broken, then she leaned on him as they crossed the road and clambered over the opposite gate.

Teresa watched them go. She wondered whether William's anxiety was genuine or whether he was trying to impress Elizabeth with his display of concern. She seemed to draw him in, handing over responsibility, believing that his pleasing response was a proof of care. Teresa thought he just looked confused.

She had the feeling that her younger sister was drifting somewhere she herself had never been. As if watching a ship leave harbour, she was seized by the vicarious thrill of Elizabeth's imminent adventure, while being acutely aware too that she was being left behind.

Not that falling in love enabled Elizabeth to understand her own behaviour any better. There are those – among whom I count myself – who feel a deep sense of self-recognition when they are in love, as if the in-love self is more intimately oneself than the not-in-love self. Of course it is a perilous trait, for who is to say that one wouldn't imagine oneself to be in love in order to induce this gratifying condition? But I suspect that Elizabeth, when in love, was troublingly unfamiliar to herself. William, however, was in control, or so she thought: he was eight years older and in important respects, it's true to say, he seemed to be in control. He asked her to marry him. The new young master of Sweynsend Hall asked for the hand of Elizabeth Fairfax – imagine! A dream come true! And why ever not? They said they were in love.

# Chapter Seven

THERE HAS BEEN an unsettling development. While I have been going about my business, back and forth to London as usual, pausing every now and then with my laptop to imagine a little more of the situation at Sweynsend preceding Lucas's appearance – while I've been doing this, I have been outflanked. Circumstances have made a damn fool of me.

It appears that Lucas was here one afternoon last week.

What am I to make of that?

Teresa told me herself as we were getting ready to go out to dinner with some people who live near Market Harborough. 'You'll never guess who was here today,' she said, as she fixed up her hair with two tortoiseshell combs.

I said I could not.

'Lucas.'

'Lucas?'

I knew she had a thing for him long ago because she'd told me all about that now. But they hardly behaved like long-lost buddies when he came to visit a few weeks back.

'What did he want?' I asked.

'I don't know. He'd just got off a plane at Luton and took a taxi here.'

'Why?'

The answer she didn't give was, *To see me*. Instead, she shrugged. 'He's like that, I suppose.'

'Is he?'

I'm glad she told me. I don't think there is any rekindling of her feeling for him, but how would I know if there were? Would she tell me like that, pat, while putting in her earrings? I can't help feeling uneasy. What would I feel if Iris suddenly showed up? I can't imagine talking about her with Teresa.

'Oh, Jimmy,' she said as she stood up, 'You look worried. It's all right!' She put her hands on my shoulders and kissed me on the lips – fondly. 'Now I shall put on some lipstick,' she said, and sat down again. 'What did you think? That I would tear his clothes off on the lawn and force him to make love to me?'

I was not thinking of that. I was thinking of Iris – with her long blond hair and her eyes of blue. But it is understandable that Teresa should presume I was (she is sweetly thoughtful), since the last time Lucas had been mentioned between us was when she told me how in love with him she had been. Note the tense, Jimmy. Why be suspicious?

We were in bed when she told me about Lucas. Pillow talk. And she began, 'Jimmy, how much do you know about girls in love?'

I was on my back and she was looking into my eyes, propped on one elbow. 'I know you,' I said.

She kissed me. 'Yes. That's true. And I do love you, very much. But it's a different kind of love. More spacious. Less greedy.'

'A love that isn't love, then?'

'Don't put words into my mouth. No.'

'I know what you mean.'

Teresa's dark eyes registered a possible meaning to my remark, but she was intent on what she was going to say. 'It ought to be a relief to you. What I mean is a sort of mania that would be exhausting to live with. I would not wish it on you.' She rolled onto her back. 'Have you ever encountered unmanaged obsession in a girl? For your sake, I hope not.'

I wondered if she thought 'unmanaged obsession' was any easier in men.

It began, she said, two days after the engagement was announced; when, after all the lavish expressions of pleasure, they had gathered to think about the wedding itself. Teresa had joined William and Elizabeth and her parents in the passage-room, as if it provided a desirable formality which the evening sunshine on the lawn could not. William's parents were in Hong Kong but they had been spoken with, and they sounded pleased. Tom and Marie were careful to avoid any suggestion that Elizabeth's marriage would give them any claim over Sweynsend, but it was understood that the link would in some way legitimise and justify their love for the place.

'But we must get married in this church. It's William's family's,' said Elizabeth.

Teresa refrained from pointing out that the Carews' domains did not actually include the church, however they might behave as if they did.

'It's up to you, but it does seem a bit funny when you're a Catholic,' said Tom.

Elizabeth was sitting well back in the Major's chair to the left of the fireplace, her soft yellow hair loosely pinned with a black plastic slide that shone like a diadem on top of her head. Her legs kept crossing and uncrossing beneath her long cotton skirt, as if she were about to lean forward and then decided not to. The furtive thrill of imminent possession pervaded her manner. Although nervous, she was enjoying herself. Tom sat where he had always sat, on a low, armless chair with a curved back and worn green velvet upholstery from which several buttons had worked loose. He was somewhat removed from the others, beyond the low table where the Major used to lay his pipe and the *Spectator*. Teresa was sprawled on the *chaise longue* by one of the windows, and Marie sat to the right of the fireplace, in front of the other window. William hovered near Elizabeth, awkward about touching her in front of her parents while being aware that it would seem odd if he didn't. From time to time Elizabeth took his hand, demurely tucking hers into his and then holding decorously still as if they were about to be photographed. Or she touched his leg with her fingertips, suddenly exposing herself to her sister as a lover. Having always been blind to their relationship, Teresa found when she looked back over the last few weeks that they were spiked with little deceptions.

'I don't want to force you, Lizzy, I mean it's up to you,' said William.

Teresa disliked the way he had taken to calling Elizabeth Lizzy. He said it was after Lizzy Bennett, as if he might be Darcy.

The high mantelpiece behind his shoulders was still arrayed with pale photographs in sooty, cracked frames from the Major and Mrs Carew's day. Small children in V-necked sweaters and walking shoes. Forced into the edge of the gilt-framed mirror were warped postcards from long-dead friends. Its surface was covered with half a century of nicotine and grime, but the back of William's head was still obscurely reflected as he shifted from one foot to the other. The discussion seemed pointless to Teresa. She knew that their own Catholic church meant little to Elizabeth beside her desire to be married in the Sweynsend church. Elizabeth was going to be the squire's wife, and she was taking to the role as if she had been waiting all her life to be enfolded in this drama. There was the sense too that William's family would value her concession. She wished her performance to be seen as irreproachable.

But it also mattered to her parents that she be married as a Catholic.

'Can't you get married in both?' Teresa said, and yawned.

'Teresa, that is not helpful,' said Marie.

'If one of them is a blessing though . . .' said William.

The telephone rang. William crossed the room to the table beside Teresa, on which Mrs Carew's needlework box still stood. With his back to the room he picked up the receiver. 'Hello? . . . Lucas! . . . Yes . . . Yes, it's quite true. To the . . . Yes, to the girl-next-door. Elizabeth . . . Actually, it's not a good moment now, no . . . But you must come and meet her . . . When can you come? . . . The weekend after next? Good . . . Come on Friday evening, in time for supper . . . Brilliant! . . . Yes, see you when we see you then . . . I look forward . . . Bye.'

William replaced the receiver. 'That was Lucas,' he said slyly to Teresa, 'who you were so keen to meet. He's coming in a couple of weeks.'

Teresa did not answer.

'Look! She's blushing!'

I was lying in bed with Teresa. 'While he was speaking to Lucas,' she said, 'I felt a rush of blood, like vertigo, as if I were walking along a path in the dark and suddenly a shaft of moon-light showed that I was on the edge of a cliff. I had a vivid intu-ition, based on nothing but that glimpse of him at the Major's funeral and the way in which William spoke to him, of Lucas pushing ahead – the opposite of William's anxious circling round everything. Something in me was taken possession of by the *idea* of Lucas, a fantasy but – I wanted him to be here amongst us, shaking us up – there it was. And I knew it was all so transparent!'

Teresa's vehemence hung there, with a presence of its own, like a guest in the house; not necessarily troublesome, but needing to be circled, and weighed, and accommodated within the usual terms of our exchanges.

'Did you know that his real name is John?' I asked.

'John?' I felt her head turn sharply on her pillow. 'You're mak-ing that up, Jimmy.'

'I'm not. What do you think his surname is?'

'I can never remember. Something unpronounceable and Polish.'

'It is Lukasiewicz.'

I first met Lucas in the lounge of a Moscow hotel, when he immediately wrong-footed me. I was perhaps thrown by the directness of his look as he stepped up to greet me. 'Jimmy Hood?' He was shorter than the average, but there was none of the deference you usually get with people pitching for work, the slightly rounded shoulders and the strained confidence. He looked as if he had known all along that it would be me. He smiled and sat down opposite without turning, black hair swept back by a casual hand after getting out of bed; humorous eyes and a sense of energy even when still, as he now was. He waited until I had taken him in, his good looks and his ability to enter a space with presence. 'Lucas Lukasie —' I began, and he rescued me: 'Lukasiewicz.' I replied, 'That's a lot of Lucas,' and he laughed. 'My real name is John, in fact, but people have always called me Lucas. I don't bother with the 'John' except on my passport and other KGB forms.' This might have been performance, a speech he made in all situations like the present one, but then he added an afterthought — as if it had only just struck him (though it cannot have done so); it seemed to be for my benefit, an unrehearsed disclosure prompted, I suppose, by some receptivity he detected in me — 'Like the logician.'

'Excuse me?'

'There was a Polish logician called Lukasiewicz.'

'I'm afraid I don't know him.'

'He persisted, in the teeth of all evidence, in believing in the freedom of the will.'

Of course, this made me think of Iris. Still, at that point, in the grip of hopeless love for her, I often wondered what was going on, psychologically I mean. I did not want to be captive in this way, or so I thought. I wanted to be free. That was why I moved away from the US, and hadn't I exerted my will by doing so? I regularly remind myself of this: that I tried hard, honourably as I thought, to get away from thoughts of her: I moved country, moved life, moved on. I pulled myself out by the hair. Yet still I thought of her all the time. Nothing she did was holding me, it all seemed to come from myself, as if it were somehow necessary for me to stay in love with her precisely because it was hopeless, a condition from which there was no escape.

Now here was some guy sitting in front of me talking about the freedom of the will. Whichever way I looked at it, I was caught. If I didn't ask him to do the research I needed, wasn't I turning away the prospect of escape, wilfully locking myself in tighter, so to speak? And if I did, wasn't that succumbing to a childish notion of fate? Not a good basis for hiring someone, you might say, but it is on such whims that the best connections are made, and – professionally speaking – it certainly turned out to be a good one. The man was not formally qualified, after all, but at that time, in that place, nobody was. You either had it – the language, the skills, the experience, the connections – or you didn't. And Lucas did. He had been busy in the nine years since he was last seen at Sweynsend.

Teresa said it was strange to think of him as John. She did not believe she had ever heard him referred to as such, although William must have known it.

'Oh shut up, William!' she had answered then. 'Of course I blush when you make faces and stupid innuendoes . . . Honestly!'

She leaned back against the cushions on the *chaise longue* as the others resumed their discussion, staring at the murky ceiling, wondering if it had once been white. It was quite possible that the mottled yellow-brown (it matched the panelling on the walls) was a coat of filth from years of the belching fireplace and the Major's pipe. It struck her how strange it was that they all took it for granted that Elizabeth would be married from the Hall. William had never spent more than an evening or two with them at the Manor: it was always Elizabeth and her family who came to him. Nobody, least of all Elizabeth, questioned this. It occurred to Teresa that this discussion ought to take place at the bride's home, the home from which he was taking her. Although her family knew the Hall very well, wasn't their behaviour a cheeky pre-emption of fate? She thought that if she were in Elizabeth's situation she would not like discussing her wedding with her fiancé and family in her fiancé's house unless his family were there too. For as long as it was just her own family, she would expect him to come to her house, to her ground. Crossing the fields with a pack on his back; braving bears in the woods if necessary . . . She wanted him to come to her.

With nothing to contribute to the talk, Teresa was suddenly aware of feeling cast down by the residue of smoke and stuffiness that had been allowed by habit and indifference to clog the room for so long.

'I'm going back,' she said, and swung her feet to the floor.

'There's nothing wrong?' said her mother.

'I want to do one or two things for tomorrow.'

Outside the front door Teresa breathed deeply, relieved by the stillness and the warm fresh air. Although it was evening, the scents of a hot summer's day in a rich garden still lingered. There was no work she had to do. She didn't know what she wanted.

With the thick, uncut grass groping at her ankles, she walked up the bank to the edge of the ha-ha and looked down. At the bottom lay decayed bricks which had come loose from the retaining wall. She wondered if they would ever be removed and the ha-ha repaired. Or would the bank on which she stood slip a little further each year into the ditch, until at last there was nothing to separate the front of the house from the sheep paddock? She was about to walk along to the left towards the garden but, realising that she would be visible from the passage-room, she turned right instead. She jumped, anticipating the softness of the earth when she landed. For a moment she stayed crouching, as the sheep collected themselves by the ash tree and turned to watch her. She stood up slowly, taking care not to alarm them again, and tried to approach. There was a bolder one at the front and she looked her in the eye, willing her to stay where she was so that she could touch her. The sheep backed off with a little hop, then stopped again when Teresa paused. The animal's head was almost black and she was smaller than the others. Teresa wanted to run her hand over the fleece and feel the ears twitch against the palm of her hand. A thistle was scratching at her ankle. When she moved forwards again, a ripple of unease passed through the little flock, then they decided not to trust her and they turned and ran, wobble-arsed, towards the hedge by the road.

Teresa walked past the collapsed pen where, years before, Mrs Carew kept chickens, to the little gate into the front yard. A piece of frayed orange string held it shut, which broke when she tried to undo it. The shabbiness of everything suddenly infuriated her. As she wrenched the gate back over the tufts of grass, she imagined Lucas coming to this rotten gate. She had a clear picture of him testing its strength with a single touch and, not wasting time trying to open it, taking to the air in a weightless vault. Retying the string she could almost feel him behind her, laughing at her struggle.

The news of Lucas's visit clarified the restlessness she had been feeling since the engagement. She was ashamed of herself, of her trapped selfishness, because she wanted to feel pure goodwill towards William and her sister. How had she been so blind? She had taken it for granted that Elizabeth would confide in her. Now she felt betrayed. Why had Elizabeth not told her? They must have misled her deliberately, hiding their feelings in her company; talking and laughing about not letting her know, congratulating each other on their secret. She thought of them romping about the house while she was at work and then, when she appeared, catching one another's eyes and giggling at her stupidity. Teresa believed Elizabeth to be prettier than herself, and knew her to be a flirt, but because Teresa was older she had always assumed that she would be the first to marry. Not that she wanted to get married now – she wasn't at all convinced that the institution was worthwhile anyway – but she was nevertheless outraged that Elizabeth was doing it first.

Teresa peered through the encrusted windows of the School House. When the opacity shifted she realised that a chicken was sitting on the windowsill, pressed up against the glass. She tapped: it rose in a bustle of feathers and flopped to the ground, where the rest of Jed's brood were pecking and squawking. Why had she disturbed the silly creatures? She had no wish to look inside, like a child. Instead, she walked round to the well-trodden track which led past the Kennels to the Manor. Was Elizabeth going to have babies then? She imagined her sister's raucous children running about their lawn, and suddenly she felt sick with envy. What did Elizabeth know about the place? She, Teresa, knew far more about it; of the two of them, it was always she who took more interest. And when they were comfortably settled, where would she be? Would she become a shrewish maiden aunt making vats of unwanted damson jam in the old kitchen, irritating them more and more as the decades passed with shrill pleas and unwanted suggestions?

She opened the Manor's front door. She would leave them to their solemn discussions about which church they were going to get married in. Elizabeth was too foolish to know the difference anyway, and so was William. Teresa knew this was unfair and was disgusted at herself for thinking it, but, like running downhill, she couldn't stop. She had allowed herself to think some bad things about Elizabeth; the momentum had gathered; and now they tumbled uninvited into her consciousness. Knowing that she must intercept herself and escape, she went to her room and inspected her books. An image came of herself as a teenager wallowing in a story about a lady falling in love with a pirate. For a couple of minutes she wondered if she had invented it, then she snatched out *Frenchman's Creek*. Turning it over, with creeping delight she saw from the blurb that the pirate possessed 'boundless passion' and 'a soul as unfettered as her own'.

She went to the bathroom, locked the door and turned on the taps. Even as she undressed she began to read: 'When the east wind blows up Helford river . . .'

# Chapter Eight

L<small>UCAS ARRIVED</small> earlier than expected. Elizabeth and Teresa were upstairs, making his bed, of all things, like vestal virgins. He just walked into the hall and shouted, not expecting anyone but William to be there, or not caring.

'William, you asshole, where are you? Who's been crucifying squirrels in the woods?'

The girls looked sidelong at one another, cautious – knowing who it must be, but unfamiliar with these antics.

'Jed's squirrels,' Teresa said.

Elizabeth hurried from the room. Her new shoes clattered on the wooden stairs like a cascade of jam jars from a sharply-opened cupboard.

Teresa heard him say, 'You must be Elizabeth. I'm Lucas.' A brisk voice, as if she, not he, were the interloper.

Resting her hand on the wide banister, Teresa waited at the top of the stairs.

'You made good time,' Elizabeth said. 'We didn't think you'd be here for ages.'

'Listen, who the fuck goes nailing squirrels to trees round here? It scared the shit out of me!'

'Ugh! I don't know. Maybe Teresa . . .'

'Who's Teresa?'

'My sister . . .'

'She nails squirrels to trees?'

'No, no! But she may know something about it, she's . . .'

Confused, Elizabeth turned towards Teresa, who was coming down the stairs. 'This is Teresa,' she said.

'You don't look like a squirrel-killer to me.'

He was lean and unshaven. He held a black crash helmet loosely in one hand. The skin around his restless eyes was soft, like a girl's, suggesting a delicacy that was belied by the knowingness of his blue eyes. He wore jeans and a worn black leather jacket which he unzipped with a jerk, revealing a faded, blue cotton shirt with a frayed collar and missing buttons. His inspection of Teresa was overt, almost gaudy. She felt undressed by him, yet his regard somehow did not feel sexual. The thought came to her that he probably looked at old men, motorbikes and tables in the same way, assessing their value to him.

'No. It's Jed,' she said. 'He's a sort of unofficial gamekeeper. He sometimes does it. He says it keeps them down.'

'Keeps them up, more like.'

'You can't keep a good man down,' she added, like catching a ball coming at her from the blue.

Elizabeth squealed her squeal. Teresa stared bug-eyed at her feet.

'It would keep me down, being nailed to a fucking tree.'

'I'll go and see if I can find William,' Teresa said, propelled out of the front door by embarrassment.

She half ran across the lawn, up the slope to where the shrubs converged at the fringed arch in the yew hedge, the entrance to the great walled garden. Dozens of pieces of plastic drainpipe were sticking up from one of the plots nurtured by Jason, a successor to Mr Joy who kept order in the kitchen garden in return for the use of half of it.

Fretting about how to face Lucas again, replaying their exchange in her mind, Teresa registered that they had been so intent on answering his questions that they had not thought to ask him how he knew about the squirrel. It was true that Jed would sometimes nail up a dead squirrel in the copse between the School House and the Manor, but it was done where no passing visitor could notice. Even Elizabeth and William were not aware of it, so why should Lucas know within minutes of arriving?

'William! William!' she called.

There was no sign of him in the potato patch at the far end of the garden, opposite the skeletal greenhouses, and Teresa turned round wondering how she had missed him. Why did she expect to find him there? She had fallen in unthinkingly with what Elizabeth said, never a good idea. Returning, Teresa looked for impressions of her shoes in the warm grass, but it was dry and tough and there was no trace of her own steps.

Approaching the house, she saw Lucas and William with Elizabeth on the lawn. She veered off and skirted round the other side of the house towards the yard.

There was Lucas's motorbike, parked near William's car. She walked up to it and brushed the sleek blue tank. It was still warm. How did he know about the squirrel? Nearby were the two red-brick garages, their steep pitched roofs stripped of lead years ago by some nocturnal marauder. They were overhung by the tall trees of the copse behind. Like a cat lightly changing direction after a momentary pause, Teresa slipped alongside the furthest garage, where no one ever had reason to go. From there she immediately saw the squirrel nailed to a tree, out of sight from the path twenty yards beyond. She looked down and saw a wet patch at the base of a tree: Lucas had climbed off his bike and come here, in a hurry, to piss.

Amused by her furtive discovery, Teresa took the shortcut back into the garden, through the lobby under the rat loft.

Lucas was strolling across the lawn with a croquet hoop in each hand. 'Of course it'll work,' he was saying, 'how can a croquet set not work?'

William was examining a mallet. 'This mallet's a bit . . .'

'There are plenty of mallets!'

'I know, it's the balls really, they're a bit chipped.'

Lucas rammed a hoop into the ground. Seeing Teresa, he straightened up and said: 'Are you going to play croquet? You and me against William and Elizabeth.'

Teresa felt exposed, as if Lucas had somehow divined her private knowledge of him and unaccountably gained an advantage over her because of it. 'I'm terrible, I'll miss the ball. I'll make us lose,' she said.

'I bet you're better than the rest of us.'

His attention tugged her across the lawn to the lavender bush near the dining-room door, where the mallets were leaning. He handed her one and she swung it two or three times, out of the habit of its weight. 'We're black and blue,' he said. 'You go first. Blue.'

Elizabeth emerged from the house carrying a round tray with glasses and a bottle of wine, which she set on the grass. As she poured, she whistled 'Imagine'.

'Thanks. I can't believe you don't play all the time,' said Lucas, gesturing with his glass towards the pitch as if making a toast.

'Lucas came out here, took one look, and asked if there was a croquet set,' Elizabeth explained to Teresa.

'Seeing this lawn, in this light, I just thought, "Croquet!"' said Lucas, and he placed the blue ball in front of the first hoop for Teresa.

'Oh crumbs, do I have to be first?'

'Yes. I also thought, "Music!" Have you got sound in there?' he asked, nodding towards the drawing-room.

'Help yourself,' said William. 'It's true,' he added, reverting to Lucas's first remark, although Lucas was already half way across the terrace: 'I don't know why. We never really think of playing, although my grandfather used to play all the time, until his sight went.'

Teresa lifted the mallet back between her legs and brought it down in a straight line with the ball and the hoop.

'Fluke,' said Elizabeth.

'Skill,' her sister replied, and hit her ball again.

Over the road, the church had softened to honey in the evening sunshine. Its edges had melted, and the distance foreshortened, so that the shadow of the dovecote on the nursery wing wrapped obliquely over the wall and crept towards the porch. It was silent in the village. The *tock* as Elizabeth hit her ball, and the immediate metallic ring as it collided with the hoop, were clear. 'Damn!'

'Never mind,' said William.

Loud music erupted from the house. William smiled. 'Good choice!' he said, as Lucas reappeared on the lawn; and to Elizabeth he added, 'I haven't listened to this for ages. We used to play "Sweet Jane" in our band.'

Lucas bent over his mallet. He struck: when his ball went through, his limbs relaxed as if a spring had been released. With his extra turn he tried to hit Teresa's ball but missed.

'Now,' said William, already lined up behind his ball. He took a high practice swing, then tensed himself and hit the yellow ball clear through the hoop. 'Phew! It wouldn't have done for both of us to be left behind.'

'All right, all right,' Elizabeth grumbled. 'So who played what in this famous band of yours?'

'Lucas did vocals and rhythm, I was the bassist. You don't know the lead guitarist or the drummer.'

Teresa knew Lucas was watching as she hit his black ball with her blue one. 'Perfect,' he said, 'brilliant.' She was about to jump off from him when he intervened. 'No, you can hit them both through from there.'

'Not a chance!'

'Sure you can. Try.'

She tried; and hit them both wide. 'There, I told you.'

He prodded in front of the hoop with the top end of his mallet. 'Uneven lawn,' he said.

At the other end, Elizabeth failed to get through the first hoop again. 'Oh! Can I have it again?' she cried. 'It'll be a better game for you if I catch up a bit. Please!' She smirked, pleased with the logic she had contrived to disguise her threatened sulk, knowing that she wouldn't be refused.

'Elizabeth, my darling . . .!' William wouldn't deny her, but he looked to the others for permission.

Lucas shrugged. While Elizabeth steered her ball through the hoop, he swivelled round to survey the house, like the captain of a paddle-steamer looking up fondly into the rigging of an ancient galleon. 'So tell me more about your accident of fortune then, William,' he said.

'Eh?'

'How come you inherited?'

'Oh. Well, my father is the oldest but he already has as much house as an ordinary chap can use. So, doffing the hat to primogeniture, it came to me.'

'Not exactly an accident,' said Lucas. 'I mean, it can't have been altogether unexpected.'

'It was an accident in the sense that it's completely accidental that I happen to be the one it came to.'

'You what?'

'Accidental that it was me rather than anyone else.'

'Isn't that like saying that it's accidental that a rabbit is born with four legs, two ears and small enough to fit down a rabbit hole?'

'Is it?'

'Well we're not talking four cousins tragically killed in a motorway crash, are we?'

Teresa was laughing because it had always seemed strange to

her that William didn't anticipate the situation, or so he said. 'You feel guilty, don't you, William? Your social conscience keeps you awake at night . . .'

'At college,' Lucas said, 'I had no idea you stood to inherit this pile. But then I didn't have much impression of a social conscience either. Perhaps it's all part of your artistic sensibilities?'

Suddenly energised by being teased, William swiped cheerfully with his mallet towards Lucas's ankles. Lucas hopped to avoid the blow, accepting that he deserved it by making no attempt to counterattack. 'You're a dangerous man, William.'

'Whose turn is it?' said Elizabeth.

'Lucas,' Teresa said.

'Lucas,' Elizabeth repeated, 'it's your turn.'

'Yes, Lucas, concentrate on the game, will you?' said William.

'If you'd only stop trying to cripple me then —' He lunged at William, who retreated too fast and tripped back over a hoop. 'There.' Leaving William to pick himself up, he hit his ball towards the third hoop. 'But seriously,' he resumed, 'what have you inherited? It's more than this house, isn't it?'

To Teresa's surprise, Elizabeth laughed when William fell backwards. Then, afraid that she might seem to have betrayed him, she hurried to help him up. 'Tenants,' she said. 'He inherited a tenant's daughter, didn't you?' And she kissed William tenderly, her hand spread on his chest.

'Good God! The *droit de seigneur*, alive and well . . .!' And Lucas thrust back and forth to the music.

'No, no!'

Lucas ignored him. 'The liberal conscience nowadays,' he said. 'Deplorable.'

'The house,' said Elizabeth, 'the house where we've always lived is part of it all. We always looked after his grandfather.'

'Young squire marries daughter of faithful family retainers . . . How touching!'

Teresa was enjoying Lucas's interpretation, but she sensed that he might upset Elizabeth if he persisted. Although part of her would have relished this, she chose to head him off by telling him that there was also some land: 'The big field on the other side of the road, and the woods beyond. And there's a huge Kennels.'

'Kennels?'

'For a Hunt,' William explained. 'Yap yap. Foxhounds. And horses.'

'It was the largest Hunt in Leicestershire,' said Elizabeth.

'*Maşallah!*'

'Pardon?'

'Sorry, an Islamic blessing was the best response I could come up with.'

'Fair enough,' said William. 'Anyway, so there's lots of buildings and stuff. But they're all falling down.'

'But you'll build them up again?'

'That's a little easier said than done,' Elizabeth observed.

'No!'

'Lucas can be a bit simple,' William said in a mock aside to Elizabeth and Teresa.

'Or does your liberal conscience forbid you from repairing your accidental inheritance?'

'Ooh!'

'Are you a friend of William's?' Teresa asked, suddenly protective.

'You ought to have a look around before you criticise,' said Elizabeth. 'Anyway, he didn't inherit any money.'

William said affably: 'Pay no attention to him, he's just a bum.'

'Yes, tell us what's so great about you,' said Elizabeth.

'A bumptious bum,' William added. 'Where's my drink? I completely forgot about it!'

'I thought you were jittery,' said Lucas.

'Fuck off. Now, tell Elizabeth and Teresa about being a bum, Lucas. I'm looking forward to this.' And he drank appreciatively.

It was Lucas's turn and he made a great show of aiming for Teresa's ball, which was neatly positioned in front of the fifth hoop. As soon as he struck, he raised his head and smiled, flutter-eyed. 'Actually, I'm an advertising consultant.'

'Crap,' said William.

The black had gently kissed the blue. Lucas lined up both balls and jabbed, without following through. They both went through the hoop: Teresa's rolled right on beyond the final hoop, while his own stopped short of the central post. It was a superb shot, for Elizabeth's ball was in the vicinity and now, as he carefully hit her, he said, 'Actually it's not crap. I am going to be an advertising consultant.'

The music had stopped.

'I don't believe you,' said William.

Lucas hit his ball at a wide angle to Elizabeth's, so that hers went a short way to a point between the last hoop and the post, while his own ran several yards beyond Teresa's. Now that they realised what he was doing, the others watched in silence.

'Yes,' said Lucas as he considered his next shot. 'When William refers to me as a bum he means that I don't have a nine-to-five job, but he doesn't seem to understand that that doesn't mean I don't work. There is a little word – not as little as "bum", but he's a writer and will no doubt understand – which William needs to be introduced to: freelance. I'm stopping being a freelance now though, and going to work for a company in a couple of months.'

He had hit Teresa's ball and knocked them both through the hoop. Now he used Elizabeth's ball to improve his position behind his partner.

'All right. I believe you, if you insist so forcefully,' said William. Lucas's ball knocked against Teresa's again, then he tapped them both against the finishing post. 'I do,' he said, grinning, surprised and pleased by his own performance.

★

Last night Teresa dreamed of Lucas. She did not wake me to share the news – she knows I am not interested in dreams, as a rule – but when I asked in the morning how she had slept, she answered that she had woken early, disturbed by a dream about Lucas. She did not elaborate, and I did not enquire. Where can we be private, if not in our dreams? Let her tell me if she wants. I could have countered her admission (if that is what it was) with the information that I sometimes dream of Iris. Of course I did not – it would open up a box of questions that I prefer to remain closed. As I said, where can we be private, if not in our dreams? Sometimes, bed is the most glorious, solitary haven for me, even while I lie there beside my wife. There is silence, stillness – and I watch the curtains draw back across my mind's stage: my own, undisturbed space where memory and fantasy cavort in freedom. Dreams take wing from these reveries; are peopled by the figures I have conjured up, and acted out with exquisite surprises. In this nocturnal domain, Iris is queen. It is she I dream of, as I have ever since I first saw her in her stripey skirt at Fanny Goodman's old apartment in Greenwich. I can't help that I dream of her. And it is because she occupies my subconscious like this that I take note of her in my conscious life. I mean, what should I make of it all? If she is there for me when I sleep, how can I deny that she matters to me?

On the other hand – and I know this stinks coming from me, who dreams of Iris – I'm not sure I like the idea of Teresa dreaming of Lucas. Is the figure in her dream the old Lucas, arrested in time, or the present one? Does she still dream about me, I wonder, as she used to in the early days? Lucas may have business with me, but what business does he have in my wife's dreams?

It is hard to know precisely what to make of Teresa's descriptions of him. The dreams will have cast their peculiar illumination over her memories. Her impression now is that he moved about the pitch without faltering; lithely, in control of the game and of

109

those around him. There is Lucas crouched over his mallet, eyes flitting to the other balls, to a hoop, to his own ball, then concentrating on his target, confident of strategy and tactics; and there he is speaking and joking with unfamiliar, demanding authority. And so it seems to her that he must have won their game without effort. But I believe that these images play Teresa false. It may be true that she and Lucas won, but I suspect their victory owed more to Elizabeth's incompetence than to Lucas's skill. Despite the confidence Teresa associates with Lucas, I doubt he was a better player than the others. As for the 'advertising consultant' bit, that – unless the mistake is Teresa's – is a fancy answer, so far as I understand. At that time he had just been taken on by a consultancy to do some market research for them. William wasn't so wide of the mark when he said that Lucas was a bum, although the epithet didn't sum him up: he may have been a layabout, but he was a luminously attractive one. He was a free-lance copywriter who had got some work as a researcher. It was another five years before he outwitted his own boredom by brushing off his school Russian and going to court the grafters of St Petersburg.

They were in the passage-room now. Lucas was standing in front of the bookshelves, glancing along the spines. He touched the glass top on the cupboards beneath and inspected his fingertips, then rubbed them together to get rid of the dust. He was moaning about his lack of direction, how his contemporaries put effort into things and got results while he still farted about.

Teresa had been determined to do the washing-up herself after supper, but William and Elizabeth forestalled her. Telling her to leave them to it, they went off together to the kitchen. It made her prickle with humiliation to think that she was being set up. Did they think she had no pride? If they thought that it was agreeable to Lucas, did Lucas think that she had connived at it? After her secret delight during dinner, watching the lift of his eyebrows and the stroke of his fingers, she had been shoved into a situation from which she dared not escape for fear of revealing how it upset her. So instead of assuring him that persistence was over-rated and that his achievements weren't less significant but different – trying, moreover, to keep the conversation harmless; besides, she was curious – she asked, 'And what about William?'

Lucas swivelled round, his eye pausing for an instant on a picture as he turned. 'What about William?'

'He doesn't seem to depress you.'

'Why should he?'

'I thought you said it depressed you, comparing yourself to contemporaries.' She took a box of cards from the needlework table and emptied it into her hand.

Lucas reached into his pocket for some cigarettes and held the packet towards her. She shook her head. He lit one for himself while Teresa clumsily shuffled the cards.

'The thing about William is that he manages to be happy by doing nothing,' he said. 'That could be depressing, if you want to look at it that way. But I find it interesting. How does someone who has no aspirations – and I don't count poetry because, well, have you ever read any of his stuff? – manage to be so bloody cheerful all the time? I really believe that he's not without imagination, but he flogs the same old horse in the same old way, indifferent to whether it's alive or dead, and he doesn't get bored. Maybe it's I who have no imagination, after all. But even if I change horses, so to speak, I do get excited from time to time. What the fuck gets William going?'

'He's about to get married to my sister.'

Lucas stared into the dead fireplace and drew on his cigarette. 'That's true.' The smoke furled round the mantelpiece.

'Maybe you should allow him his poetry.'

He shrugged. 'Don't get me wrong.' His eyes were vivid as he looked up at Teresa. 'Although I don't understand William's stability, I am fond of him. That's what intrigues me. I respect his stability.'

Lucas drew on his cigarette and went on, 'His father once asked me if I believed in Original Sin. William and I were doing something about the Romantics at school. I said no, of course not, why? And he said, didn't I think we all went about life as if we had lost something? And if, like Shelley, you no longer believed in God, then wouldn't the unfocused sense of loss translate as a reverence for the Antique?'

Teresa felt the slyness of his appeal to her, but she still wished she knew how to give him whatever it was in William that he sensed he lacked.

Elizabeth and William returned at last. He bore a tray with coffee cups and a jug of coffee; she had an unctuous, insinuating smile.

Teresa sat through five minutes of chatter while they tried to work out if she and Lucas had got anywhere, then she decided she had had enough of their game.

As she was leaving the room, Lucas called out: 'Will you show me round the place tomorrow, Teresa? I'm sure you'll do it much better than William!'

His request startled her. With her hand already on the door she looked over her shoulder and said, 'If you want.'


Teresa was woken during the night by a loud crash. Sleepily investigating the noise, she encountered her father, who had also been woken, pulling his dressing-gown about him after switching on the landing light. Tripping at the top of the stairs, Elizabeth had knocked a vase from a shelf as she reached out in the dark to prevent herself from falling. Frozen in the sudden glare, she crouched among scattered shards and the spilled contents of her handbag: and there, like a cat's trophy mouse deposited on the drawing-room carpet, was a packet of condoms.

'All right?' said Tom. 'Glad to see you're in one piece. Too bad about the vase.' And he went back to bed.

Elizabeth shrugged at her sister. She finished picking up her treasures and proceeded to her room.

When Teresa came down to breakfast, Lucas and William were already leaning back against her mother's Aga, each with a mug of coffee. Lucas was telling Marie some piece of nonsense about motorcycling. He did not know about the night's clamorous revelation, nor most likely did William, although he would have understood if he had known about it. Still, the amiability of the scene surprised Teresa.

Elizabeth was still asleep. 'We'll leave her,' said Marie. 'Poor Elise, it's such a difficult time for her.'

When she described this to me, I told Teresa that I didn't see why it was such a big deal.

'To you, whose mother turned down the covers of the spare double bed for her adolescent son when a girl so much as set foot in the house, it must be hard to comprehend,' she said primly. 'But this was the nearest Elizabeth had come to acknowledging to our parents that she might not be a virgin on her marriage. Although she and I both knew that for anyone of our generation to be chaste at the altar would be unusual, if not deviant, we also felt that our parents would and even *ought* to disapprove. They couldn't condone it. Yet here they were confronted by indirect – but unmistakable – evidence, and they said nothing. For me –'

'Surely they would have been pleased to find that she was using precautions?'

'I suppose so. But that would be outweighed by their conviction that nice girls –'

'But it wasn't?'

'Wasn't what?'

'Outweighed. In fact, what you're telling me is that they didn't care at all.'

'No, that is absolutely not what I am saying! They cared very much.'

'But they didn't seem to care.'

'Exactly.'

'To a good New Hampshire boy, that is a fine distinction.'

'I can't help that. The point is, while my parents chatted away as if they were accustomed to people like Lucas informally joining us for breakfast, I was all fluttery – afraid of invoking the scene in the night, but also not knowing if Lucas had remembered that he'd asked me to show him around. I remember spreading a thin skin of butter into the corners of my toast, then pressing in my mother's orange and ginger marmalade . . .'

In due course, Marie asked, 'Is William going to show you around then?'

'I hope so,' Lucas replied, and Teresa avoided his eye.

Although he didn't exactly change position, his feet shifted as he rubbed first one instep, then the other, with the opposite foot. He flexed his ankles and forced his toes back into the angle of the floor and the Aga. His fingers flicked and tapped around his mug.

'Do you really want to be shown around, though?' William asked. 'After all, you've been here before.'

'Yes, but I've only seen the main house – and only a bit of that. I've never been here, or to the Kennels . . .'

'I don't believe William himself has looked round all of *this* house,' Tom said mischievously.

William frowned, withdrawing his chin into his collar.

'Aren't you curious?' Lucas asked.

'Well yes, I suppose so.'

'You ought to look, you know,' Tom went on. 'Half of it hasn't been used for twenty years, since Mrs Bromage died.'

'Nobody's been in there for twenty years?' Lucas repeated.

'My husband –' Marie waved at him – 'he goes in there sometimes to look.'

Suddenly Lucas addressed Teresa. 'Have you finished now, Teresa? Sure you wouldn't like another slice or two, another loaf? I want my guided tour.' It was the first indication he had given of recalling his request of the previous evening.

The others laughed. Teresa did not think she was being watched as she ate. 'Oh dear, was I being very greedy?'

'I wouldn't want you to come out feeling hungry . . .'

Her chair scraped on the stone floor as she stood up. 'No. I'm not hungry any more.' Was she fat? She had never considered herself to be fat, but perhaps he dreamed of anorexics.

Tom cleared his throat as he stood. 'William, since you're here, can I have a word with you, please?'

'Of course.'

'We'll go on out,' said Lucas.

Tom smiled at his daughter: she had the impression that he wanted to come out to the Kennels too.

'See you later,' Lucas said to Marie, and left without waiting to see if Teresa was following.

Teresa began to clear up the breakfast, but her mother intervened: 'Go on, Teresa, off you go.'

'But all this — it'll only take a couple of minutes.'

'Exactly. So go.'

Lucas was walking backwards away from the house, looking up at the façade. When he saw Teresa coming out of the front door, he called: 'Stop there!' And he held a hand up. 'Wait!' Then he relaxed and she joined him, puzzled. 'A perfect tableau,' he explained. 'It's actually a much prettier house than the Hall.'

Although the Kennels adjoined the house, there was no access from the side. They had to go out through the copse as if they were going to the Hall, then go in by the main gate.

'What was that all about?' said Lucas.

'All what?'

'The atmosphere. The "Can I have a word with you, William?"'

'Elizabeth woke us up when she came in, at four o'clock. She knocked over a vase or something.'

'And her being out late is William's responsibility?'

'Yes, sort of. My parents are quite old-fashioned Catholics.'

'Good Catholic girls! William and his bride shouldn't be doing the nasty yet, is that it?'

Teresa laughed, never having heard this phrase before. 'It's partly a matter of being discreet,' she said.

'What the eye does not see . . . Right. Well, each to his own . . .'

As they entered the Kennels compound he stood still, with his hands by his sides. Teresa was side on to him, holding the corroded gate hook. She could see his eyes pass along the dilapidated barns to the left and up the long line of kennels to the building opposite, on the other side of the mossy yard. His gaze rested for a moment on the overgrown, shed-like structures in the centre, then strayed to the side of the Manor before coming back down to the old smithy in the bottom righthand corner and the row of stables which veered in to where they stood.

'Christ,' he said.

A large section of the roof of the nearest barn had collapsed altogether. The edges of the hole were buckled so that the slates looked as if they were being sucked inwards: throw a stone and it would surely all come shuddering down to the ground.

They took a few steps into the yard and then, with a furious barking and rattling, one of Stan's febrile mongrels came at them. When he reached the end of his short chain he jerked, half throttled by the iron collar, and howled. Stan called him Tip, but Teresa refused to use this name. He was the last of several dogs to have fallen into Stan's clutches. Their plaintive barking had been one of the constant sounds of her life, and she had never grown used to it. But at least this old dog recognised her. 'Ssh,' she told him, and he lay down flat, his head between his paws, ears laid back, watching them and whining.

She explained to Lucas how the place was occupied by Stan. He had been ill lately, she said, in and out of hospital. His son or grandson came to feed the dog and the old nag they could hear snorting in one of the stables beyond. They didn't come as often as they should, only once every other day early in the morning, and the suffering of these wretched animals upset Teresa. She wanted to feed them herself but was afraid it would create trouble.

'You want to keep out of range. He'll bite, if you give him half a chance.'

Lucas looked up from the craven animal. 'First, crucified squirrels, now a rabid dog. This is the sort of place you find dead bodies.'

He leaned back on a gate, elbows crooked between the upper bars, one heel hooked over the lowest. From this new perspective, he considered the Kennels again.

'So what's going to happen to this place?' he asked at last. 'What's the plan?'

'I don't know.'

'William must have ideas?'

'It depends on Stan.'

'Why?'

'William has to get him out before he can do anything.'

'It will all just be rubble soon. I mean what could be done now with fifty thousand quid will cost half a million in a couple of years, especially if there's a gale or a heavy snowfall. Up there –' he pointed to a roof on what was once living quarters for grooms: the slates were all there but they had a crinkly texture, as if they were all loose; they needed to be taken off so that the roof could be overhauled, and then put back – 'one dark and stormy night, not very far off, the whole caboodle will gently slide off and smash to smithereens. Slates are expensive.'

It had been falling apart steadily all Teresa's life. Usually she avoided thinking about it. 'Does William have that sort of money?'

'He may not have it sitting prettily in his own bank account, but if he seriously wanted to renovate the place his family –'

'There's the main house too, which is crying out for someone to spend a fortune on it.'

'Are the Carews short of fortunes?' Lucas laughed. 'What better project to spend them on?'

'I think they'd be sorry if the Hall fell down,' Teresa conceded, 'but I can see why they might think there's not much point slinging money at it.' Teresa was feeding him the line that her parents used to justify the Carews' neglect. She didn't know if this was their own view, but they had become reconciled to it. She herself had never been invited to think otherwise. She had even used the explanation to console William, who did not want the property to fall into total ruin, and recognised that responsibility for preventing this was his alone but wished it weren't so. And what could she do?

'It's the only part of the whole place that would give a return on the money they put in,' said Lucas.

He walked into the middle of the yard. As Teresa drew level with him, he pointed up to the first barn. 'Workshop,' he said, and stabbed towards the next: 'workshop. What do those stairs go to?' He was pointing at the external stairs leading to Stan's tiny flat.

'Caretaker's office?' Teresa answered, already sensing his drift.

'With site shop below. Then each of the kennel units can be made into a small workshop. And that building at the end, with the forecourt, could be a couple of offices. Or make it into a little house if it can open out the other way . . .' He turned and pointed back to the stables. 'More workshops – one two three four – larger. And what's that in the corner?'

'The smithy.'

Suddenly William was beside them. 'What are you sounding off about, Lucas?' he asked. 'I could hear you spluttering and grunting from fifty yards!'

Teresa moved a step away from Lucas.

'Why didn't you tell me about this place, William? It's fucking amazing!'

William rolled his eyes. 'It's in ruins, in case you hadn't noticed.'

'Bollocks. Well, it needs money spent on it, but it's not ruined, not yet, you could do a million things with it.'

'Let it fall down, to start with.'

'You can't be serious?'

'Come with me.'

William set off wearily across the yard and the dog woke, barking and dragging his chain across the cobbles as he lunged at William, who hopped aside. 'Shut up! Stupid animal!'

'You could make it into workshops,' Lucas called after him as he followed. 'You're slap in the middle of England, you couldn't ask for a better location, you've got a sodding great yard, all amenities... You're sitting on a fucking gold mine, William!'

'I don't want an industrial estate on my doorstep.'

William picked his way through rubble and nettles to the steps leading to the upper floor of the building that Lucas cast earlier as a house. The bottom steps had crumbled away and he hauled himself up to the higher ones by clutching thick weeds that grew from the brickwork. When he was safely up, he extended his hand down to Lucas, who sprang up beside him: 'And once you've done the roofs and the walls, all you have to do is bring power to each unit, and water . . .' He turned and helped Teresa up.

William pushed open the rotten door. 'Look.' The floor inside had fallen in except where it clung to the main beams, so that they could see through to the ground. He pointed up to the beams beneath the loose slates. 'They're all rotten,' he said.

'A detail,' said Lucas. 'Replace them. What makes it a nice building is there, the old red bricks, the slates, the space. Here you've got outside access to the upper floor, so you could divide it that way instead of losing space by putting in a staircase . . .'

'Lucas, for Christ's sake, it's a wreck!'

'I can see it's a wreck! But if that's all you can see, then the inside of your head's a fucking wreck, William!'

William turned to Teresa with a weak smile. He took it for granted that she agreed with him.

Treading warily on the remnants of floor, Teresa peered up to the roof. It looked filthy up there, but how could William tell that it was all so rotten? 'Have you ever thought about it, though?' she asked him.

'Not you too, Teresa?' he said.

'Well, wouldn't it be worth thinking about it? You always say you don't know what to do with it.'

'Lucas, have you been corrupting my sister-in-law?'

'Sister-in-law-to-be,' Lucas corrected him.


After lunch, while they were drinking coffee on the lawn with the girls' parents, William admitted that no harm could come from thinking about Lucas's suggestion. But he said the yard depressed him.

Elizabeth happened to be passing behind his chair with the coffee pot and she touched the side of his neck. He must have shaved with a blunt razor because it was scraped raw. 'Poor William, are you feeling got at?'

'Poor lamb,' said Teresa. She did not know what her father had said to William, but she saw that Elizabeth was determined to act as she pleased.

'Ssh, Teresa,' Marie said. 'Engagement is not an easy time.'

Lucas's mouth flickered. He looked intently at his hands.

Teresa couldn't understand why her mother insisted that life was so difficult at the moment for William and Elizabeth. They were in love, they had a beautiful house. It seemed to her that two people could scarcely be better provided for.

As soon as Teresa told me this, I replied, 'Were you jealous?'

'It all just seemed too convenient.'

'And do you think the same is said now about you?'

'I don't give a shit. People will say anything.'

'But you were contemptuous of Elizabeth.'

'Well I understand now that things were not so straightforward. My mother may have been referring back to difficulties during her own engagement. Also, unfortunately, events proved her right.'

'When did you come here, Marie?' Lucas asked all of a sudden. 'Wasn't it just after you were married?'

'Just after, yes, we lived for a few months in town, and then when I was expecting Teresa we came here.'

'It must have been strange.'

'The Carews, William's grandfather and grandmother, they were very kind to us. But yes, I don't know, maybe it wasn't so easy.' Unused to such questions, she turned away to Tom, who shrugged elaborately and smiled, as if dissociating himself from her feelings. 'It was very cold,' she added. 'I remember it was very cold.'

'I've heard they weren't easy people,' said Lucas.

'Is that what William says? They were always very good to us.'

'She was one of those people who seems more awkward to her family than to others,' said Tom. 'I think that's fair, isn't it, William?'

William nodded. 'It never ceases to amaze me that you all managed to keep out of her clutches.'

'She had us in her pocket anyway,' Teresa remarked. 'It wouldn't have been much of an achievement to get us in her clutches.'

'Teresa, what is the matter with you?' said Marie. But Teresa was cross with her mother for being so passive.

'There may be something in that,' Tom remarked. 'She was a snob, that much one cannot deny.'

Marie behaved as if any criticism of Mrs Carew amounted to outright attack, not only on Mrs Carew but also, by extension, on herself. She turned haughtily to Lucas, hoping that he would change the subject.

'Tell about your scheme for the Kennels,' said Teresa.

Lucas put a cigarette in his mouth and leaned back, probing the tight pocket of his jeans with two fingers. Extracting his lighter, he flicked his cigarette alight and stood up. Although everyone else was sitting, he remained standing. He spoke chiefly for Tom's benefit, seeing that he was amused, and paid no attention to William's silence.

'I think he must be mad, William, your friend!' Marie interrupted at one point.

'It's none of my business,' Lucas concluded, 'but to me the place is full of possibilities.'

'But as you say, it's none of your business,' said William.

'No harm in a little fantasy,' Tom said quickly, to appease William; then to Lucas he added, 'I must say, I think it's a marvellous idea.'

'But it's a castle in the air! I mean, who's going to pay for it?' William cried with sudden, agitated contortions of the right side of his face, like half of a sneeze.

Lucas laughed. 'Don't panic, William. As you say, it's a castle in the air.' He patted him on the shoulder.

As he removed his fingertips from William, Teresa saw that his attention had shifted: he was gazing up at the nursery wing. Before lunch, when showing him round the inside of the house, she had tapped on the end wall of the empty nursery flat, where her parents originally lived, and said, 'I'll show you the other side later.'

Teresa could see that he was connecting what he saw now with where they had been inside. He looked at her for confirmation. She said, 'Yes,' and set off towards the door.

'Hey!' he called, ambling after her.

The catch clacked up and the old door rattled open. This was where the mower was kept; in this season it smelt of grass and petrol. The door giving out to the yard on the other side was closed now. As Lucas slipped past her to open it, he touched her elbow. She didn't know if this was unintentional, or a polite way of getting her to move so that he could get past without pushing. He saw the yard, the grey cobbles glinting in the sunlight like gun-metal.

At the foot of a rickety staircase was an open doorway, obstructed by the mower. Rusting petrol and oil cans stood on the bottom steps. Stepping over them, it occurred to Teresa that her long white skirt was a ludicrous garment for this enterprise.

The rat loft used to frighten Teresa as a child. She had never even come across a mouse there but she imagined malevolent, sharp-toothed creatures crouched among the rubbish. Now the worst surprise she imagined was a sprained ankle. 'Be careful where you tread,' she advised Lucas, for there were holes in the boards on the landing. 'My dad says there can't have been a stable boy here since before the First World War.'

There were two cobwebbed rooms, each with a small dormer window set awkwardly in the steep roof. One was stacked like an ossuary with derelict furniture. In the other, light squeezed through grimy glass in weak trapezoid panels, highlighting a three-legged chair with a broken cane seat and a knot of encrusted, mangled books. All around was an ankle-deep mess of papers, leaves and twigs. Teresa had always wondered how the leaves and twigs got up there, and it struck her now for the first time that they were the remnants of old dried-up birds' nests, collected perhaps by the Major as a child, or one of his brothers.

Lucas bent down and picked up a mildewed book.

'They're old almanacs and diaries,' Teresa said. 'Diaries without any appointments.'

He riffled through a sheaf of torn papers, holding them up to the light, brushing at the skin of dirt. 'Old adverts. Invalid chairs. Doctor William's Pink Pills For Pale People. Zambuckrubitin. What on earth is that?' And he dropped them.

'The Major said that his children and grandchildren used to come up here looking for stuff, in case there was anything valuable. It looks as though nobody's been here for a hundred years, but it's been picked clean.'

'Picked dirty.'

'Yes, but you won't find an envelope with a stamp on, or any Old Masters. All that's left is exactly what it looks like: rubbish.'

At the bottom of the stairs Teresa stepped carefully over the mower. She was anxious not to get oil on her skirt. In the lower room were racks for tack and harness, the only relics of the room's former purpose. Although it was August, it was cold. Crumbled white stuff filled the fireplace. She pointed to a post in the centre of the room, a length of crudely trimmed yew jammed under the beam that held up the ceiling.

'I wonder what would happen if you kicked that?' he said.

'I wouldn't want to be in here, that's for sure.'

Lucas peered underneath a worn table with broken chairs piled on top. He pulled at something. Teresa heard metal grating on the stone floor. He stepped back, dragging into the light a contraption which she knew was for marking white lines on grass, though she hadn't seen it before. He kicked at the wheel and it shifted. 'A bit of oil and a clean up, some whitewash. All it needs,' he said, and dropped to his knees again to see what else was hidden under there. He reached back through the heaped junk. 'Hey!' He tugged gently and then passed back a net from hand to hand.

'It's a tennis net,' he said. 'I wonder if it's in one piece. Let's take it out to the lawn.'

He scooped it up and hopped over the mowing machine. Teresa followed but, as if dazzled by his enthusiasm, she didn't watch where she was going and her skirt snagged on a protruding lever. There was a loud rip; she felt a stab at her shin and stumbled noisily against the machine. 'Damn!' A four inch strip of skirt hung loose below her knees, but in her eagerness to join Lucas she inspected no further. Lucas must have heard the commotion but he didn't stop.

He was already laying out the net and the others were coming over to see what he was doing.

Teresa's appearance startled them. William let out a high-pitched giggle. 'What on earth's happened to you, Teresa?'

She looked down. The lower part of her right leg was bloody. The bottom of her torn dress was red. Seeing it, she suddenly felt weak, and remembered the scrape. 'I think I cut myself.'

'I think you did,' said Lucas.

Elizabeth laughed nervously.


Where the previous day they had played croquet, there was now a tennis court. Lucas and Tom were playing against William and Elizabeth. Teresa was lying on the grass near one of the posts which held up the net. A bandage was wound tight round her right leg, just below the knee.

It was a deep cut: when the blood was washed away, a little gobbet of flesh the size of a redcurrant was found to have been gouged out. Marie said she couldn't be sure if the wound was clean, however much TCP was sloshed on it: the mower was filthy. 'Hospital,' she said, but Teresa would not go. 'Well, don't expect sympathy from me when it goes septic,' said her mother. 'It doesn't even hurt,' Teresa replied.

When at last she got back to the lawn, the others had marked out a court and begun a game without her. Teresa was relieved at not having to excuse herself, rather than disappointed. Although she had not been lying when she told her mother that her leg didn't hurt, it tingled now.

The tennis switched to and fro in front of her. Nobody was much good but Teresa was paying scant attention to the game itself. It was Lucas who occupied her. Afraid she was making an exhibition of herself, she tried to drag her eyes away. If she couldn't avert her gaze then she ought to go elsewhere, but she felt pinned down by his presence, compelled to watch him by some unprecedented hormonal cannonade.

I have known this inner compulsion since I first met Iris. She turned up with some friend at Fanny Goodman's, where I had gone with Alec, I forget what the occasion was. She can only have been eighteen or so. She was wearing a rainbow-striped skirt that fanned out around her as she sat on the end of a low, broken sofa with such composure that you would have thought that the sofa had been adapted to suit her. There were hardly any chairs and, would you believe it, I sat cross-legged at her feet. Like the sun in my eyes, she filled the room and everyone else dropped into obscurity. It has been like that every time I've ever met her. She opens oxygen valves at my arteries so that I am alive in a different way, and she responds to it and knows me as no one else does, not even Teresa: and no one could, because it isn't there for anyone else.

Did Lucas know that she was watching him? Although she was aware of what the others were doing, she felt that her interest must be ridiculously apparent.

She wasn't following the game at all but she wanted it to continue. It existed as a frame for Lucas to move in, for her to watch him as he jumped, waved his arms, shouted, laughed, bounced a ball on his racket. And he called out to her: 'How's the leg, Teresa? Did you really not feel anything?'

Marie brought tea out to the garden. The sun hung low over the rat loft and Lucas's shadow lengthened, covering Teresa as it approached, veering away as he collected a final sliver of cake. He was playing singles now with Elizabeth. Teresa's greedy eyes were screened by a book.

The evening chastened her. She knew from the writhing in her guts that this was no ordinary attraction. It had no relation to anything she had felt before. She had been dealt a joker.

Peter Aaron himself once said, 'Once a man begins to recognise himself in another, he can no longer look on that person as a stranger. Like it or not, a bond is formed.' The same applies even when that person is my wife, who is not exactly a stranger anyway. (I wonder, incidentally, if Aaron has experienced something of the sort with Iris, his own wife?) This inner recognition is not what is meant by falling in love of course. It is something else – and not exactly welcome, since it involves perceiving how my wife was once in love with someone else in a way that she never was with me. It has to do with recognising that a capacity for betrayal must lurk in her. Yet it consoles me a little to think she has this thing inside her too. Having stumbled into this net and been snatched up by an unseen hand and suspended above the street, you can observe the activities of others and be seen but you cannot engage with them directly unless you get out. Release only comes if the love is returned, or dissolved. Some people spend their life inside that net. That, for them, is reality. For if they doubt that the resolution will be in their favour then they will resist putting themselves to the test in case they have to abandon the last shred of hope that tethers them to life, or sanity. But there is comfort, of a kind, in seeing someone else in a similar net. Such people are only recognisable to one another.

In due course William emerged from the house with two bottles of white wine in a cooler, and glasses. The evening ritual had commenced. Everyone drank. But today – let the young ones enjoy themselves! – Marie prepared supper. William's kitchen was still the Major's kitchen, which was her domain. And they went in to eat. Asparagus. Veal, which Elizabeth would never touch; mushrooms, potatoes mashed with cream and butter, glazed carrots. Mountains of food.

Teresa wasn't hungry.

She felt full and drained at the same time, exhausted and impatient. She felt ashamed, and she resented her shame. She wanted Lucas – and why should she be ashamed of that? Yet it was hopeless unless he wanted her too, and how would she know if he wanted her? How could she make him want her? She was ashamed of her need to make him want her. Beneath the inhibiting eyes of her parents, and William and Elizabeth's flattening smirks, she was inert. She couldn't look at Lucas any more. How would she behave if she were alone with him? There would be no opportunity to find out. Her body felt tied down, her voice stifled.

Lucas was oblivious to her disquiet. She wanted to shout it at him, but she also wanted him not to notice so that she could go on seeing him as he was, energising the laughter and chatter of the others. She loved it that he made them all seem so happy, she wouldn't have him stop for the world. Why should he be concerned if she was isolated in the midst of it?

Teresa thought with dread of the future, beginning from the moment of his departure tomorrow. He would leave ignorant of her covetous heart. He wouldn't squander another thought on her, while she, tortured and alone – she would long for him. Perhaps it was better that he didn't know what she felt, rather than suffer a change in his behaviour if he didn't feel the same. Not wanting him to stop being as he was, concealment was her only option.

She wanted him, but she would not make a fool of herself.

After supper, she left with her parents.

Three abreast, they followed the hopping beam of Tom's torch, past the School House and through the spinney. 'Are you all right, Teresa?' he asked.

'Yes, fine, why?'

'I thought you seemed a little subdued.'

The next morning, her leg ached. From the look of the cut she would have expected a sharp local pain, but there had been none. It was a more general slight pain, a dull pressure.

She was reluctant to go over to the Hall alone, convinced that she would give herself away. Instead, she stared at the Sunday papers in the drawing-room, waiting for Elizabeth to get up, listening for William or Lucas to rap on the front door. But they didn't come and it was almost midday by the time she got there with Elizabeth.

When she saw them playing chess in the passage-room, sadness seared her. Could it really be that he preferred to play chess with William? Was she worth so little? He wasn't even curious.

They exchanged good mornings and then turned back to the board, unwilling to be disturbed. Elizabeth looked about, huffed, sat down, stood up, then startled Teresa by pulling them away. 'Why don't you show me what's for lunch, William? Teresa can get vegetables and show Lucas the greenhouses. I'm sure he'd like to see the greenhouses. Then we girls can do the lunch together while you boys go on with your game.'

William pretended to cringe beneath the sardonic tone with which she concluded, but he obeyed without discussion and Teresa suddenly found herself outside on the gravel with Lucas, a battered basket in her hand.

As they walked, she explained that the greenhouses were still in use, although perilous, when her parents first came to Sweynsend.

The complex occupied the far left-hand quarter of the kitchen garden, in the corner of which was the verge where Mrs Carew once kept her vegetable stall. Twenty yards from them as they walked down the central path was an exposed wall, which was the rear wall of the hothouses; the fixings were still discernible at the top. The ground below was thick with undergrowth, forcing its way among the broken glass and the multiple gallows of smashed frames. Iron rods protruded like stripped bones, from which you could infer a sophisticated system of screws and levers to open up sections of the glass. Lucas clambered over a low wall and Teresa saw him raise a piece of iron grille from the cracked brick path with his toe. Weeds had broken the pipes below. The carcass of a crucified peach tree was still splayed on the wall behind.

At the bottom of the path she turned left to the bow-roofed potting shed in the corner, where she collected a fork. An odd dwarf turret with widely-spaced bricks butted up against it, which she pointed out to Lucas as a beehive. It was full of old flowerpots now, and he didn't believe it was for bees. Backing on to the hothouse wall was a long, slack lean-to structure, filled with pots and leaves and an ancient wooden barrow with one of its handles broken off. The near end was divided off like an office. Inside were numerous pretty little drawers and trays for seeds. It was all tumbled and rotten now. At the end of the lean-to was the dark, rank mushroom house. Choked stairs led down beneath it to the boiler room. Lucas leaned into the musty gloom and wondered aloud if the mechanism would work again.

'I don't think it's worked for over seventy years.'

'I thought you said it worked when your parents came.'

'No. The greenhouses were used, but like husks. The heating was already shot to pieces.'

'The whole lot can't have been built much more than a hundred years ago. They thought they were setting things up for ever, and it scarcely lasted a generation.'

'Perhaps they couldn't make things grow here.'

Lucas gestured at the thick, tenacious weeds: 'Not the right things, anyway' – then at the shambles around them – 'but it wasn't for want of trying.'

Another long greenhouse stood opposite, between the path

and the garden wall. Unlike the others, it had not collapsed, but it seemed to be supported from within by thick banks of vegetation which sprouted from the shattered windows in huge clumps of deadly nightshade. Teresa thought of Mrs Carew's fabled vegetables and shook her head.

In a modest bed further along she let Lucas dig some potatoes because her leg ached, then he took the fork back while she picked peas from a great blossoming stand in the centre of the garden. He came back by the central path and she watched him stop and turn, looking at the wreckage again in amazement. When he joined her, the mauve and pink flowers nuzzled at his face while his fingers darted and ducked among the greenery. She wanted to tell him that she loved him but it sounded so incredible. Tell him that she didn't want him to go, that she wanted him to return? That was feeble, pitiful. But how then should she begin to convey what she wanted him to understand? Or should she have reached through the sweet peas and pulled him towards her by the belt, kissed him among the soft flowers?

As she turned away, a flash of pain ignited in her calf.

And so Lucas left after lunch, unaware of my Teresa's longing.

# Chapter Nine

I HAVE BEEN travelling a lot lately – Moscow, St Petersburg, New York – and this has made it possible for me to keep on going with this tale; and perhaps accounts too for its muddled nature. I take my laptop with me everywhere and tap away in hotels, airport lounges and at 36,000 feet. From time to time I see my wife. This is not always at home. She came to St Petersburg for a few days a couple of weeks back and we had a good time together wandering through those mind-blowing palaces. One of the things that impressed me most was the Soviet restorations after World War Two, when the Nazis left most of the palaces blackened wrecks. I mean, why would Stalin want to restore in such loving, no-expense-spared detail those monuments to excess and private wealth? It makes no sense to me.

Teresa is pregnant. She found out before she came to Petersburg, and it was partly in celebration that she joined me. She ate an enormous amount of caviar. I've heard of cravings but this tops them all. For the short time we were in the land of cheap caviar it was no big deal, but I'd have to mortgage the house for seven months of caviar in Leicestershire. I suggested it was just a question of the salt content, that roll-mop herrings might do as well, but no, it seems it has to be caviar. For the moment. Well, I suppose it's nice to be able to show my appreciation. It makes me laugh too because although I would say she has good taste, she's not generally one for fancy goods. In fact, she is pretty disgusted by her own sudden desire for caviar, particularly when confronted by poverty at every step in Russia. Hard to decide whether satisfying the desire stokes the shame or appeases it. We tell one another that it's not high on the scale of human iniquity. Perhaps St Peter will judge my amusement at her distress with greater severity.

In view of this news it may sound perverse that I have been travelling a lot, but the idea is to do it now so that I can cut back later on. Whether this is practicable, as new situations and opportunities open up, we shall see.

It is strange finding out all this stuff about Teresa. You think you know someone well, then you discover that they have this whole other history. I sometimes wonder, what is the point of finding out about it? Then I reflect how it is with me, that in this chasm between the pointlessness of remembering and the struggle against forgetting lies the core of me. Oh, I know it's futile to think of Iris, worse than futile because it distracts me from my chosen life, yet there is this blind urge to think of her because not doing so is akin to cutting out my own flesh. It's an ache that grows worse and you get weary of the pretence: what is the point of denying your flesh like this? And so it must be with Teresa – who is my wife: so why would I not want to know this about her too?

The world in which she woke that Monday was new. It was a world in which she loved an absent man, who did not know she loved him. Her previously unfocused imaginings had gathered witlessly about him, like dew on a thread. Awareness of him was like a dazzle on all her thoughts and deeds; behind it crept the shadowy knowledge of his separateness.

'The Major used to say that weekend visitors were like dogs: tolerable if house-trained and sometimes even amusing, but on the whole one was thankful that they belonged somewhere else.' We were leaning on a stone balustrade looking out over the glittering Gulf of Finland from the gardens of Peterhof. 'When I was still quite small,' Teresa continued, and her cheeks were pink in the icy breeze, 'my father explained that I shouldn't believe everything the Major said. Not because he was lying, nor because he was wrong, but because sometimes he was just stating an opinion. When I was older, he said, I too would hold opinions with the Major's assurance, and I shouldn't expect everyone to agree with them any more than we always agreed with the Major – or the Major expected us to agree with him. I forget what provoked this advice. I suppose the Major had upset me with one of his remarks at which an adult would have known to smile. But he didn't stop to clarify his obscurities for children, and so he was liable to confuse them. I've forgotten exactly what he said, but I remember recalling my father's words as I woke that morning to a new and unnerving loneliness. Nobody knew about it, and I felt that I had to keep it that way because they would try to purge me of something vital.'

As soon as Teresa got out of bed she knew that her leg wasn't healed because it hurt when she put weight on it. There was a dull ache which didn't surprise her, but, riding her bicycle into work, the pain spread from the restricted area below her knee to her thigh and then down as far as her ankle, where it felt as if a flame had entered behind her shinbone and was scorching her every time she pressed down on the pedal. She tried to cycle slowly, working hard with her left leg so that her other one could relax, whereupon she became conscious that the entire limb throbbed. The slight gradient into town was usually unnoticeable, but now she felt herself sweating with the effort of turning the pedals through the pain. She was afraid to dismount for fear that walking would be just as difficult: she would be stranded. It seemed essential that she reach the office without giving in. She thought of her sister and William tripping off to London that morning because he wanted to see an exhibition of new printing techniques. He had some notion of starting a printing press at Sweynsend. Elizabeth said he had enough claims on his attention, but he was excited. Teresa couldn't help thinking that it would never get beyond a few brochures, although she liked the idea in principle. For Elizabeth, the pleasure of going to London was wholly in buying clothes.

Teresa wondered if they would see Lucas while they were there. She pictured the three of them in a restaurant, and with them was a fourth: a laughing girl whom Lucas turned to and kissed. Did she exist? Wobbling away from the traffic lights, Teresa thought how ridiculous she would seem if he saw her in her present condition, yet part of her wanted him to see her, as if the pain she was suffering was on his account.

Her colleagues wished her good morning and Teresa joined in the chat as usual. Although the painkillers she had taken appeared not to have made the slightest impact, she found that by moving with care she could contain the pain in her leg, and stand and walk without drawing attention to herself. It occurred to her that it was just the bicycling which disagreed with her, that perhaps she had only pulled a muscle. It was odd not to have appreciated it before, but she persuaded herself as she sat down that such was the case. She had probably tensed up her leg after cutting herself, predisposing the muscles to strain. She felt ashamed of herself for feeling the pain so acutely when she was riding her bicycle, and banished the idea of seeing a doctor. How foolish of her... Lucas would scorn her if he knew... Her thigh felt heavy on the seat of the chair. When she moved, there was a tingling down her leg like a swoop across the keys of a xylophone. As she stood up she felt again a burning in her lower leg which surely wasn't a pulled muscle.

Teresa's mind was a thicket of confusions as she worked. She knew she ought to see a doctor but she didn't want to interrupt the day. Her leg felt increasingly, peculiarly clumsy, but she told herself that she was overreacting. It was certain to feel better soon. Perhaps she had done something really serious to it, in which case she would find out sooner or later because she would collapse: then she would not have to make any more effort because someone else would have to take care of her. She wanted Lucas to know; then she wanted him only to discover afterwards, when she was better or dead, so that he could marvel at her fortitude. Since the injury had occurred in his company there was an immediate link to him, and it lodged in her mind that all the pain was in some way *for* him. If he knew, then he would feel just a little sorry, but she would be strong; she wouldn't allow him his pity: in the end he would have to love her.

Whenever she stood up, the abrupt pain made a knot of unease tighten within her, only to be shredded in the claws of her muddle. And as the day progressed she began to feel as if she were getting flu.

She was not accustomed to feeling ill. It made her indignant. A pulled muscle or a cut in the flesh was inconvenient but tolerable. She set her teeth against it, determined to chase it from her system with the force of her will, as she'd surely done on previous occasions. But she could not avoid the fact that she was uncomfortably hot and crumpled, as if paint were shrivelling on her skin. She was angry with this queasiness for distracting her from thinking of Lucas.

As she cycled home, she was sustained by the thought that giving in to the pain would amount to giving up all hope of Lucas. Not that this feverish equation was so coherent or baleful as to make her pain the measure of her worth to him, but a childish superstition was at work: 'If I get home without treading on the lines between the paving stones then there will be cakes for tea', or 'If I get home then I will get Lucas.' And by the time she reached her front door it seemed of the utmost importance that she get through the evening too without surrendering.

This was made easier by the arrival of a guest, who suspended her self-absorption and diverted her parents' attention from her. His name was David Groat and he had lived in the Servants' Hall flat while he was a postgraduate student at Warwick University. Now he worked in California, but he was back for a few days for a conference in Coventry. It was many years since the Fairfaxes had seen him. Tom and Marie were pleased that he had taken the opportunity to invite himself because they were fond of him. Unlike most people who ever lived in the Servants' Hall, David had managed to get on amicably with the Carews. Living at such close quarters demanded patience, imagination and a sense of humour. He had been there for nearly three years at the critical period leading up to Mrs Carew's death, and he had formed a bond with the Fairfaxes which survived his years of absence. Teresa had been looking forward to seeing this character from her childhood, so her fury with herself for feeling ill was aggravated and she was determined not to let discomfort impinge. All the same, she found it hard to concentrate on the conversation and several times she chopped across the flow with a sudden question to which she should have known the answer, and which she asked more from a desire to be friendly than from real curiosity.

'What did you say you did, David . . .? I mean, I know you're a scientist but . . .' He blinked and there was a flake of dry skin on his eyelid. His fair hair was brushed back in stiff crests, like egg-whites.

'I don't think I did say.'

'Tell us though.'

'I'm a seismologist.'

'You're not expecting any earthquakes here, are you?' Teresa asked.

Tom laughed uproariously.

Teresa's lower lip was glistening. Marie looked at her daughter and asked if she was all right.

She wasn't, but she thought it might be just a fit of nausea although she had hardly drunk any wine. She said she was fine and took a sip of water, hoping that the dizziness would pass.

'I met a man at Stanford who said he'd been to Sweynsend,' said David all of a sudden. 'You wouldn't believe. He was a bishop or some such. He came to the consecration of Coventry Cathedral. All the bigwigs who were asked had to be farmed out to stay with local worthies. This fellow, together with two or three others, drew – not the short straw; let's say the corkscrew straw – and was dumped on the Carews. Said he'd remember it to his dying day. They were using Georgian glasses like gas station tumblers, and the Major boasted about his bottle of Jefferson's port.'

Teresa was feeling very sick. She stood up shakily, a spear of pain thrusting from her right hip to the ankle, and left the room. In the passage she put a hand against the wall and tottered along to the loo. She was consumed by a nausea whose only possible conclusion was vomiting, but her throat remained empty. She wondered if it was a side-effect of the useless painkillers. In the mirror she saw that her cheeks were suffused with green, and her forehead between the two swathes of black hair was bone white. She pushed her hair back from the scalp; her temples were damp and there was a glaring highlight on her cheekbones. She leaned on the basin, half expecting bile to rise in her throat, hoping for the relief of being sick. Seeing herself like this in the stark light worried her, as if it had not really occurred to her before that she might be ill. Suddenly she understood clearly that it wasn't flu, nor was she drunk on half a glass of wine: something was wrong, and whatever she had been trying to prove by pretending it wasn't was now surely proved, or else irrelevant. If Lucas could see her now. She limped awkwardly to the dining-room, knowing

138

what she had been afraid to admit all day, that her confusion and sickness was a result of the injury to her leg.

'I'm sorry. Mum or Dad, I think I need to go to hospital,' she said.

Leaving Tom with David, Marie took her daughter off to Casualty in Rugby. Teresa thought her mother would be tight-lipped, but she said it was a relief when she asked to be taken to hospital because she had been looking increasingly ill during the evening. 'Anyway, David and Dad will have a nice time together,' she said.

'You told me to expect no sympathy if my leg went septic.'

'*Tu es bête. Voilà.*'

At Reception they were told that Teresa might have to wait for at least an hour. From high on one wall of the waiting-room, a light shaded from beneath cast an aqueous gloom below. Seated on cold plastic chairs, Teresa saw that there were several other people silently nursing their pain. The bones in her right leg now seemed like hot iron rods. She scrunched her eyes for a moment, wondering how to bear it for another hour without relief. Then her mother began to talk.

'Poor Teresa. Does it hurt very much? You're so stubborn. I used to worry something terrible would happen and you would not tell me. Not because you didn't want to tell me but because you thought you could make it go away if you refused to admit it.'

'What are you on about, Mum?' Teresa said, and she shuddered, or shivered. She looked up, thinking someone had left a door open because all of a sudden she was cold.

'You used to do such dangerous things,' Marie went on. She was sitting upright, with her hands folded across her handbag on her lap. 'Perhaps it wasn't possible to avoid them very easily at Sweynsend, there are so many loose things about, rusty nails and I don't know what, and you couldn't be supervised all the time. I used to worry so and try to stop you going about the place so freely, but your father said you must be allowed to wander and find out for yourself. So I watched you running about, along the path by the bonfire, where there were old tin cans and rusty springs from an old mattress, Lord knows, and I wanted to stop you and I had to stop myself from stopping you. And you, Teresa, you didn't seem to look where you were going, you just ran, and my heart was in my mouth . . .'

'Mum, what are you telling me this for?' Although half aware that her mother was making an unparalleled admission, Teresa could not concentrate at all. She wanted her to save her speech for another, more suitable time; to shut up and leave her to her pain. But she didn't have the energy to confront her and tell her so.

'Elizabeth used to watch where she was going, and weigh things up. But if you wanted to get somewhere, you didn't look at what lay in your path or worry about any obstacles. As if by ignoring them they would vanish. I used to worry that with your eyes on the horizon you would one day walk into quicksand . . .'

'Mum, please! If you're going to talk, can you at least talk about something nice?' She wanted to bend forwards and put her head between her knees, but her leg was seized with agony when she tried, as if the bones were being wrenched apart.

Marie laid her forearm against her daughter's. Teresa had not noticed that her mother was wearing the Indian bracelet that Mrs Carew had given her years ago, a soft golden bangle with two facing tigers' heads. She rarely wore it: she must have put it on for David. Liverspots had recently started to appear on the backs of her hands. 'I'm sorry, darling,' said Marie. 'You're so determined to be strong, to be in control, that I don't know whether to ask . . . Is it very painful? I could see that you didn't want us to interfere earlier on, but I knew that you were battling with it. You were starting to behave very strangely.'

'You make me sound like Mrs Carew,' Teresa said, and for the first time she apprehended from her own pain something of what it might have been like for Mrs Carew. The thought of any resemblance, however, was immediately appalling. The spectre of herself behaving in middle age towards Lucas as Mrs Carew had towards the Major reared into Teresa's mind's eye: her slim girl's figure bloated into a heavy, granitic mass, source of glares and erratic commands, disallowing the exercise of his will.

'Please Mum, tell me something nice.'

'What . . .?'

'I don't know! Tell me about when you first came to live at Sweynsend or something, I don't care.'

'But you've heard all that before . . .'

'I know, but I want you to distract me.'

Gamely, Marie began to describe the early days at Sweynsend, and at first it calmed Teresa. But the stories were already familiar and Teresa's attention wandered away. When she closed her eyes she saw the pain in her leg like the heart of a bonfire; the image of Lucas flickered against it.

They sat there in silence until Teresa was called into the surgery. And the doctor said, 'No wonder it hurts. Look how your leg is all inflamed around the wound.'

A lurid puffiness had spread for three inches in each direction. The knee was swollen and the whole of her leg was faintly dis-coloured, as if it had been sweating profusely. In the centre, where the doctor picked away the old dressing, was a mess of gore and tiny shreds of torn skin. Teresa wondered now how she had failed to perceive the deterioration in her leg, or to recognise its taint. It wasn't that she hadn't looked, but it seemed as if she were blind to her own condition; as if it absolutely required someone else to point it out before she could see it for herself.

Teresa was instructed to stay at home for a week with her leg up. Her only outings were to be a daily check-up at the hospital.

The gravity with which her injury was viewed surprised her, but it was also comforting:

'I no longer felt that I had made a fuss about nothing,' she told me. 'I remember hobbling off to collect my antibiotics. Although it still hurt, it was already a relief to know that I had reason to hobble. As Mum took me home, a lightness stole through me. I was tired, my leg throbbed and my head was fuzzy, but I was strangely excited. In the week ahead I saw an unexpected opportunity for continuous contemplation of Lucas. And there was this sense that my extreme event in one sphere must presage an extreme event in another.'

I'm aware that this must all seem a little odd; as if Teresa and I never speak of anything other than this business. Of course it is not like that – I am selective. Then again, we talk about it a great deal. For me, there is an eerie sense of seeing a period of my own life reflected in Teresa's narrative. And it is heading – or appears to be heading – towards a climax which never in fact occurred in my case, so it seems that by continuing to listen I will relive those events in my life and be offered a different outcome. Never mind that the outcome did not happen, it is enough just to see it unfolding.

If this explains why I am eager to listen, it does not explain why she is so keen to tell me all. Naturally, since I am happy to listen I do not question her motives. But the question arises, nevertheless. Does she sense in my readiness to listen a drawing-together? Perhaps she feels that she is strengthening something between us, establishing a new bond by entrusting me with this intimate story. For me, however, our separateness is redefined as she unwittingly draws up between us this thing from my past.

The pain in Teresa's leg receded soon. If she stood up and walked around, it felt as if the steel jaws of a mantrap had closed upon her. But sitting back in the sofa with her leg raised on a chair in front, there was only a mild ache, which she could ignore. She had made a sort of nest for herself in the drawing-room with cushions and a rug. On a low table at her side were a couple of Daphne du Mauriers, her walkman and a bottle of Lucozade. She should have been comfortable; she *was* comfortable, in spite of her mother's suffocating kindness. For Marie kept popping in and offering to turn the TV on, or feed Teresa, or bring her a *tisane*. Did she want a cushion under her heel? Teresa's comfort nurtured a growling impatience that was aggravated by her mother. All she wanted was to be left alone.

Her immediate situation was an acute and constant reminder of her remoteness from Lucas. Not only was she in a different place, in a separate life, her feelings not even divulged let alone reciprocated, but also she was trapped at home as surely as if a rope were tied about her neck. Her immobility mocked her restlessness. In her frustration, she marshalled all that she knew of him and let her imagination elaborate, as if peeling back the petals of a rosebud with her fingers, opening them out into an artificial spring.

I regret that when Lucas came to visit us in April we made no effort to find out more about his background. Just how little Teresa knew was revealed by her surprise when I told her his real name the other day. She knew there was some Polish, or Russian connection, but no more than that. Her information was based on what she had from William, and at that age, or at the age when William and Lucas became friends, what matters is the music you like, the dash of your wit and the way in which you respond to immediate circumstances. No eighteen-year-old ever cared about their friends' antecedents. Only later do they come to seem relevant. As for me, my relationship with Lucas is professional and I never had cause to inquire about his personal life. But I could have done so then, when he was a guest of mine. What could have been more natural than to ask as we sat round the dinner table, 'So tell us a little more about your Polish background, Lucas'? Yet as I imagine doing so, I realise that it would have been awkward. His demeanour, his manner of being, does not invite such questions. I don't mean that delicacy, on account of some suspected horror, makes one wary, but that he is always engaged in the present. He tells anecdotes for entertainment, not psychological illumination. He is good company because he takes you out of yourself; he takes you as he finds you, and therefore one does the same with him. He is not coy about being personal – on the contrary, he relishes it; he is quick to make personal remarks, and they are often very funny – but, now I come to think of it, he deflects questions about himself with a self-deprecating word or two, a joke that is at the same time a caution against prying. It is noteworthy, for example, that we managed to spend thirty-six hours together, and they were a merry thirty-six hours, without a single reference to the immediate causes of William's death.

If I put together the scraps I have gleaned from our encounters or from other people, I find that I believe Lucas's father was a Pole, who perhaps came to England during, or just after the war. I believe he died when Lucas was in his teens, but I cannot say this for sure. Perhaps I only think it because of Teresa's comment that he had some money -- not that it would follow from this. His mother is English and he has two younger sisters, but I know nothing about them. I first came across him in St Petersburg in '92 when I went to him for some market research. He had contacts there, including some media access; he had an ability to think on his feet, and a talent for presentations. But how he came to be there I cannot say. You don't ask questions like that, especially in frontier markets.

Teresa says that part of what drew her to Lucas in the first place was the unexpectedness of his friendship with William. Lucas is a restless person and the idea of himself as such may have a sombre appeal to him. But if this were all then he would be just another irresponsible egoist, which neither Teresa (all those years ago), nor indeed I (now), quite believe he was or is. The difficulty and the interest lie in the impression that he does not admire himself for his restlessness. He acknowledges it in himself, but he also longs for stability. His reticence about his background reflects not lack of curiosity but awareness that its connection with himself is tenuous. Rejecting the hollow comfort of an ancestral fatherland, he finds himself alone and loose.

It isn't hard to see why William liked Lucas: he thought he was a handsome, glamorous figure, everything that he wanted to be himself but was not, and he was flattered by his friendship. But Lucas's fondness for William is harder to fathom. William was surrounded by every outward sign of stability, and he had been so from birth. Yet for all William's solidity, Teresa says that Lucas saw a feebleness in him, and was fascinated by this combination. He wanted to see just how far William's props sustained him. Lucas's character was always more powerful than William's; without doubt, William was in thrall to him. This was unproblematic when the girls first met Lucas at Sweynsend because William had both a fiancée and a grand home: there was charm in his reverence for his drifting friend. But if the power were abused then it could provoke bitter jealousy, as they discovered. And despite the challenge of later events, Teresa's impression that Lucas was genuinely fond of William never faded. He didn't always respect himself, but he was at least honest, even about the desperation that underpinned his fondness and ensured that William simultaneously attracted and repelled him.

Teresa did not wonder why Lucas had come to Sweynsend. It didn't matter. He had come, and he had gone. The question was, how was she to see him again? This was her preoccupation. And though she knew that he might return to Sweynsend at some date, she wasn't content to rely on chance.

On the second day of her incarceration it occurred to her that she should write him a letter. *Dear Lucas, I so enjoyed meeting you when you came to Sweynsend.* She sensed his restlessness. She knew that the nimbleness that she saw would be seen in him by others with more opportunity for gaining his attention. If she wished to be anything to him then she could not afford to wait. *In fact I haven't been able to stop thinking about you.* But it seemed like an act of mad foolhardiness to write to him. She sat back in the sofa with her leg up, silent headphones clamped to her ears, staring at the wall. She was three years younger. She had only met him over the course of one weekend; and she had no reason to suppose that he saw anything special in her – how ridiculous to write to him! *I don't suppose you've thought much about me, and you'll probably think it's very . . .* Very what? Foolish, cheeky, forward? What else was she to do? She was laying herself open to ridicule and cruelty, but she thought of his boyish, neat nose and trusted him. And even if he wasn't in love with her now, was it impossible that she should jolt him into it, that she could write it into being? He would see her courage and respect it. *I hope you won't despise me.* And if he did despise her then she would have lost nothing because without her declaration, despicable or not, she would get nowhere.

These impossible moments in a life. Impossible because you are faced with claiming the person you want more than any other in the world, but with some hard edge of your being you suspect that you will fail. (And I use 'claim' advisedly, because a recognition has occurred: *this* is the person by whom I will henceforth be occupied, by whom I am *pre*occupied.) Impossible too because henceforth you will have to live with this moment, it will accompany you down the years as the moment when you made your claim. Whatever your subsequent achievements, this moment is fundamental because it is when you were nailed to your solitude. This too is a love that dare not speak its name.

146

There was a nocturnal bus ride with Iris which I repeat over and over in my head, when we talked all through the sliding darkness. And though we didn't touch and nothing was said, I knew from her movement, her rhythms, and her curiosity, that it was not all on my side; that things were possible between us. But we arrived and were met by friends, and nothing was said. Later we walked for an hour on a stony hillside with the ground slipping beneath our sandaled feet, and things were said, half said, and she turned away with that grinding kindness, let us be as we are: friends. With Teresa and me it was different. We were already reconciled to our emptiness, at least I was to mine, and if I did not then know of hers then perhaps I sensed it. Oh, I don't mean we didn't love one another – or that we don't now, in our way – but we accepted one another with some awareness of how different it might all have been. Hearing now about Teresa's desire for Lucas, naturally I will reflect on my own experience, but I also wonder what she felt as she married me. And in the shadow of her sister's woeful tale too.

Teresa struggled to her feet. With every step, pain slashed down her leg. It wasn't that she wanted to go somewhere particular: she wanted to go anywhere at all. She hobbled into the hall and started to climb the stairs, pulling herself up by the banisters and swinging her leg clumsily round so that she did not have to bend it. The pain and ungainliness of the manoeuvre exasperated her and she burst into tears.

Immediately, her mother appeared. 'Teresa! Oh my darling! Did you want something? Why didn't you call me?' She had rushed up the few steps and put her hand to her daughter's back.

'I didn't want anything, I just . . .'

'Then why . . .?'

Teresa shook her head, unable to explain why she had left the comfortable sofa and begun to climb the stairs without purpose.

Marie escorted her back to her wretched seat. 'Is it something else?' she asked, in the special tone she reserved for speaking about menstruating.

Teresa shook her head again, her lips clamped tight lest she blurt out the truth. She was tempted to speak just for the relief of sharing her burden, for the possibility of being able to discuss what action she should take, but she knew that her mother was the last person she could do this with.

After her return, Elizabeth showed off her new clothes and told everybody about her trip – a visit to Joseph, a bargain at Hobbs; dinner at some restaurant or other – and Teresa was surprised when later she came and sat on her bed. She had assumed she would go to William.

'Mum says you were all upset earlier on,' said Elizabeth.

Teresa said nothing.

'It's Lucas, isn't it?'

Teresa twisted her head.

'We saw him when we were in London. He told William that he'd chosen the wrong sister.'

'What on earth did he mean by that?'

'I suppose he meant he fancies you.'

'Me?'

'Uh-huh.'

Teresa considered this information in silence. It could mean what Elizabeth said, but it could also be a polite way of telling William that he didn't think much of Elizabeth. She did not dare believe the first, but she rebelled against the other interpretation too.

'He said that?' she asked.

'Yes.'

'I mean, you heard him?'

'No, he said it to William, but William told me afterwards.'

'He told you?'

'He meant it as a compliment, I think.'

'Funny kind of compliment.'

'You know – that he loves me, whatever Lucas might think.'

'Very pretty, I'm sure.'

'But I'm sure he said it.'

'And if he did, then what?'

'I'm sure he'll come here again before long.' There was a pause, and then Elizabeth said, 'You should phone him.'

'I can't do that.'

'Why are you so afraid to do what you want to do, Tee? You shouldn't be. We shouldn't let other people tell us what we want. Or wait for other people to ask us what we want.'

This was an unlikely speech to hear from Elizabeth, who tends to tailor what she says or does according to what she thinks people expect of her, especially if they are men. Teresa wondered whether it was she who had proposed to William.

During the next four days, however, Teresa persuaded herself that if things were to turn out as she hoped then she must try to influence them instead of waiting passively. She imagined how her words might thrill Lucas into wanting what she wanted, and he would come back to find her. The alternative was a fog of inert air, a future where she sat and watched and waited for something to materialise. She had no choice, it seemed, but to write to him.

As for what Teresa wrote – who knows? It's not the content of the letter that matters, after all, but the fact of it, and its after-effects. Perhaps she remembers but does not wish to tell me, but it is more likely that she doesn't remember at all, even though the act of writing it is probably ever-present for her among the images each one of us has of moments when something happened to close off other options; moments that are kept vivid for us by the myriad pinprick illuminations of events in the parallel worlds lying behind them. Yes, there was a moment when I declared myself, if you like, to Iris, but what I remember above all is the limpness of her pale hand in mine, a hand which I was used to seeing mobile and sinuous, a shaper of things, an instrument. And it is this involuntary, unmeditated transformation in her hand, which no doubt I palpated repulsively in my anxiety, more than anything she said or any visual expression, that I recall of that encounter. That, and a certain quality of seaside light that cunning memory has bolted to the occasion – for it did not take place anywhere near the sea.

# Chapter Ten

AND SPEAKING of the sea, I gather from Alec that Iris and her husband are coming over to Europe. They have taken a house in the South of France for the summer, a summer that starts around now (April) apparently. Aaron must be earning a decent living from his books. Good for him. It turns out he has not been charged for 'aiding and abetting the Phantom of Liberty', but there have been unpleasant remarks in the right-wing press. I suppose they're coming over here to get a break from it. Iris told Alec, 'Maybe I'll get to see Jimmy. He could come over and visit with his wife, I've never met her' – those were her actual words, according to Alec. Maybe she was only saying it to make conversation with him. She knows he is still a good friend of mine. But it's possible too that she is curious to see me (and Teresa). I never doubted that she wanted to regard me as a friend, and it may be that those earlier days have been gilded with innocence for her by all this recent trouble over Sachs. After the limelight of seeing her husband dragged through the press because of his association with a terrorist, and the nightmare of a federal investigation (albeit one that was aborted – which is not to say that it couldn't be started again, such cases are never truly closed), Iris's earlier life, and whatever I represented in it, must seem sublimely carefree. I don't flatter myself that she regrets anything, but just knowing that I wouldn't be unwelcome is powerful news.

I don't quite see how we would get there, though. Living in

America, she assumes that the South of France is like the next county to England. It's true that I could probably make the time to go for a week – there is some advantage to being freelance, even if at times I get very busy indeed – but it will be a bit harder to present it to Teresa. She has never heard of Iris, after all, though I expect she's heard of Aaron since she's a novel reader. What would I feel if I saw Iris now, and what sort of half lies would I need to tell everyone to protect myself, and her? And to protect them from me? Better perhaps not to go at all than to forge an anodyne new social relationship where Iris and Teresa talk to one another about suntans and shopping (not Teresa's best topics, nor Iris's either, but they would be uncontentious for women who don't know one another, and don't want to know one another). Meanwhile I suppose Aaron and I would swap anecdotes about football or politics – or, even worse, novels.

'There was no reply, Jimmy. No reply came.'

Teresa had been telling me about her letter to Lucas when Alec rang. For a moment I couldn't think what she was talking about – we were in the drawing-room, daubing swatches of paint on the walls – and I guess I was distracted by Alec's news. But I switched back to her story with revived interest, especially since she did not quite seem to regard what she had done as ridiculous, despite being ready enough to laugh at her younger self.

'Lear's claim that nothing would come of nothing always seemed to me the loaded assertion of a vain, manipulative old man,' she said. 'For plainly despair would come of nothing. Now despair had come to me for doing something, and it struck me that "doing nothing" was only a reflection of the speaker's values. If I'd done nothing, i.e. not written my letter to Lucas, then I would at least have avoided that particular form of disaster, which would have amounted to something since it was a very painful disaster. In short, I felt I *ought* to regret my letter. And yet, somehow, I didn't.'

That period of waiting for Lucas's response was a strange limbo for Teresa. Everything in her life seemed to have led to this, and it was the future's pivot. By writing, she had dismissed the past, rendered the present irrelevant and committed herself to a future which, until she knew Lucas's reaction, she could not begin to predict.

At first, she imagined him telephoning at once. When he did not, she reflected that the phone was an inadequate, trivialising gadget, and he would be right to send a letter instead. The prospect of a passionate epistle brought her hurrying down to breakfast the next day. Her only anxiety was how to smuggle it away and read it in secret. But there was nothing. Although disappointed, she saw how foolish it was to expect a reply by return: it would take longer to compose something suitable.

The time for a quick reply passed and she persuaded herself to be more cautious in her expectations. Evidently he had decided on a different tack. Why wouldn't he wait for a few days? And why should he behave as she, in her impatience, wanted him to behave?

Still she had not been rejected, and the misgivings jostling within her were tempered by a dogged core of hope which, like a tapeworm, developed its own habits as the days passed. Although part of her knew that he would have replied already if he was going to, she would remind herself each evening of a thousand possible excuses for his not having written and convince herself that tomorrow would be the day of her deliverance. In the morning she would dress slowly, taunting herself with visions of his letter, delaying her arrival at breakfast in dread of finding nothing. Later, returning from work on her bike, trying not to think about the second post, she pictured coming into the house and removing her jacket as normal – a bright, desirable girl whose attentions would surely flatter any man. She goes into the kitchen with a smile. She happens to glance at the straw basket where the letters are put, and there is a letter flamboyantly addressed to her. It's obviously from an admirer and she chuckles, for she has many admirers competing for her attentions; she can clap her hands and they'll do whatever she asks . . . But reality never matched the daydream beyond the moment when she took off her jacket. Foreboding gripped her then: she trembled as she entered the kitchen. When she found no letter from him, she went into free-fall from her state of suspension.

This waiting was almost physically painful, like lining up each day and volunteering to be punched. She despised the idea of unrequited love because of the futile self-mockery it must entail, and because it seemed like a failure of will. She did not blame him for not loving her. It was her own fault, she thought. She should not have sent the letter; should not have written it, should not have thought it.

And Elizabeth's silence bewildered her. Although Teresa had no desire to talk about it with her sister, she knew something was in the air and it wasn't like her to say nothing. It seemed suspicious. Perhaps she had discussed it with William. Had William spoken to Lucas? Were they all sniggering behind her back? If so, would Elizabeth tell her? Or had Lucas kept it to himself?

He must have realised how his silence tortured her, but he did not trouble himself to send so much as a kind note. It was nullifying, as if she had no more claim to a response than a complete stranger. She knew from Elizabeth that he was in London, and therefore she could not doubt that he had received the letter. If it was really so unwelcome to him, then what could he do without humiliating her more than she had already done for herself? Even a negative response, he must have thought, would nurture her hope; and when she examined her own feelings, she realised that he would have been right. Any response at all would have stirred her up, so wasn't it better to leave her alone? It was true, moreover, that she would have been mortified to learn that he and

William were laughing together at her expense. Wishing to avoid this, he had refrained from mentioning it, which was at least a kind gesture.

Teresa can be strikingly articulate. It is being a lawyer, I suppose. But you would not get an American lawyer speaking this way: 'The more worried I was by rational doubt, the more obstinate grew the clamour of irrational hope. My parents must have known that something was up, but we weren't in the habit of discussing intimate emotional concerns and it would have unsettled me to have done so.' It is to do with being English then, or having read a great many novels. Or is it to do with her relationship with her parents, especially her father, with whom she has a very good understanding? He is himself highly articulate if he chooses to show it (schooled, allegedly, by the Major). She values that and, consciously or not, has emulated him. This trait in her, this facility, instantly appealed to me when we first met, because it displays a thoughtful and ordered response to the world. I could make a life with someone who talks like that, I thought. The mistake – and it is one that many people make – comes in assuming that this kind of language has no emotional content. Elizabeth's emotional life is trivial, at least it has no interest for me, and her only means of articulating it is by ranting, or brandishing other people's empty axioms. Teresa's emotional life is by contrast complex and profound, and her mode of speech is a subtle instrument developed for the precise purpose of articulating what is inside her. Yet occasions may arise where this degree of sensitivity inhibits communication that clumsier individuals would manage without difficulty. So now, if Teresa had spoken about her predicament to her father she would have violated an unwritten contract that did not exist with Elizabeth. Teresa is a private person, who always appreciated that her father respected her privacy but was ready to talk if she chose. But there was a further sense that it would somehow have been improper for a father to initiate intimate conversation with his daughter. They would have identified their carnal natures to one another and, in so doing, the distance between them would have been revealed. A closeness would have been dissolved, and it was precisely his closeness that was the most valuable support to Teresa. No doubt Tom was vaguely aware of what was happening – more so than she supposed – and he subtly let her know this. It takes no more than a word to express sympathy for someone who is unhappy; thereafter, a combination of restraint and attentiveness – a reproach left unspoken, passing the salt – is enough. Teresa was grateful that he did not blunder about with assumptions about what she felt, wielding patronising consolations ('Never mind! There are other pebbles on the beach!'), as if he wanted her to be cheerful for his own benefit.

While Teresa was content to maintain silence with her father because of his implicit sympathy, it frustrated her that her mother was so unreceptive. It was natural that Lucas's name should be mentioned from time to time, not just because he had recently spent the weekend at Sweynsend but also because he had taken such an interest in the place. William had still done very little and, with the autumn now upon them, Tom was anxious. Regardless of grand projects in the Kennels, there were urgent mundane repairs to be done on the Hall, such as overhauling all the gutters and drainpipes. Hoping to spur William into action, Tom sometimes reminded him of the ideas that Lucas had produced. He wasn't praising Lucas for Teresa's benefit: he was trying to make William feel excited about looking after his own property.

During a high wind towards the end of September, hundreds of slates cascaded from a barn in the Kennels, just as Lucas had predicted. For twenty-five years Tom had watched the place decay. He had hoped that William would halt the process, but nothing had been done and the slates were smashed. In his disappointment, Tom was angry. Even if William had no wish to repair that barn, he could have removed the slates and sold them. Tom is gentle and kind, not the sort of man to speak harshly to his prospective son-in-law, but in his exasperation, he said: 'It's such a waste! It's just what your friend Lucas told you would happen! He was so full of enthusiasm!'

'It wasn't his responsibility. He could afford to be enthusiastic,' Marie said at once.

The conversation was swiped off its feet. Tom felt indignant on Teresa's behalf; and while William was embarrassed to be openly criticised by Tom in the first place, to be defended in such a way by Marie confused him further. Elizabeth wavered between sympathy for her fiancé and her sister.

As for Teresa, she took her mother's remark to be directed entirely at herself. Although she knew that she must have been aware of Lucas's recent influence on her, she had never acknowledged it, which baffled Teresa and sharpened her isolation. Marie made no overt attempt to understand the circumstances, nor did she offer any sympathy. She behaved as if the only thing to have happened recently to her daughter was the injury to her leg. She was determined not to let her solicitude over that spill into other troublesome areas. Now her words implied to Teresa that she knew perfectly well what was going on: Lucas was an irresponsible show-off, and Teresa was a fool for fixing her sights on him; she didn't want to hear anything about it.

'Now,' says Teresa, 'I can see the anxiety behind her remark. But at the time I saw that she was cross with my father for using Lucas as a stick with which to beat William, and I didn't understand why.'

Elizabeth and William's wedding was set for February, four months away, but Marie was already exhausted by the preparations for it. There was a great amount to deal with and it irked her that Tom was agitating about the barn, which was irrelevant to the wedding. Not that she didn't want William to show more activity: she did, but she wanted him to start with the places the wedding guests would see. She wanted the damp patches in the house cured, the cistern in the downstairs loo fixed and, ideally, another loo installed; she wanted the chimneys swept and the drawing-room redecorated. Nobody could accuse her of fussing in the circumstances, for these things were not details. Fields of mould had spread on the ceiling near the porch and in one corner of the dining-room, although summer was only just over. At a February wedding in what was assuredly the coldest house in England, the chimneys needed to be functional. Yet they belched smoke and periodically coughed up soot. Wallpaper hung off the walls in the drawing-room in swags like unfurling sails.

If Teresa came to recognise why her mother resented time spent considering Lucas and the barn relatively soon, it was much longer before she came to appreciate her more serious and general concern. It is perhaps unusual for a mother to see so much of her daughter's fiancé during the couple's engagement, but here it was inevitable. They were constantly in each other's homes. Everyone saw William pottering about; he did it very charmingly. At least, he was charming – but what did he *do*? Perhaps he wrote a bit of poetry and maybe its quality really was not important, but the question of him doing any work was never addressed. Everything was put off until after the wedding. If the original point of his coming to Sweynsend was to do the place up, not to live there and go out to work elsewhere, why delay all renovations until after the wedding? Did he in fact have any intention of beginning after the wedding? By now, the Fairfaxes knew William too well to believe unproved pieties about his perfection: they knew him well enough to doubt him.

Marie was less bothered about his commitment to Sweynsend than Tom. She was more concerned about his commitment to Elizabeth, and hers to him. Perhaps Tom would have been, had he doubted it. But he no more presumed to encroach on Elizabeth's emotional affairs than on Teresa's. He trusted Marie to provide guidance where necessary. In her dismay at her mother's apparent lack of concern for her, it did not occur to Teresa that she might be worried about William and Elizabeth; that, compared to their situation, she regarded Teresa's as one of childish infatuation. The problem wasn't even that she doubted William's commitment to Elizabeth. One can usually comprehend dimly, at least, what an engaged couple see in one another. He may not seem the most attractive of men, but you let this pass because it's a personal matter; he may like fishing, but happily she likes painting rivers; she likes spending money frivolously, so does he, and fortunately they have some to spend. Some compatibility is usually evident. If you know one of the partners much better, and are very fond of them, you are apt to search the other one for positive signs. You will be ready to see them, but if you don't then you will be more worried than if your affections weren't involved. Marie was undoubtedly delighted by the idea of Elizabeth marrying William and, ever since his arrival at Sweynsend, she couldn't have been better disposed to like him. To begin with she took him on trust, but as she got to know him better, she grew puzzled by what her daughter saw in him. Not that he wasn't agreeable and so on, but it seemed more and more surprising to her that he was the sort of person Elizabeth could love. Elizabeth is shallow. She likes bad pop music, magazines with other people's fantasies, films with rich loverboys. Put her in a sun parlour with a magazine, her Walkman and a video and she would be in heaven. Where was she going to find that at Sweynsend Hall?

# Chapter Eleven

IT WOULD BE misleading to suggest that the Fairfaxes led an utterly secluded life. Situated in the fork of two converging motorways, three miles from a junction with each, Sweynsend is easy to visit for anyone driving north. It was a pleasant place to break a journey because William was hospitable: a telephone call in advance would guarantee a visitor a good meal; a drink was always available. It wasn't only friends who appeared but also members of his family. His father and one of his uncles lived in Yorkshire despite working in London and, though they usually travelled by train, a car went by from time to time. William's impending marriage provided many reasons for them to drop in, chief among which was curiosity about Elizabeth.

One Sunday in October, Hal and Vivienne stopped off on their way south. Everyone gathered for tea in the passage-room, behaving with careful joviality.

'I suppose you'll want to put a new roof on, won't you, Elizabeth?' said Hal with a grin. 'Being a Catholic.'

'Oh, Hal!' cried Vivienne, drawing attention to her husband's mischief even as she appeared to reproach him for it.

Hal enjoyed fluttering his witty intellect. It didn't much bother him if he wasn't understood: he expected to be challenged, and it was all the same to him whether he was called upon to defend his point or to explain it.

Vivienne didn't understand Hal's jibe, but she knew that no

one else understood it either. It was a form of showing off for her husband, and of testing his future daughter-in-law. Having suffered from his cleverness herself in the past, it amused her to see how others coped, as if it were her due.

Elizabeth had once known the rules of this game well enough from the Major's sparring, but now she seemed to have forgotten them. She was afraid of offending Hal by challenging him, and she did not appreciate that nobody else had understood him better than her. She blushed and smiled, at a loss how to respond.

'Dad likes a bit of theological banter at teatime,' said William. 'It's well known.'

'I eat cake. Ergo my will cannot be free. Justification by cake,' said Hal.

Tom cleared his throat. 'I used to say it to your father,' he told Hal: 'By their works shall ye know them.'

'A misunderstanding!' cried Hal. 'The first of many from Geneva. It's the Catholics who are materialists.'

'Coming from you, Dad!' said William.

Then Elizabeth interjected: 'Does it need a new roof?'

Everyone laughed briefly, indulgently, as if Elizabeth had countered Hal to some effect – which, in a sense, she had, because the house did not in fact need a new roof and it sounded as if she were telling him very sweetly to mind his own business. Nevertheless, everyone could see that she had missed the dialectical point, whatever it was; and when Vivienne proffered her cup to Marie and said, 'Is there any more tea?' there was a brassy gleam on her voice as if she had produced a cunningly withheld trump.

'I'll fetch the kettle,' Teresa said, and hurried from the room.

She found the spectacle of Hal and Vivienne trying to prove something to her family bizarre. Even if they felt themselves to be socially superior, richer, cleverer, it was scarcely polite to point it out. It angered Teresa to see her sister being humiliated. She might not understand exactly how or why it was happening, but she could feel that it was. It was cruel, a cat playing with a mouse.

The kettle boiled. Teresa returned with it to the passage-room, her feet loud on the flagstones. She wondered if William's parents would always behave like this towards them, and whether it would be rude of her to slip away. She was dimly aware of the front door opening and William greeting an unexpected visitor but, sunk in her gloomy reflections, she did not think who it might be.

Teresa entered the hall just as Lucas came into the house. It was like falling through a trapdoor and finding herself in a different story in which events ahead were suddenly glimpsed like explosions from a casually ignited fuse unrolling into the future.

For surely he had come for her.

Lucas was dressed in leathers. He had just pulled off a crash helmet and his hair was pulled forward. He smiled.

Teresa's mouth strained, then it occurred to her that he was smiling at William, who stood between them. Still clutching the kettle, she ducked into the passage-room. Through the window she could see his motorbike. Another helmet was strapped to the back. She had never been on a motorbike before and she was curious. She could imagine tunnelling through the wind, the feel of him braced in front, her arms about him.

Hal and Vivienne stood up. She had forgotten that she wanted more tea. 'It's about time we were on our way,' she said; they had already stayed far longer than they intended, the idea had been just to pop in and say hello, but it was always such a pleasure because she was so pleased about William and Elizabeth, Elizabeth was such a charmer . . .

'Viv, turn the tap off darling.'

Vivienne looked startled, as if her husband had pulled her hair. In another instant she was smiling again. 'My husband! He is naughty!' she said and, turning to Elizabeth, she added, 'I wish you better luck with yours!'

After Vivienne had said her goodbyes, Hal twizzled his hand with outspread fingers, a gesture towards the idea of a wave. Teresa liked him. He was spiky, but a man who could not even let a wave go without an ironic charge, however purposeless, was interesting to her.

The Carews seemed to back out of the front door in a rush, embracing William as they passed and shouting hello-goodbye at Lucas.

Lucas had taken off his outer clothes. He was now in jeans and a stretched black jersey. William ushered him towards the chair nearest the fireplace in the passage-room, but he stepped aside at the last moment and turned, plucking a biscuit from a plate on the trolley. Everyone was talking at once, commenting on Hal and Vivienne's speedy departure and asking Lucas how he came to be passing Sweynsend. He said something about the rain, about riding a motorbike on wet roads. But when Teresa looked outside she saw that it wasn't raining and inferred that the rain was a hasty excuse to disguise his real purpose. All that time and anguish wondering why he hadn't replied to her letter evaporated. Now it was perfectly clear: not wanting to write, he had waited until he could drop in personally. Of course it was what he would do. She should have known better than to expect a letter. The delay could only be because he couldn't come before.

Otherwise, how would he dare to show his face?

Teresa could feel the blood surging at her temples, her heart drubbing her ribs. She told herself he was just a man, like any other. But his presence alone frazzled her skin. The effect he had on her was weirdly, shockingly physical. She felt there must be a coil of smoke issuing from her collar: she did not dare look at Lucas lest she blush in front of everyone. William asked if he would stay for supper and he said, 'That's very kind, why not?' which seemed to confirm what she knew to be true, that he had come to Sweynsend deliberately, for her.

Remembering that Lucas came into the kitchen garden with her on his earlier visit, it occurred to Teresa that he would follow her if she went there now. He would find an excuse. Gathering her composure like remnants of discarded clothing, she left the room.

It was raining again outside, very gently, like a soft and cooling mist in the air, not unpleasant. She stumbled across the green lawn waiting for his voice behind her, listening for the clump of his step on the grass. If he reached her by the time she got to the yew hedge, it would be all right; if he didn't catch up till they were in the vegetable garden, it would end in disaster.

It was dry in the arch of the yew hedge, relatively dry. She would wait for him there.

She could hear drops falling on each side of her shelter as she peered through the drizzle back across the lawn towards the house. She shivered, although she wasn't cold, and muttered to the spiders that she must give him time to get away. But she was impatient: Come on Lucas, come on, I want you, don't you know that I want you; stamping her feet as if that would make him join her sooner. And suddenly she saw him.

He was ambling, despite the rain, with his fingers stuffed into the pockets of his jeans. He looked up at the ilex tree, from which a large bough had lately split away. Only when he was quite close did he see Teresa. He gave her a surgeon's brisk smile but did not change his pace, and for the first time since his arrival Teresa was afraid. The sudden doubt was like an incapacitating drug. She imagined holding out her arms and leaping into his embrace, but she was rigid.

Lucas's hands stayed rooted in his pockets as he joined Teresa in her musty bower. Raindrops glistened in the tussock of his hair; tiny sparkles of moisture were caught in his black eyelashes. She looked down at his feet and he flexed one ankle, pressing out

164

against the inside of his boot with the arch of his foot while his toe bit sharply into the earth.

'Your letter must have been difficult to write,' he said. 'You must have been wondering.'

Teresa nodded, hugging herself as if she might break apart, like the ilex tree. Whatever he was about to say or do was already beyond her influence, but she knew that it would take its place as a feature in her life: she could only wait and watch whatever happened unfold, like the moment between realising that a ball is going to come down on the roof of a greenhouse and after it has struck.

'I've never had a letter like that. I was very flattered.'

An image of running away and sparing herself this scene flitted across Teresa's mind, but she dismissed it, for above all she wanted to be with him, with his turquoise eyes and sharp-toed boots, his loose black jumper and narrow lips. Disgusted by her own slavishness, she could not resist a sardonic interruption: 'But.' Even as she said it, she knew that it would only irritate him.

He looked up obliquely, considering whether to remark on her sour tone. 'You took me by surprise. I had no idea that you thought of me like that. I'm not used to people throwing themselves at me.'

When Teresa did not respond, the smile flickered out of his face. 'It was so brave of you,' he persisted. 'I couldn't believe my eyes when I read it. I can't think what I did to deserve it!'

'But?'

'You're not going to make this easy for me, are you?' he said, and brushed an overhanging branch of the hedge with his knuckles so that a little shower skittered down on each side of them.

'Easy for you? What about me?'

He looked at her candidly, as if to point out that it was she who set this up, but he refrained from saying it and she was grateful. He breathed deeply and then started talking again. 'I know, of course it's difficult for you. You must have been in torment ever since you wrote your letter. It doesn't make it any easier to be told you've made a mistake but, believe me, you have, and it's better for you if I tell you. You've set me up as some kind of paragon. After just a few hours with me you've jumped to a rash of wrong conclusions and made me into something I'm not. Your letter was so . . . I don't know . . . so pure . . .'

'Ha!'

'Well, it was pure in a way. It was direct and honest, and it made me feel ashamed of myself. You see I'm not what you think, Teresa. You want someone who will respect your love for what it is, return it in the spirit in which it's offered, and I wouldn't do that. It's not that I don't think you're attractive – you're lovely. Who wouldn't find you attractive?'

'Stop it!' she cried, raising her hands to her ears. He reached out and the tip of his middle finger touched her elbow. She backed off instantly into the prickly hedge. 'You don't have to start telling me how attractive I am now!' she assured him.

'I'm not so jaded,' he said, 'that your letter didn't move me.'

'Move you!'

'Yes, it moved me. If I were sensible, no doubt I would try to pretend to be the sort of person you think I am. Reap the benefit, in the hope that I would change.'

'Spare me this, at least!'

Teresa turned towards the kitchen garden as if to walk off quickly, but her intention was washed away by the first drop of rain on her face and she stepped back again into the shelter. She knew it was futile listening to Lucas any more, and that he couldn't be enjoying the performance either, but she felt obstinately determined to hear him out, if only to push him into a little more discomfort of his own. She imagined the warmth of his breath behind her; she wanted to stay there with him still. 'Reap the benefit,' she repeated. From where she was standing, everything looked so bedraggled. In the corner of the garden were the splayed bones of the broken greenhouses and the dilapidated sheds with their sagging roofs. Dripping saplings lodged in the remnants of the gutters like garlands in a mortuary. Strewn on the desolate earth were sodden vegetables that nobody wanted. 'So my letter fell on barren ground.'

'As I said, it bowled me over. I wanted to come back to you at once but . . .'

'But.'

'You keep saying "but"!'

'But rain stopped play.'

'I did want to, it seemed the least I could do. *But*, as you say, I didn't. And the longer I left it, I felt that I should come and see you face to face. Which is why I'm here.'

'I thought you were here because of the wet roads.'

'You think I should have announced to everyone that I came to answer your unilateral declaration of love?'

Teresa looked out over the garden to the arched gate in the crumbling wall at the far end. The opening invited the eye, as if beyond lay an enchanted wilderness, the secret garden she had read about as a child, but she knew that there were only a few sheep on a patch of ground in the fork of two roads. She was afraid of meeting his eye lest she burst into tears, and she didn't want him to see her cry.

'How many love affairs have you had?' he asked suddenly. 'One? Two? I've had lots, Teresa. I mean twenty or something. Lots. I know that when you want someone, only that person will do. If it doesn't work out, it's terrible. I know, it's terrible. But things change. You'll get over it, Teresa: you'll see I'm a shit after all, then you'll laugh and see how ridiculous it would have been to love me. You'll find someone who will be worth it, you'll have children and he'll be a good father, just as you will be a wonderful mother, and it'll all be fine. Whereas I, well, I'm sure if I wanted to settle down, if I was tempted by the prospect, then you would be the best possible girl. But it isn't me. I'm not that type. It would be irresponsible of me to let you think I was. I may be restless, but I'm not altogether irresponsible.'

Teresa had the vague sense that something in what he said was wrong, but she didn't know what and she didn't have the energy or the clarity of mind to work it out. She was tired of his voice explaining and telling her things as if she ought to agree, and she wanted to walk away. But she could not even summon the power to do that: although clouded with hopelessness, she was mesmerised by him, as if staked to the spot by a freak sunbeam. It was a relief when he took her arm and said, 'Come on, let's go in.'

'I don't really remember what happened after that,' Teresa said, rocking back onto her heels – she was weeding one of the flower beds in front of that same yew hedge, while I sat on a stone bench in a niche that I cut. A garden like this one at Sweynsend is a lot of work, especially in spring when you can practically see things growing, it changes so fast. I had spent most of the morning mowing, and I still hadn't begun on the paths in the kitchen garden.

'Don't remember?' I said. 'That doesn't seem likely.'

'I think it stopped raining before long, and Lucas left, but I have no memory of what was said either before or after his departure. Nobody commented, but the general nature of what had occurred must have been fairly obvious. I know that I was unable to follow any train of thought, or focus on anything except the image of Lucas talking to my back while I stood in the arch there' – she pointed her trowel towards the gap in the hedge – 'and watched the rain falling on the kitchen garden.'

It wasn't so much the fact of his rejection, which didn't altogether surprise her, she explained, as the finality of it. For as long as he hadn't answered her letter there was a glimmer of hope that, if confronted by her, he might succumb. It might have been an unfounded hope but, for as long as he hadn't actually rejected her, she could pretend to herself that he might not, and it wasn't until this opening was closed off that she realised how much light it let in. He might have avoided Sweynsend altogether and spared her the explicit rejection which until then had never even registered with her as a possibility. In the event of his coming, she imagined him evading the burden of a relationship, or getting tired of her and cheating, 'but I never thought he might flatly decline the opportunity of fucking me.' Men, she said, had all sorts of ways of avoiding responsibilities, but they tended not to turn women down. But Lucas appeared to have taken the responsibility, and she was stunned by this. He could have stayed away, but he had come to Sweynsend specially to tell her that he didn't even want to fuck her. When she recalled him telling her how attractive she was, she shivered with humiliation and wondered what was wrong with her that she had failed even at that level.

Overwhelmed by this single fact, she was slow to wonder about the details of what he had said, to sift the ashes for an ember to lighten her gloom. She expected to find nothing with which to reproach him, nor did she want to remind herself that it was she who had fallen in love with him and written the letter – that it was her fault. He had been patient with her; he had not laughed or chattered about it to anyone else. She had given him such an opportunity to take advantage of her but he had refused it, and this implied at least some respect for the impulse, however foolish, that had driven her to do it. It was her problem that she was hurt and insulted, and she despised herself for it. She knew that he'd done the right thing if he had no feeling for her, if the right thing was what her father would have called the decent thing; he had even bothered to come to Sweynsend to tell her. She knew all this, and reminding herself of it only made her feel worse. But when she began to reflect on his words in subsequent days, she was surprised to find things which, instead of forcing her grudging admiration, made her seethe with venom.

It occurred to her first that he had lied about his reasons for coming to Sweynsend. He had said to the others that he was on his way from somewhere to somewhere on his bike, and he'd stopped off because of the rain. Why shouldn't she believe this too? He had not told anyone in advance that he was coming, nor tried to confirm that she would be there; and he had left as soon as the rain stopped. It was easy for him to say he'd come to see her, but then why had he not come before? Even supposing he had vaguely intended to meet her face to face, he had waited until the accident of encountering rain on that stretch of motorway before doing so, which wasn't the deliberate visit he had presented to Teresa. No sooner had this doubt nipped her than she believed it, and wherever she cut into the memory of his words she found them likewise infected, as if the very act of her looking produced the poison.

For in everything he had said, she now realised, he had adopted the voice of Experience towards Misguided Innocence. From the moment when he began to compliment her on her letter she had felt uneasy, as if it wasn't him talking to her but a more calculating man with a smoother tongue. How dare he claim to know what she thought or felt? Was he really convinced that she loved not him but an idealised creature extrapolated from him? Or was saying so a dodge to justify his coldness? It infuriated her to be told bluntly that she had made a mistake, because it implied that she had a choice. He misunderstood and devalued her love by suggesting that it was contingent on his positive response. She knew it was not something she could just withdraw because he told her that she was unwise, like the offer of a loan, for she doubted that wisdom was or should be her guide. It was nonsense to think that he knew what she felt because he had had twenty love affairs. Twenty affairs maybe, but not of love. It was inconceivable to her that she could feel the same for twenty people in a few years. Hard enough to imagine that it could happen more than once in a life. Nor did she believe that he himself would necessarily love wisely, whatever he said. She remembered him saying how attractive she was, and saw that it was a despicable thing to say. And how smug to tell her that her letter 'moved' him. Consoling her with the announcement that, had he been thinking of marrying and having kids then, no doubt, she would be the right woman – this was scarcely credible! She couldn't understand her passivity at the time; she despised it in retrospect. The feebleness of his description of domestic bliss was sufficient evidence of its abhorrence to him – but why did he imagine that she coveted it? Throughout their meeting he had made assumptions about her which he had no business to make, assumptions that insulted her and revealed his own limitations.

But it was no use Teresa persuading herself that Lucas was insufferable, because she could not reach the corollary that it was better to be scorned by an unfeeling brute than by the man of her dreams. The worse she made him seem, the worse she felt, for she was ashamed of denigrating him: in the end, she did not believe in his failings, however much she catechised herself with them. She could re-run in her memory all that he had said as often as she liked and interpret it in his absence with surging indignation, but in her heart she knew that at the time of hearing it, influenced by his voice as if he effortlessly struck harmonics, and by the commitment of his presence, she was upset but she wasn't outraged. In the cold dawn of analysis he seemed patronising, devious and cowardly, but at the time she had felt the reverse. And she trusted what she felt at the time because, when all was said and done, she still wanted him. So in the chilly, narrowing dawns of autumn, she alienated even the restorative warmth of her venom.

# Chapter Twelve

IT WAS A COUPLE of days later and we had taken our coffee out to the terrace after breakfast to ponder what to do about the shattered de Morgan tiles. Most had long since been removed but a few remained, separated by compacted earth and tufts of self-seeded lavender. I say coffee, but Teresa had given up coffee since getting pregnant and was drinking some kind of chicory stuff. I don't know why, but it annoyed me. Quite unreasonably, I see that.

'William and Elizabeth. . .' she began.

'Teresa, Honey, remind me why you are telling me all this,' I said. Only the previous day, I had arranged to visit Iris in France during the summer. In due course I will tell Teresa that I'm meeting a prospective client in Paris, and I'll slip south for a couple of days. If she wants to speak to me she'll ring me on my mobile and never know where I am.

Grotesquely, I felt irritable after fixing up this deceit.

Teresa laughed. 'I rather gathered you were interested.'

'I didn't say I wasn't.'

'I'm telling you, I suppose, because what happened here weighs on me, and Lucas's appearance – his reappearance – has given me the opportunity to share it with you.' When I said nothing, she added, 'Or perhaps you mean, what did all my heartache over Lucas have to do with William?'

I shrugged, and she continued, 'I might ask you why you have been listening so patiently.'

Now I laughed myself. I mean, it was a fair question. It's not every man who would want to hear his wife detailing her unrequited passion for another man. She might believe it was over, but I do not look on things so simply and my acquaintance with Lucas makes it all, at the very least, intriguing.

Lucas did not do anything to make Teresa fall in love with him. Had he made a great effort to impress her and win her over, I suspect he would have put her off. All his actions would have seemed laboured, his behaviour deliberate, when part of what attracted her so much was a kind of challenge he represented. He was friendly and attentive towards her, but so he was towards everyone. He didn't single her out, and if he flirted with her then it was no more than a light-hearted response to her own flirting. He did not try to present himself to her in a different light from that in which the others saw him. Yet she threw herself at him.

There was a time when a man could have blamelessly taken advantage of such an event. What does the broad expect if she throws herself at his feet? It's her problem if she gets upset: women do get emotional, boys will be boys, and she started it anyway. I say 'there was a time': but if Lucas had in fact done this, who would have blamed him? Sooner or later the charade would have been exposed, one of them would have dumped the other and her passion might have faded. A satisfactory result all round.

But he chose not to. Is this why Teresa chose him – because she sensed that he would reject her? Was this story latent within her, requiring only Lucas, or someone like him, to awaken it? In which case, is this all that happened between me and Iris? Is she no more than a foil?

He might have take up with Teresa cynically, and Teresa thinks he didn't because he isn't that sort of person. She thinks she would have sensed it if he had been, in which case the situation would never have arisen because she wouldn't have fallen in love with him. He would have looked different in some way, his voice would have been less compelling perhaps or his movement less fluid. He wouldn't have seemed so beautiful to her. And who, in youth, does not reach out to the challenge of beauty? How wrong can it be to remain true to it?

There is an infinite number of possible explanations for the behaviour of men and women, but the one that interests me here is honesty. I imagine a girl who knows that her so-called lover has stayed in town to tup his secretary, or gone on a trip with another man's wife. She knows because he doesn't try to conceal it and, though her misery flows unabated, she cries to whoever is interested, 'At least he doesn't pretend!' And the world thinks, 'He doesn't even have the decency to hide it from her.' Well, it's true that no woman wants a man who is feeble, but bullying isn't a sign of strength and it's sad to see a woman confusing the two. In the same way, because a man is shamelessly duplicitous or flagrantly cynical he isn't therefore honest. Nonetheless – despite whatever accusations of hypocrisy I may have opened myself to – there is a point to this plea of honesty in deceit which should not be ignored. A man may conduct his life openly or, on the contrary, he may be secretive, but honesty's scales have many weights and gauges, and openness is no proof of a just balance. God knows.

'And what do you think now?' I asked her.

'What do you mean?'

'Do you think he was honest?' For though it may be true that he didn't screw her for the hell of it, it's false to say he wouldn't have. Perhaps she believed this at the time to justify her own behaviour to herself; maybe she tended her bruised self-esteem by persuading herself of his virtue. But the fact of the matter is that it's precisely the sort of thing he would have done. Teresa may not know it, but he has a reputation for playing around with women. You only have to look at him to see that he has spent years fixing women with his suggestive eyes and leading them to his bed – or a haystack, or up against a wall for all I care; I gather he is open-minded – as frequently as he can, lying and shrugging his way through affairs that the poor girls think are 'relationships'. Without doubt he's been successful in these terms. He exudes sexual experience and must have done so even back then, making him seem jaded beside William's naïveté. And yet, and yet . . . I say that he has a reputation and he has, but it is not just as another womaniser: there is a mystery to him, as if he has worked out something about women which other men have not; as if they see something of themselves mirrored in him that distracts them from the crudeness of his masculinity and permits them even to indulge it a little. And where in the past I suspect he disregarded or overrode a great deal in his pursuit of sex, his avoidance of sex with emotional attachments now proceeds from a recognition of their danger, which he respects as one might respect another person's faith. But he is slightly bored by these murky waters. I think Teresa hazily recognised that Lucas steered away from the risk of getting bored with her. She called this honesty, and was excited by the challenge it represented. But while this behaviour may be more honest than, say, Aaron's (who is bored but pretends not to be), Teresa is wrong to attribute honesty as a motive, for the motive is distaste.

'Who cares?' she said. 'It's ancient history.'

'Is it?'

'What's that supposed to mean?'

Certain things, if not utterly forgotten, might as well have happened yesterday: they retain a presence in the mind that haunts our solitude and shadows us in company. But I do not want to say this to Teresa, for what would be the point? I do not want her to think I do not love her; I do my best, and why would I not love her? She has twilight in her hair, a fine straight nose and a look of unforced truth like the feel of sunshine on the back of your neck in April.

I took her hand in mine and said, 'Say what you like, I don't understand why Lucas did not want you.'

'I was obsessed. It's not hard to see why he steered clear of me.'

She was aware, she said, of the drag that her disappointment exerted on William and Elizabeth's happiness. She had no inclination to discuss it with William, but the matter was more complex with her sister. In the end, she told herself that she should let Elizabeth enjoy this period of her life without unloading her own disappointment on her. Now Teresa wonders whether this glib attitude didn't conceal both the worry that she wouldn't be understood, and also a deeper fear for her sister.

She remembered how Elizabeth had encouraged her to phone Lucas. Perhaps she really had misunderstood him, but it seemed more likely that Elizabeth misled Teresa from a desire to supply the answer that was wanted. She likes people to think and behave in ways that she understands, and if she does not understand then she would think nothing of misrepresenting their thoughts in order to make them comprehensible to herself, without a thought for the consequences. By substituting patterns of her own where she sees none, instead of discovering what is obscure, she maintains an illusion of control that consoles her wonderfully, though it bears a poor relation to the true nature of a situation. It was typical of Elizabeth to tell Teresa that Lucas liked her on no evidence at all, only because she wanted it and thought it ought to be the case. So heedless was she of the possibility that her sister might be hurt that Teresa wondered if she imagined it really was possible to shrug it all off without a word. It could only mean that she did not know what passion was. Should Teresa then tell Elizabeth – who was engaged to be married and therefore *surely* in love – that she did not know what love was?

She had no proof for this shocking notion, nor did she desire it. On the contrary, William and Elizabeth behaved as if they loved each other very much. There was the poetry, for example, which embarrassed everyone else, and baffled them too since there was no reason to suppose that Elizabeth was able to distinguish good poetry from bad. Perhaps this was the saving grace, in the circumstances, for the fact is that William wrote love poems and read them aloud to her, which she appreciated whether or not they were good; or at least she thought she appreciated it, for people in love did this sort of thing, didn't they? 'My sister is the kind of woman who believes that a gift of flowers is a demonstration of love,' Teresa told me one day. She crushed a head of lavender between her fingers and held her fingers to her nose. 'Not that flowers aren't nice, of course.'

William did other things, however, which were touching in their peculiar, rather feckless way. Having hitherto paid no attention to the roof, the chimneys, the heating, the windows, the drawing-room walls, or any of the other urgent problems with the fabric of the house, he now started throwing money at projects which Tom, in a sad attempt to keep his exasperation in check and enter into the spirit of Elizabeth's happiness, dubbed the PILLOW, Programme of Improvements and Labours for the Love Of Wife. 'How's the Pillow?' he would ask with heroic jocularity. It wasn't very funny but it enabled him to refer to everything while keeping it at a distance, to subsume it all under one title without having to think too hard about any of it.

The little room which is Teresa's dressing-room, where I found her alone listening to music all those weeks ago – come to think of it, she said Lucas 'always' referred to that song as 'the perfect pop song' but surely she only met him a handful of times? How often had she heard it? Or did William play it, declaring each time what his friend thought? – anyway, the dressing-room was deemed too small for Elizabeth by William. It would do well enough for himself, he reckoned, as it had for his grandfather, but it contained no proper hanging cupboards, nor space for any. The two wardrobes in the large main bedroom apparently satisfied old Mrs Carew, but William didn't think they would meet the new Mrs Carew's needs. He opened up the sealed connecting door into the next bedroom, the 'blue room', which had been Jem's and still housed a few of his unwanted jackets and ties in its wardrobe. On the walls were dim photographs of school football teams with boys whose shorts came to their knees. Those with straight hair had it groomed against the scalp, while those with curls had it pressed into improbable ridges. Jem smiled out confidently from every picture, although he looked much younger than the others. William removed these pictures and the clumsy painting of a favourite horse called Jackanapes, the horseshoes and the stuffed birds, and he ousted the iron bedstead from the corner. Then he called in a salesman from Coventry who persuaded him that a wall of cupboards in laminated board with chrome fittings, interior 'eezy-pull' drawers, and full-length mirrors on the backs of the doors, was what he required. And though William did not in fact require any of it, he nevertheless wanted it very much and needed to be told that he required it in order to feel comfortable about buying it. Pink wall-to-wall carpeting was laid one morning the following week, then the entire monstrosity was installed in the afternoon by men who, sensing a generous tip, obligingly moved the beautiful walnut wardrobe to the nursery. The result was ghastly. It ruined a delightful room. But Elizabeth − for whom all this was a surprise − was thrilled. Blinded by love, perhaps, and anyway destitute, I believe, of taste. She either couldn't see or didn't care about the room's proportions. They did not deter her from parking that ugly juggernaut in there; she said it was practical. And she preferred soft pile carpet beneath her tender feet to cold boards and slippery rugs. It occurred to neither of them that Elizabeth didn't possess enough clothes to fill a quarter of those cupboards. Nor did it seem odd to them that they should need so much more space than his grandparents. Such delusions of grandeur: where did Elizabeth get them? Certainly not from Tom and Marie. From magazines, I suppose, which told her she was owed them. Nor did she worry that this gift might not be an improvement, or a sensible way to spend money. She accepted it with gratitude, as a token of William's love – which, perhaps, it was. And it seemed right to her that he should do such things.

Encouraged by this triumph, William turned his attention to the bathroom. In the cupboard in the corner, where the airing-cupboard is now, there used to be a boiler. He kept that. In the middle of the room, between the two tall windows, Teresa says there used to be a gorgeous great big wallowy cast-iron bath with claw feet. He replaced it with an oval cream-coloured plastic fitting, probably called something like 'spring blossom water-lounge' in the brochure. It turned out that Elizabeth had once commented on the brown rust stain near the old bath's plughole. At each end there once stood a wide basin: His and Hers for the Major and his wife. To be fair, one of them was cracked. William removed this altogether and replaced the other with a curved 'utility' to match the bath. To the right of the door there used to be a chest of drawers and a large free-standing linen cupboard, while to the left there were two further low sets of drawers. These were all expelled, and a hulking walk-in airing-cupboard was intruded. It was a room in itself. It chopped off a third of the old bathroom, occupying the end vacated by one of the basins and the old linen cupboard. One of the handsome windows was almost occluded. Of course, the old bathroom was not modern but it worked perfectly well; with all that space and light it is one of the best rooms in the house. William banished its charm (it has been restored, I'm happy to say) and introduced mischief of his own. It must have cost as much as Teresa used to earn in six months; and he did it all in misguided homage to Elizabeth's femininity.

Next it was the kitchen's turn. In this venture he had more support, for it certainly needed attention. The pockmarked oatmeal linoleum floor needed replacing, and all the thickly varnished seventies cupboards were cumbersome as well as ugly. Replacing the Aga with a state-of-the-art gas cooker, however, was improvident, for though the Aga was ancient and temperamental, it was the only substantial source of heat in the house. The rest of the kitchen survived the ordeal of improvement quite well – the designer tried her best to make a pleasant room, and it was probably William's insistence, not hers, which led to the aberration of the cooker.

Elizabeth accepted the results of these exploits uncritically. It was Teresa who thought they were dreadful and, while he tried to keep his opinion private, she was aware that her father thought so too. Marie seemed uninterested in the quality of the changes. She understood that William was doing them for Elizabeth's sake and she believed that this was sufficient justification. It was different when he bought a motorbike and started driving around with Elizabeth riding pillion. It suggested that her new son-in-law had more money than sense.

I wonder how many people there are who can point to a single terrible event in which they weren't directly involved and know that the sequence culminating in that event was set in motion by a decision of their own (or lack of it) over which they had control? Aaron, of course, who knew about Sachs and did not inform the police. And Teresa too. She will be dogged forever by the thought that she could have said no. Had she done so, none of what followed would have occurred. And she wanted to. But William was so eager that she was afraid of offending him, so she went along with his scheme like a good girl. She disliked almost every aspect of it, but she gave in to *his* idea of what she might want, to please *him* – without even the excuse of being about to marry him.

Of course, Teresa is hard on herself. She did not accept William's offer solely to please him. While it may be true that in normal circumstances she would have done her utmost to refuse, the circumstances were not normal; had they been so, then he wouldn't have made the offer.

On Saturday mornings Teresa used to get up as if it were a weekday. She could only ever sleep in on Sundays. One morning in mid-October, about a month after William had bought his bike, she went downstairs and sat, as usual, in the comfy chair near the Manor's Aga with a cup of coffee. She drew her knees up inside her dressing-gown, wedging her heels against the front edge of the seat. Then she opened her book and, with a little sigh in anticipation of her forthcoming hour of contentment, began to read. But her coffee was still too hot to drink when Elizabeth joined her.

'You're up early,' Teresa said.

Elizabeth pushed her hair behind her ears and grumbled that she could not get back to sleep. She poured herself some coffee and sat down at the table. After a moment she asked, 'What are you reading?'

A caustic rejoinder was on the tip of Teresa's tongue ('If you weren't preventing me, I would be reading . . .'). But it was most unusual for Elizabeth to express any interest at all and so she answered her (Walter Scott? Angela Carter?). Elizabeth nodded but she made no comment, and Teresa's eyes reverted to the page.

'Is it good?' she asked.

Teresa frowned with exaggerated ferocity. Elizabeth knew, in an abstract way, that Teresa loathed this sort of interruption and that she was not deceived by the pretence of being interested in her book. But since she herself regarded reading as a last resort where all interruptions were welcome, she did not hesitate but disguised her determination to proceed with a brusque apology. 'I'm sorry.'

Teresa closed her book.

Elizabeth's shoulders sagged inside her unfastened dressing-gown. Her slightness and her unbrushed hair made her seem forlorn, exposing the neediness which had brought her downstairs to find Teresa without any of her habitual attention to her own appearance. 'William's gone off to meet Lucas today,' she said.

Teresa digested this information. If William had gone away to meet Lucas, it must be because Lucas wished to avoid Sweynsend on account of her. And it surprised her that William should go and join Lucas without Elizabeth. While she knew in a general way that boys might go and do things on their own, she had no experience of it. Now she realised that she had taken it for granted that wherever he went Elizabeth would henceforth go with him. 'Where?' she said.

Elizabeth shook her head and managed a wan smile. 'Some bikers' thing.'

'Well it would be daft going to all that trouble and expense and then never bothering to use the bike.'

'I know. That's what he says.'

'But you don't like it?'

'Oh, I don't mind the motorbike.'

'What then? You're jealous of him going off with Lucas?'

Elizabeth drew in her breath as if about to reply. Then she paused and looked into her mug again before saying, 'Why do you think he bought the bike?'

Teresa shrugged. 'Why do people ever buy motorbikes?'

'No, but why William?'

'I agree, he's not your obvious biker.'

'It's so that he and Lucas can go biking together,' said Elizabeth, as if this amounted to a revelation.

Teresa said she was grateful, in the circumstances, that William had the tact to meet Lucas away from Sweynsend. But she realised that she was evading the point of her sister's remark.

'I know, it sounds silly, doesn't it?' Elizabeth continued. 'Why would he want to go riding with Lucas, particularly . . .?' And the additional 'When he's got me', though unspoken, was pathetically clear.

'Elizabeth, you can't really take umbrage just because William wants to go off biking with Lucas occasionally. Anyway, do you really want to go with him?'

'That's not what I mean, Teresa,' Elizabeth said, tearful now.

Then it dawned on Teresa what Elizabeth was trying to tell her. 'You don't really think . . .?'

'I don't *know*. But there's always more going on between them than one thinks. They talk on the phone . . .'

'You can't conclude from that that . . .'

'He's always sort of copying Lucas. When they've done whatever it is they're doing, they tell each other how they ought to have done it. They're always in competition.'

'So they are men.'

'But it means more to William than to Lucas. I mean Lucas is more relaxed about it, as if he's just playing along for the fun of it. Whereas William is serious. He goes out of his way to impress Lucas.'

Teresa put her hand flat on my chest, a curiously intimate gesture as she turned towards me. We were kneeling on the terrace among the fragments of tiles. 'We were so ignorant,' she said. 'Even if Elizabeth didn't exactly think they had a sexual relationship, she didn't know that they didn't. Neither did I. I couldn't just dismiss her worry as the result of jealousy, though that is what I think it was. In retrospect, I have no more reason to think they were having an affair, but it doesn't matter. The suspicion was enough.'

Once voiced, however, the suspicion was immediately buried.

The girls did not know how to deal with it, but Elizabeth needed the fiction to justify jealousy which she dimly understood to be, in itself, inappropriate; to gain sympathy for something that did not deserve it. And Teresa didn't have sufficient confidence to challenge her sister. Besides, if Elizabeth were making it up then Teresa felt sorry for the insecurity that caused her to do so.

'Anyway, I think for your sake that William should stop seeing Lucas,' Elizabeth declared, as if she were trying to enlist her sister's support against her fiancé; as if taking up sides in this way would somehow remedy something.

Teresa was starting to feel uncomfortable on Elizabeth's account. She had the feeling that something was wrong, and that Elizabeth was flailing in the dark to see what it could be.

The following morning, Elizabeth had not come back home since being collected the previous evening by William on his motorbike. He had taken her off to a restaurant somewhere. Teresa was sitting in the kitchen with her parents, the Sunday newspapers spread out between them, when there was a knock on the door followed by William's voice: 'Hello! Anyone in?'

'In the kitchen,' Teresa called.

'Teresa,' he said as soon as he was in the room, 'I've got a suggestion.' He clapped his hands together. 'Good morning, by the way. Good morning, Marie, good morning, Tom.'

Teresa's parents smiled at his shambolic heartiness and said good morning. 'Help yourself to some coffee, William,' said Tom, waving him towards a chair.

'Thanks. Now then, Teresa, I want to give a party for you.'

'What!' she cried, as if the idea were a dead mouse that had been thrown at her.

William smiled. 'Now listen,' he went on, 'I knew you wouldn't agree at once, but let me tell you what I've decided. I would love to give a party for you – over at the Hall, I mean – and it could be a sort of dry-run for our wedding reception too.'

'But . . . It's very kind, William, but . . .'

'So what do you want to do on your birthday? Go to bed early with a book and a mug of hot chocolate? It's going to be your quarter century – why don't you let us celebrate it?'

'There's a conspiracy here, isn't there?' Teresa said.

She had meant a conspiracy between William and Elizabeth, but she suddenly understood from her parents' benign silence that they had colluded too. It had all been cooked up since her conversation with Elizabeth. She supposed one of her parents had been round to the Hall before she woke up.

'If only I'd insisted,' Teresa told me. 'If only I'd insisted that I really didn't want a party thrown for me. But I was flattered by William's grand invitation. And I didn't mind that Elizabeth had obviously had a word with him because I felt sorry for whatever kind of problem she was having to deal with. I felt sorry for him too, because whatever doubts we may have expressed about him clearly had no bearing on his good will towards Elizabeth. It was confirmed by this gesture towards me. It was reassuring to see that Elizabeth was able to touch these springs in him, as if it proved their love for one another. My parents were pleased with William's gesture too, and they wanted me to accept his invitation in the spirit in which it was given. It was oddly moving that they were prepared to go to so much trouble for my sake (for I knew at once that they would be involved) so soon before Elizabeth's wedding. All the wrong reasons, perhaps. Anyway, I let myself be persuaded.'

They spent the rest of the day discussing the scheme and drawing up a guest list. During her lunch hour on Monday Teresa bought a hundred stiff cards with 'requests the pleasure of your company' printed across each one in flowing cursive script. That evening they filled them out: 'William Carew requests the pleasure of your company to celebrate the twenty-fifth birthday of his future sister-in-law Teresa Fairfax at Sweynsend Hall at 8.30

on December 10th 1985.' It struck Teresa that the wording on the invitation was unusual, and she reflected that it was strange too because the party would be more significant for her in respect of Lucas's absence than her own birthday. But she let this frail spark of insight drown in the comfortable, sluggish confluence of her vanity and the benevolence that she felt towards William and Elizabeth. Telling herself that she must not be so ungracious, she posted the invitations the next day.

# Chapter Thirteen

ALEC INFORMS me that Iris is in France already. He has given me her phone number. Apparently she went there with Aaron last week, to a house near Sanary. Sanary. I have no idea where Sanary is, other than being beside the sea, nor what happens there. But at once it has a claim on me. Whenever I hear the name in future it will mean one thing only: a place that is inhabited, or has been inhabited, by Iris, and if I should go there many years from now, long after her departure, I shall wander its streets or shore observing the houses and wondering which one it was that Iris occupied; seeing her shadow at the threshold of the boulangerie, a flutter of her skirt smoothed down by her long-fingered hand, a glimpse of her calves; and the shopkeepers will be people who have talked to her; and the beach will have been trodden by her, and the view out to sea will be familiar to her, perhaps loved.

I can't help noticing how her relative proximity inflames me. There is a renewed sense that our paths might cross; that all, perhaps, is not over.

I do not think of Iris in terms of physical attributes but rather as a destiny. Not that I discount the possibility that, if she and I shared a desert island, I would fight with her, repel her, or get mad at her: but even if this happened, I do not believe I should wish to be elsewhere for it would feel as if this was what was intended for me.

How did it get to be like this?

The question leaves me floundering. Intended by whom? It just is so. It has been so ever since I first met her. Everything that has happened away from her – my life – has not seemed altogether real: it belongs to an interim existence, which is perhaps ironic if I consider how my life has been occupied by material things, envied by others. Ironic, too, that Teresa would understand, though I do not fool myself that understanding would amount to complicity here, nor perhaps forgiveness.

It is ridiculous of course, but there it is. And, knowing that it is ridiculous, I have made other arrangements, attempted a more feasible reality.

Speaking of which, Teresa is now four months pregnant. 'I'm nearly at the end, Jimmy,' she said to me last week – but she meant the story of her curtailed parallel life, not the term of her own gestated reality.

Shortly before her birthday, Teresa's father gave her money to buy a party dress. He assumed she would buy a frock in Rugby, but she went instead to London where she bought a pair of loose silk trousers in a deep peony pink, almost cherry-coloured in a certain light. There was a little matching top like a camisole, and she got a short black jacket to go with it. Unable to find any pink or red shoes which didn't clash, she got some expensive black satin ones that she justified on the grounds that she would be able to wear them with other clothes in the future. Never in her life had she spent so much money on a single outfit. I asked if she still possessed it, and she answered that she did – except for the shoes – but then she patted her stomach and said that she doubted, at the moment, if she could wear it. I took her meaning but I was surprised, for I had not noticed any thickening of her waist.

She had imagined herself coming downstairs, feeling like a

million dollars as the party began. Early arrivals would look up as they took off their dark coats, and there she would be – resplendent, radiant; beautiful. But in the event she came down early, before any guests arrived, because she wanted to inspect the preparations again and see that everything was in order. She was nervous about all those people coming on her behalf.

Descending the stairs in her finery, wearing new red lipstick, she felt like a gawky impostor, for by dressing in one of the bedrooms for her own party, as she had, she was behaving as if the Hall was her home. She was acutely aware that it was not, but was soon to be Elizabeth's. She remembers her obscure trepidation as if, when everyone recognised her pretence, terrible things might occur. But she never imagined it would be the last evening of William's life.

It did not seem like the Sweynsend Hall of her childhood. The ground-floor rooms had been cleaned and warmed for the party. Flower arrangements altered the light. The dusty gloom of the Major's last years had receded and the ghost of terror inspired by Mrs Carew had withdrawn. Two more of their grandchildren had come to stay for the party: Sam, William's younger brother, who had been energetically moving furniture since his arrival the previous day; and Josephine – Jem's older daughter – who had taken charge of the flowers. The only reason for them to do this was simple good will, for which Teresa was grateful. The Carews had always been generous, in their way, and she was ashamed of her own surprise at remembering this.

As she came down into the hall she saw Sam advancing along the passage towards her, carrying a large bowl of fruit punch which he had made. He whistled and cried, 'Whoa!' pretending to wobble the bowl. 'Knock 'em dead, gorgeous!'

She grinned.

He came past her and put the punch on a table that had been covered with a white damask cloth and employed as a bar. A hundred glasses twinkled on it, their stems demurely pointing up. To the brackets of the shaded wall lamps were fixed clusters of holly with bright red berries. The dark wooden floor glowed. The chest near the dining-room door with the funny upward tilt seemed to smile. The heavy oak stool beside the front door was like a sturdy friend's shoulder and, above it, William's hunting whips hung slackly like antique curios from the brass hooks where once the Major's matchlocks rested. There had never been curtains on the tall windows: on their recessed seats, Josephine had placed urns salvaged from the old kitchen, and she had arranged in each one an imposing display of foliage with great chunks of holly and yew. They were discreetly lit from beneath on the other side and, when Teresa went outside earlier on she saw that the colours were visible in the blocks of yellow light. The hall looked warm and inviting from outside. A clump of mistletoe hung from the light in the porch.

Teresa went past the right-hand window, through the door opposite the passage-room and into the small dining-room, where supper was to be served. It had been thought too complicated to seat everyone in different rooms and they decided in the end that people would prefer a buffet anyway. A table was pushed to the edge, with enough space for someone to get behind it to serve. Plates and cutlery were laid out on a round table near the door. In the fireplace, clear now of bees, its chimney swept, a fire was smouldering. The Georgian glass glittered like sculpted ice on the shelves to each side. Teresa had dusted and cleaned both the glass and the shelves herself, and the whole aspect of the room shifted as if, after years of stillness, the air had begun to circulate. They had talked about taking the glass away but William said, 'Is that really necessary, Teresa? Are your friends all hooligans?'

One of the caterers entered from the other door carrying a large plate with various kinds of cold meat covered in cling-film. He was called Phil and he had a high, gleaming forehead. He set the plate on another small table and parted his fleshy lips at Teresa in a smile, then he went out. Marie had tried to stop William getting in caterers, insisting that she had produced food at Sweynsend often enough for parties. But he said that they would all have to help her if she was doing the food, and he wanted her to enjoy the party. His view prevailed but Marie still fussed around, unwilling to accept that the caterers had brought with them everything they would need. She kept on showing them where the serving dishes were kept or where they would find a knife-sharpener, a lemon-squeezer, a reserve coffee-pot, a spare colander.

Going out towards the kitchen, Teresa could hear a voice straining with suppressed impatience, 'Thank you, Mrs Fairfax, we have enough tea-towels at present but I'll bear it in mind in case we do run short.'

Besides Phil and his wife, Beverley, who were middle-aged, there were two girls and a boy in their early twenties. They were the same team who did the food after the Major's funeral, so they were acquainted with the house and some of its peculiarities. Nevertheless, Teresa was impressed by their efficiency. It was obvious that they preferred Marie to be out of the way, so when Teresa entered the kitchen she made out that she had been looking for her.

'Hello, there you are, Mum! I want to know what you think about something.' She left the room quickly, trying to think of a pretext and hoping that her mother would follow.

'What is it, Teresa?' Marie said with a trace of agitation, stepping half into the passage.

'I want to show you something.'

Marie looked back anxiously over her shoulder.

'I'm sure they can manage all right,' Teresa said.

Marie shrugged, disclaiming responsibility for any disaster that ensued, and allowed her daughter to take her hand.

Teresa stopped in the hall and turned. 'I just wanted you to have a look,' she said, waving towards the hall itself and the open doors beyond, 'before people start arriving. It's looking so lovely.' Marie relaxed when she understood that Teresa wasn't drawing her attention to a problem requiring a solution. With a smile and a little ironic curtsey, she allowed Teresa to take her hand.

'And don't you think she looks lovely too?' said Sam from beyond Marie. He had been kneeling down behind his drinks table, stowing boxes of wine.

'Oh, Sam!' Marie cried. 'I didn't see you there!'

'Come on,' Teresa said, and led her mother into the large dining-room.

Chairs were drawn up to the table but it was not laid. Down the middle lay a swathe of yew and holly, with tangerines and apples and bananas tucked among the leaves. Four pairs of white candles poked through. There were more candles in brackets on the walls and in the ornate candelabra on the sideboard. Although it was a buffet, people were expected to come and sit informally in there; more chairs were backed up against the wall.

Tom was prodding in the fireplace at the far end. When he saw his wife and daughter he straightened up. Teresa had emphasised that the party was not to be formal, but he had stubbornly hauled on his dinner jacket on the grounds that he had no other decent clothes.

'I can't get this one to work properly,' he said, indicating the fire.

'What's the matter? Is it smoking?' Teresa asked.

'Oddly enough, it's the opposite. It's drawing so damn well that it sucks up anything that goes near it. You know what people are like with fires – they see a spare log and they throw it on for the sake of a nice blaze. I don't want anyone to set fire to William's chimney.'

'Maybe we should take the logs away,' said Marie, referring to the basket of fresh wood standing beside the hearth.

'They'll bring it through from one of the other rooms instead, if they want to,' he said. 'I'll warn William and Sam. It'll be all right.'

Marie raised her eyebrows. She liked his optimism, but the apparent carelessness he sometimes displayed alarmed her.

'If the house starts to burn there are plenty of doors,' he said, 'and at least it's insured now.'

Teresa laughed and her mother said, 'Tom, I wish you wouldn't say things like that!'

'Oh my! Don't you look wonderful, Teresa! Look at your beautiful daughter, Marie!'

'You sound surprised, my darling.'

'And you too, my love,' he said, touching her arm. He kissed her softly on the lips. 'You are the most beautiful of all!'

Marie averted her face, parrying him with the wall of her cheek. Then she turned away with a rustle as her hem spun on the carpet, and a flash of emerald green silk. 'Let's have a look in the marquee,' she said.

An enclosed awning led down the bank from the lawn door to a small marquee where a dance floor had been laid down. At first they had intended to have dancing in the drawing-room, but Tom observed that the music would drown all conversation in that part of the house. It was he who had suggested the marquee, adding – for his attempt at contributing to the party's expense had so far failed – that his chief purpose in proposing it was so that he could make a present. It was clear that if William denied him this then he would try something else, so it was accepted gracefully and the marquee arrived. There was no live music, however, for the band that had been engaged to play had cancelled two days before. They were friends of Elizabeth. The drummer had broken his wrist and the singer had twisted his ankle, or so they said, and a discotheque had to be hired in a hurry. William and Elizabeth were there now, talking to the DJ as he set himself up. He called himself Jonah and he was an unattractive creature with not enough chin and crafty eyes. Blobs of orange light were arcing over the marquee's ceiling.

There was a thick electrical hiss, followed by a thud; then, 'Testing. Testing. This is Jonah. This is Jonah.'

He nodded when he saw Teresa and her parents, which prompted William and Elizabeth to turn round. She was wearing a sheath-like black lycra dress that stopped curtly mid-way down her thighs. Her bare shoulders twitched and Teresa thought she must be cold, but then she raised an ankle and showed a palm as if she were about to do the Charleston. She was excited at the prospect of dancing. The promise of power in the hulking speakers and the sight of the turntables, like coiled springs, made her all shimmery. She was pleased that William would be sharing in something she loved so much: he must have seen this.

'Are the electrics all okay?' said Jonah. 'I don't want to go bang.'

'They're fine,' said William, though he had no idea.

'Where are Josephine and Lucy?' Teresa asked.

'In the drawing-room, I think.'

Lucy was Teresa's best friend from university. She was fat, which she didn't care about; she was jolly, and she was kind. She died of cancer the following year, five days after it was diagnosed. She had only been off work for a few days. Teresa had asked her to stay for the night before the party, as well as over the party itself, for she was a calming influence.

Teresa and her parents walked back through the dining-room and the hall. Sam was still hovering near his fruit punch as if afraid it would vanish if he left it alone. He stirred as Tom peered in.

'Well! That looks good,' said Tom, watching the fruit dip in the carmine eddies.

Sam smiled and they passed into the passage-room, where Tom immediately approached the low grate and prodded a log further back on the bed of ash with his toe. Teresa had cleaned the mirror over the mantelpiece a couple of days before, and the room now had an unfamiliar sharpness which disturbed her, as if it exposed limitations to everything that she had hitherto assumed about the room and experienced in it. She had removed the old postcards stuck in the frame when she cleaned it, and, when she replaced them afterwards, their spidery backs could be seen in the mirror. In reflection, the cargo of Carew mementoes on the mantelpiece looked like junk.

The doors to each side of the fireplace were usually closed. The cold from the great drawing-room on the left would pervade the house if the door were open, while the study door was always blocked by Mrs Carew's chair, so that anyone wishing to enter always had to shift it back and forth. Such an inconvenience in a house of this size is preposterous, but the Carews appear always to have lived in it as if they were camping. Mrs Carew's chair had been removed now, and the squalid beige carpet peeled back from the old oak boards which were now partially covered by a pair of Turkish rugs rescued from the night-nursery. Through the study door could be seen the flicker of a fire. Nobody remembered a fire ever being lit there but, when the other chimneys were swept, it seemed a good idea to have this one seen to as well. Nothing was wrong with it. The fire cleared the fusty chill and infused the room with the capacious warmth of an after-dinner haunt. It still needed all the books to be removed from the shelves and thoroughly dusted, but William and Elizabeth had moved and cleaned the furniture, and they had vacuumed the floor and wiped down all the surfaces. Josephine had also put a large bunch of asters in a Chinese vase on the Major's desk. Tom went in to inspect the fire.

Teresa looked at her watch and saw that only a few minutes remained before people were due to start arriving. She felt a tremor in her bones like a sudden draught as, not for the first time, she wondered what her friends would make of these surroundings. While some had seen the inside of the Manor and many more had seen the Hall from the outside, nobody except for those who had visited since William's arrival at Sweynsend had been inside the Hall.

Hearing Lucy and Josephine laugh in the drawing-room, Teresa followed her mother as she went to join them. They were standing by the mantelpiece in front of another blazing fire, smoking cigarettes.

'Oh! How magnificent!' cried Marie.

The grand piano had been pushed to the middle of the broad bay window. Using the same idea as in the dining-room but with greater indulgence, Josephine had covered the piano with a cloth on which she had arranged a huge nest of foliage, fruit and fir cones. She had framed it with a fan like a peacock's tail of slender yew fronds that were nailed to a crescent-shaped branch which in turn was strapped securely to the piano to prevent the whole structure from tipping backwards.

'I think Mrs Fairfax likes it,' said Lucy.

'Oh, I adore it! Josephine, what beautiful things you have done everywhere!' said Marie.

'It's nice to have an excuse,' said Josephine. She was tall, with an angular, open face and hazel eyes that promised fun. 'I've been wanting to do that for years.' She waved towards the piano with her cigarette and a twirling plume of smoke trailed her hand back and forth. She was still wearing jeans and a jersey with bark and twigs and pine needles clinging to it. 'It's all right,' she said to Teresa, 'I'll change in a moment. I just wanted to have a fag.'

Suddenly there was a pop like a gunshot from the fire and something leapt out at Lucy's skirt.

'Shit! It's that chestnut!' cried Josephine, plucking the hot bits from the floor and tossing them back into the fire while Lucy flapped at her skirt.

Lucy chortled. 'We forgot about that, didn't we?'

'Is it safe to have those out?' said Marie, eyeing a large bowl of chestnuts near the hearth.

'Not everyone's as stupid as us,' said Josephine. 'Anyway, the fire is much too fresh, it was silly of us to put it in.'

Marie bent down to inspect Lucy's skirt.

Lucy had bought a horrible navy blue skirt and a turquoise blouse especially for the evening. Teresa says that her taste in clothes was catastrophic, but it was integral to her appeal that she was oblivious to this, as if she didn't notice that nobody else ever wore clothes like hers. A garment was nice if it was clean, if it covered her, and if its colour was one of a few standard variations on the primary colours. So when she pointed to a hole the size of a small coin near the hem, Teresa said that she should be thankful for small mercies.

'Oh Teresa!' said her mother. 'Don't listen to her, Lucy, I'm so sorry! Come upstairs now and I'll quickly stitch it up.'

Lucy laughed in her face. 'Mrs Fairfax, you're mad! It's only a little hole in my skirt. But thanks all the same, I'll let you know when I need stitching up.'

Tom leaned round the open door. 'Teresa, Jed and Mabel are here.'

'Crumbs,' said Josephine. 'I'd better get changed.' And she threw the stub of her cigarette into the fire. 'I'll go out of the side door, I think, so that I don't bring my muck through the house. Will you close the curtain after me, Lucy?'

She let herself out of the half-glass door to the terrace, where the debris of her flower-arranging still lay. Then Lucy locked the door and pulled the curtain over it.


Jed and Mabel were sitting side by side on the *chaise longue,* just inside the passage-room door. They would never encroach more closely on the fire without a specific invitation because it was the Major and Mrs Carew's domain. They each held a glass of Sam's punch in their right hand, their fingers wrapped round the stems.

'Hello,' Teresa said.

Jed lifted his glass in unison with Mabel, following the upward motion of his hand by getting to his feet. He opened his mouth, revealing a depleted set of teeth. 'Well, Teresa, 'tis a pleasure to be 'ere, I'll say. I'nt it all lookin' lovely!'

His head was cocked a little to one side, and his left leg was bent at the knee. He adopted this stance in any social situation, as if locked in a skewed act of deference towards any Ladies or Gentlemen who happened to be present. His face had a fluid cheerfulness about it: he blinked a lot, and his smile waxed and waned so variously that the muscles in his cheeks and at the wings of his nose seemed to be in constant motion.

'You must come and have a look in the drawing-room. Come on, Mabel,' Teresa said, offering a hand to help her up.

'Oh, we'd like to do that, wouldn't we, Jed? We've been lookin' forward to this evenin' so much, Teresa.'

'Good. Mabel, this is Lucy, a friend of mine from university. Jed, this is Lucy.'

'Pleased to meet you, Miss,' said Jed, shaking her hand.

'Jed and Mabel have lived in Sweynsend for ever,' Teresa explained. 'Mabel runs the Post Office and the village shop. Jed looks after the animals hereabouts.'

In the drawing-room, Jed immediately noted that the damp wall had been repaired. He said that William was a good lad.

Mabel dutifully admired Josephine's display on the piano, then they went into the study.

'Nice bunch of daisies,' said Mabel. ''Aven't you made it nice in 'ere! Wouldn't the Major be pleased!'

Delighted to see the house used and cared for, they reverted to this theme back in the passage-room. They were sure that the

Major and Mrs Carew would approve of William's efforts in general, if not always in particular: they thought the removal of the carpet in the passage-room was a grave error of judgement.

'Thank you, Sam,' said Jed, as Sam refilled their glasses. 'We won't stay long.'

'Between you and me,' Mabel said to Lucy, 'we never did think it would pick up again, Jed and me didn't.' She took another sip. 'When the Major died we didn't know what'd 'appen. None of the children – not Hal, not Jem, not Hugh – not one of 'em was inter'sted, and I said to Jed, "Mark my words," I said, "they'll sell." An' Jed, 'e said, "Don't be so quick, Mabel, you can never tell, mebbe them grandchilren'll 'ave a crack at it," and 'e was right, I don't mind admittin', an' glad of it an' all!'

'It would be strange to sell a place like this,' said Lucy, 'unless they had to.'

Mabel looked at her gravely and said, 'Strange is as maybe!'

'Well, look 'ose 'ere!' cried Jed. 'Evenin' Sarah, Arthur. Hayley, John.'

'I thought I recognised that voice,' said Mabel, turning heavily in her chair.

'It was your own,' said Mr Simmonds, and chuckled.

'Hello,' Teresa said. 'Have you all got drinks?'

'Sam did the honours for us,' said Mr Simmonds, raising his glass.

Caught up with Jed and Mabel, Teresa had not noticed the Simmondses' arrival, which disappointed her. She rarely went over to Blake Farm now and was afraid that her failure to meet them at the door must seem like disdain. Hayley had become very Christian, she had heard, and her grey eyes in her pale little face looked suspicious. John's broad shoulders were stiff and superfluous in his blazer and tie. His wedge-shaped face opened nervously in an equine flash of white teeth as he smiled.

'No Michael?' Teresa asked.

'Didn't he tell you?' Mrs Simmonds raised her eyes to the ceiling. 'He said he'd told you. He was off to America last week.'

'Perhaps he did say,' Teresa answered. 'I expect I forgot.' Michael's childhood passion for machines had developed into a promising career in computer technology. Teresa knew that he must feel uncomfortable when he came home and, though certain that he hadn't let her know that he wouldn't come to the party, she didn't mind.

More people were arriving now. Excusing herself, Teresa slipped through the phalanx of Simmondses. In the hall she saw Mary, the secretary from her office, being helped out of a short imitation fur jacket by Sam.

'Teresa!' Mary shrieked. 'You never told me you lived in a mansion!' She was wearing a black skirt with a slit up the side, a pink blouse, and pounds of makeup.

Teresa laughed and said, 'I don't live here, Mary.'

'Teresa lives in the Manor House,' said Sam behind her. 'Much grander.'

Mary turned and looked at him peevishly, thinking that he was teasing her.

'Don't listen to him,' Teresa said. 'You got here all right, anyway.'

'Oh yes,' said Mary, recovering herself. 'Didn't we, Derek? This is my husband Derek,' she said, indicating a man with a moustache standing square on to them, with his hands behind his back like an off-duty policeman.

'How do you do?' Teresa said.

'How do you do?'

'We've brought you a present, Teresa. Derek, where's the present?'

A meaty paw emerged from behind him, in which was a square box wrapped in red paper with reindeers on it.

'Gosh!' Teresa blurted.

Sam said, 'Would you like some punch?'

'Wouldn't we just!' cried Mary.

'Here.' He handed each of them a glass. 'And let me relieve you of your coats. I'll take them upstairs.'

'Ooh, that's very nice of you. I'll hang on to my bag, though, if you don't mind.' She retrieved a little black patent leather bag on a gold chain. 'Go on, Teresa, open it! Where's the Ladies?' she added in an undertone.

'Upstairs, first on the right,' Teresa replied.

'I don't want to go,' Mary informed her, 'but it's as well to know, I always think.'

As Teresa laid the present aside, she saw Graham and Dawn coming through the front door. Graham used to have greasy hair and spots on his neck, and he had pursued her with morose determination. Now, considered from a depression, he seemed to have scaled peaks of achievement that were still remote to Teresa and her friends: he managed a warehouse or something near Tullworth; he was married too. Teresa had known him all her life and a party without him would have been incomplete, like a dolt whom you love to hate. In a different way, Mary was a splendid person to work with and Teresa very much wanted her to be at her party, but the thought of somebody entering now and taking these as representative of her friends presented an alarming reflection of herself. And in the passage-room were the Simmondses.

Graham was dressed in tan slacks, a navy blue blazer with brass buttons, and a tie bearing the monogram of some club. At first, Teresa wondered why Dawn hadn't managed a sartorial rescue, but the answer was apparent in the top she was wearing, a sort of sleeveless polo-neck with purple shoulders fading down to mauve around her breasts, then lilac and pink and then cream for the last three inches below the waist.

'Hello, Graham,' Teresa said, offering her cheek.

He supplied a rubbery kiss, together with a little liquid dab where his nose touched her cheek. 'We've got something for you too, Teresa,' he said.

'Have you? How kind! You really shouldn't have!'

Dawn advanced with a little packet. As she handed it over, it crossed Teresa's mind that Graham might be a bully.

'Grab a drink,' she said, pointing to the ranks of glasses which Sam had filled with fruit punch; he was circulating with the jug. 'And come through,' she added, ushering everyone towards the passage-room.

The front door creaked open again and Melanie Moore's blond head appeared. Teresa expected a yelped greeting, but her grin of recognition suddenly collapsed as she was yanked backwards: and when the door swung wide Teresa saw that her boyfriend was kissing her under the mistletoe.

Released, Melanie approached Teresa. Her smiling lips bloomed vermilion: she was as robust and healthy as ever. It was a long time since Teresa had seen her, and now she rushed forward to hug her. They had been good friends when Melanie lived in Sweynsend, but her family had moved to Birmingham when she was sixteen and they had rarely seen one another since. The soft scent of her neck was both an exquisite reminder to Teresa of childhood and a dizzying intimation of the life she herself might have had, if she were different, like gazing across a deep chasm at the sunlit shoulder of another mountain.


Yesterday, a Sunday, was one of those radiant mornings when the garden at Sweynsend seems more serene and verdant than you could ever imagine, and I am amazed at myself for having had the sense to settle here.

I went out barefoot after breakfast. 'Do be careful where you tread,' said Teresa, which of course irritated me. I wandered across the lawn, enjoying the warmth on the back of my neck, the silence of the village, the bees hovering about the rose climbing along the wall. The unruliness of the shrubs in front of the kitchen window caught my attention, and I decided to do some immediate surgery on the plasticky laurel, to give the lilac and forsythia more room to breathe. I went to fetch some cutters and brought with me also some garden shears. As I got close into the foliage it became obvious that the shears would be useless: I should have brought a saw. I laid the shears carefully to one side so that I should not step back on them and chopped with the cutters for perhaps fifteen minutes – long enough to become absorbed – when Teresa called me from the kitchen window beyond to say that I was wanted on the phone. Instead of withdrawing from the shrub in the direction from which I had approached it, I stepped round, straight onto the shears, and sliced my foot.

At first I was intensely annoyed with Teresa for 'causing' the accident by calling me to the phone, as if by anticipating it with her warning she had somehow willed it. So foolish did my barbarous response make me feel – on top of the folly of getting cut – that, when she offered to clean and dress the wound, I told her crossly that I could manage on my own. I felt taunted by a tenderness I didn't deserve, and rudely told her to get out of the way.

I knew I had upset Teresa and was ashamed of myself. As I nursed my foot upstairs, I was wondering how best to apologise when loud music engulfed the house. From its first penetrating throb I recognised the Eurythmics' 'Love is a Stranger'. That was an unexpected turn. I hadn't supposed that Teresa would remain placid, but I did not at once see what role the music had in her response, though it was certain that both selection and volume were deliberate.

The refrain reverberated around the walls as I came downstairs: '*And I want you, and I want you . . .*' Teresa was waiting for me in the hall. Seeing me descend, she strode over in a fury and shouted above the music, 'Why won't you ever let me do anything for you? Don't you understand that I *want* to?'

I have never seen her so angry. Her fingertips were quivering and her lips were taut like shards of alabaster.

She waited, glaring at me, until the song had finished. It must have been another full minute. For some reason she was missing the sandal from her left foot, so that her stance was very slightly lopsided. It was a strange moment of stand-off, with that woman's intense and dignified voice, an English voice, circling round us.

Teresa went next door and turned the music off. 'Now let me have a look at your foot,' she said, on her return; she had removed her other shoe.

She sat on the bottom step and I put my foot in her lap. 'This is ridiculous.' When she ripped off my piece of bloody sticking-plaster I snatched my foot away, stumbling. Without looking at me, she stood and turned upstairs, with her hand on the banister. 'You'd better come up and let me do it properly,' she said.

When we were both seated in the bathroom – she on a chair, I on the edge of the bath – I said, 'I'm sorry.'

'What is it, Jimmy, that makes you unable to believe that anybody – not anybody, your *wife* for Christ's sake – wants to do something for you? I know you felt a fool for cutting your foot, I'm not that stupid, but what misshapen pride is it that makes you insult me instead of admitting it, instead of laughing at it? Why is it better to be vile to me than to let me love you?'

Is it only a matter of allowing myself to love Teresa properly? She says it is pride, but it is not. Is it then just an attachment to the inner drama of loving Iris? I wonder if I would have reacted to Teresa in the same way before she told me about Lucas. Her account has reawakened something about Iris in me, which involves an uneasy sense that hers is the only love I could permit myself to enjoy; so that I make Teresa – who offers love – feel that

I have no true claim on hers. It is an absurdity considering the arrangement of our lives, the more so when I doubt whether it is the drama to which I'm attached, or Iris herself. Absence may make the heart grow fonder, but still I wonder if the fondness reflects a void in me or a direct response to her presence.

'Go on, why don't you say what you really feel?'

'It's all very well to laugh, but do you ever?'

'Ever what?'

'Say what you feel?'

'Fools, children and madmen say what they feel. We generally either try to curb them or, if we can't, lock them up.'

'And women?'

'Sometimes they say what they feel. They are more selective than they admit.'

'And men, Herr Doktor?'

'Isn't it a question of learning how to express your feelings in a way that is appropriate to a situation rather than pouring them out regardless?'

'And just now, Jimmy, were you expressing your feelings appropriately when you told me to fuck off out of the way after I offered to clean your cut, which we both knew I would do very much better than you?'

Now she pushed away my foot, which she had thoroughly disinfected and bound with a wad of gauze beneath a bandage, and looked up at me.

I smiled and leaned forward to kiss her, for I suddenly recognised that a great part of my love for Teresa flows from the very feeling that I *can* tell her what I feel without fearing that she will use it against me.

'No,' she said, ducking away from my kiss, 'answer me.'

'Obviously not.'

'So.'

'So what?'

'So Mr Jimmy does not always express his feelings appropriately, even supposing that he recognises what they are.'

'Sometimes,' I said, 'when the feelings themselves are unwanted and inappropriate, the best thing is to suppress them. It is an underrated virtue, almost taboo. And like other taboos, shitting for example, we practise it all the time; and, again like shitting, those who do it successfully have an easier ride in life than those who have problems with it.'

'Jimmy, you are full of shit.'

'Bullshit is my stock in trade.'

'Please don't practise it on me.'

'As it happens, I would say I am more direct with you than with anyone else.'

'Why's that?'

'Because I don't feel that you use what I say for your own purposes.'

'You mean you don't think I have an agenda?'

'I would never say that of anyone. But you seem happy to let my agenda exist alongside yours.'

Teresa let that pass. We were silent for a few moments before she said – and the change of subject was a peace offering – 'It was not accident that I put that song on. It was playing when things suddenly, very suddenly got out of hand at my party.'

'Tell me.'

'You don't know most of the guests, Jimmy, so there's no point in describing them.'

Giving up the idea of gardening because of my foot, I hobbled downstairs to make a pot of fresh coffee, which I took outside to share with Teresa as we sat on a bench in the sunshine. She said she would just mention the guests I knew, or who played some part in what followed.

'Attached to Melanie was Glen, her amorous boyfriend. Then there was Alix Urquhart, a schoolfriend who supplanted

Melanie in my life after she moved away from Sweynsend. Although Alix went to a different university we were still friends; she came with a new boyfriend called David Mendoza. I remember Angela, a friend from university, because she was black and Jed and Mabel stared at her as they left. She went out with a very good-looking white guy called Paul, who I recall got on very well with Ahmed, another college friend. There was Maurice Wright, of course. And then the Mintons. I remember Ian Minton sidling up to me in the hall and murmuring something catty about my having gone up in the world. I said I was working on it. He had such a self-satisfied smile. His twin sisters were both got up in black lycra, like Elizabeth, and their faces were thick with make-up, as if they had deliberately tried to make themselves look identical. I knew Cathy best because she was at school with me. She had a small, rather pinched mouth. Boys always found her attractive, which seemed very stupid to me because Alison was less calculating and she had perfect skin underneath all that make-up. Cathy gave me a present from them all. I said thank you and put it with the others on the chest. I didn't want to get involved with unwrapping parcels while people were still arriving.

'My boss arrived and I left the Mintons to Maurice. John Halloran was taller than most people and his head twisted about forlornly in search of someone he knew. He was relieved to see me and immediately introduced me to his wife Sue, whom I'd sometimes spoken to on the telephone but never met. She was small and neat and all buttoned up, as if she were here not through any choice of her own but because her husband had insisted. She smiled mechanically when I said it was nice of her to come, and I wondered if she thought I was having an affair with her husband. I liked him but he was like a giraffe, the sort of figure who makes you giggle if you think of him in carnal embrace. I took them over to my father, who would give them a drink. Meanwhile Alix's sister Susan arrived with a couple of boys we knew from the drama college, but I was some way from the front door now and the crowd in the hall was thick, so it was hard to reach them. Wishing everyone would spread through to the other rooms, I went up a couple of stairs for a better outlook. From there I saw Laura and Janice squeezing into the house together. They were both wearing overcoats, and they were carrying bags because they were going to stay the night. I waved at them: when they saw me they waved back. Laura's hand twirled above her head as if she was going to throw me a rope, which I pretended to catch and pull towards me. Then, indicating that they should follow me, I turned and went upstairs.'


Teresa showed them into the bedroom at the left-hand end of the landing, which had twin beds with pretty white crocheted coverlets. It was icy cold in there but she told them confidently that it would warm up as the party beneath progressed. And if it was still cold, there was a little blow-heater which they could use if they wanted.

'Body warmth,' said Janice. 'We'll have to find a friend to keep us warm.' She put her bag on the far bed and the springs squeaked. She stared at it in astonishment, then sat down and bounced on it. The bed complained with rhythmic screeches. 'Or maybe that's not such a good idea,' she said.

Teresa was standing near the door and she pressed down in the middle of the other bed with the flat of her hand. It didn't have the same violent reaction as Janice's bed: it seemed to let out a sigh. 'You'll have to fight it out with Laura,' she said.

'Oh, I don't mind,' said Laura. 'You have this one.'

'I might mind though, if you get lucky and I don't. I don't really fancy the idea of you humping away on these springs while I'm trying to sleep.'

Laura giggled and rummaged in her bag, pulling out clothes and laying them on the bed.

'So who have you got lined up for us tonight?' Janice asked.

'Tell us about the talent, Teresa,' Laura said, peering into her bag. To the best of her friends' knowledge, Laura had never been out with anyone. Behind her, Janice raised her eyebrows.

Teresa laughed and said, 'There's about a hundred people down there. Half of them are men.'

'And which one's yours, Tee?'

'That would be telling.'

'You'd better tell us, or this one'll get her claws in him,' said Janice, nodding towards Laura.

'I'm afraid there's nothing doing,' Teresa said.

'What? There's nothing to tell? Or you won't tell?' Janice persisted.

'Nothing. I screwed up.'

'Ah, you're a dark horse,' Laura observed.

Having emptied her bag on the bed, Janice was on the point of stripping off her jersey. She paused for a moment at Teresa's answer, debating whether to question her now or later. Then she finished pulling off her jersey and shirt together in a single, abrupt movement. 'Shit, it's cold,' she said, wrapping her arms round herself.

'Well,' Teresa said, 'I'll leave you two damsels in peace now.'

'Bitch,' Janice said.

Teresa blew her a kiss and left the room.

'I must remember the next moment wrong,' Teresa told me. 'There would surely have been lights on the landing either from the bathroom, which was the Ladies', or coming up the stairs from the party below. But as I recall it, I closed the bedroom door and stepped into darkness. Further down the passage was a patch of light high on the wall, from the bathroom's transom window. It seems to have cast no light into the passage itself, for the cocoon of light around Alix when I encountered her near the top of the stairs was like a magic lantern standing alone in the night. I suppose she chanced to be caught by a shaft of moonlight through the arched window. But if there was so much light from the moon, why don't I remember it glinting off the pictures?'

When Alix saw Teresa, with one hand on the newel post at the top of the stairs, she stopped a few steps lower down, and smiled. The left side of her face was gleaming so that her nose seemed pointed, and her neat black hair was bluish. She was wearing silver pendant earrings which trembled as she spoke.

'Hi, Tee, is the Ladies up here?'

'It's just there, up on the right.'

Events that look surprising to an outsider can appear to the person involved to have a special internal logic. Although unforeseen, they are perceived afterwards to have an inevitability. If I bumped into Iris in London, say – or anywhere else, come to that: on the moon – the encounter would have a dramatic logic for me that made it seem like something I had expected all along. Alix didn't speak her next line as if she herself particularly wanted an answer but as if it were something she was supposed to say. And as if they had been through this already before, Teresa knew the answer before Alix even asked the question.

'Thanks. Who's that guy who just arrived on a motorbike?'

'Oh. I think that must be Lucas.'

Alix didn't know who Lucas was, but she could see that mention of him perturbed Teresa for she was still and offered no explanation. She was uncertain whether to be pleased on her behalf or anxious.

Teresa just shrugged, a dismissive movement because she was suddenly bird-alert to what was happening downstairs. She heard Lucas's clear tone through the patter of voices for a moment but the words were indistinct. She pictured him in the hall in his motorcycling gear, and remembered arriving from the stairs the first time she met him. Alix's mention of him was a stimulating puff on a hoarded ember; she felt as if the blood had risen right up to tickle the roots of her hair. She thought she had smothered all hope, but abject hope now struggled up again.

Alix said something and walked on past as Teresa gazed blankly down the polished banister. The bolt on the bathroom door was like the sound of floorboards cracking under her, snapping her trance.

She realised instantly that William must have invited Lucas behind her back, but it didn't occur to her that his intentions might have been kind. She saw only a betrayal. As she wondered how to face Lucas with any composure, her panic surged with the insult. How dare William do this to her?

And why had Lucas come? How could he be so unfeeling, after all? By his presence alone he mocked her.

She turned and hurried along the passage, past the bathroom to the baize-covered door and out to the nursery landing. It was bitingly cold out there, and the insipid moonlight glimmered in watery streaks on the red linoleum floor. The rocking horse's head was picked out in precise silhouette against a window, but the body was lost in shadow beneath the sill. She felt slightly sick and was shivering; she thought she might cry. How could she go back to the party when he was there? How could she avoid it? Sitting alone up here until it was over or he was gone was out of the question because people would come looking for her. She would expose her desire in all its raw futility whereas, by pretending nothing was amiss, she might at least preserve her pride. Yet it was more than she could bear to face him at once. She was filled with the desperate rage of impotence. Why wouldn't he let her put the clock back and carry on as before? Why wouldn't he just go away? He seemed determined to entertain himself at her expense.

A great black chest stood on the landing containing dressing-up clothes, a collection of ragged cast-offs from the 1920s kept by the Major and Mrs Carew for their children. For a moment Teresa fantasised about rejoining the party in moth-eaten, shrunken gaudy. Then she considered locking herself in the loo there, but it was windowless. With its high ceiling and fluorescent light beneath the skylight, it was like a prison cell. Instead, she went into the nursery flat.

The further she got from the centre of the house, the colder it was. Her little jacket was useless. Earlier, she had not appreciated that it was a cold evening, but either the temperature had suddenly dropped or it was colder here than outside. She could see her breath in the moonbeams cutting through the huge room. By drawing attention to the emptiness, the silvery light illuminated how the occupants of this part of the house were transients: they had got clean away and made their lives elsewhere. Only a wardrobe remained in one corner, and a sagging sofa. Teresa thought of her parents living in this flat after they married, and the cold and the isolation suddenly wrenched something in her and she started to weep. Everything was desolate at this end of the house, it was a scene of wasted love and faded endeavour, and it seemed even sadder that she should feel this in the nursery of all places, which ought to conjure images of children running about. But she could only think of the cold and the excluding baize door. She pictured Lucas standing in front of the fire in the passage-room with his feet slightly apart, a natural focus of attention, chatting calmly to her guests while she was shut away upstairs stupefied with misery by the mere knowledge that he was in the house.

Reminding herself that she hadn't even seen him yet, she dabbed at her eyes with her fingers, knowing that her mascara must be running, and emerged from the nursery. She gathered some loo-paper, then went into the night-nursery where she could clean her face in front of a mirror. The room was grim and seedy in the harsh yellow light. The carpets and curtains and bedclothes were frayed and faded, the wallpaper curled and the paintwork everywhere was chipped. As she examined her eyes and wiped away the smudges, she wondered if she hadn't got it all wrong: perhaps he had come because he wanted, after all, to see her again? Wasn't it the logical explanation?

In a flurry of excitement she started down the back stairs, her mind busy with wild images of their impending meeting. He would step towards her and she'd run into his open arms, instantaneously forgiving him for his previous rejection. Whoever he was talking with now might think that he was paying attention to them, but secretly he was watching only for her. He would see her at the edge of the room before anyone else. Teresa imagined the firm feel of him as he drew her to his chest, his arms round her waist and his strong hands lifting her up.

At the bottom of the stairs there is a door. Beyond is the stone-flagged scullery area which leads to the pantry, the back door, the garden room and the rear entrance of the kitchen. The top half of the door is glass, all painted white except for a single pane – an oddity that I have preserved. Teresa now spied through it on the caterers coming and going with plates of food in a blaze of light and well-ordered activity. She hesitated before joining them, suddenly conscious that her image of herself as the-beautiful-girl-being-swept-into-her-lover's-arms was just a theatrical fantasy. Her face must look a mess. She didn't want anyone to see that she had been crying.

Teresa was just returning up the dark, cold stairs when she heard Elizabeth's jaunty steps clipping down the landing on the other side of the baize door. It swung open. With her tight short dress and glittering eyes, Elizabeth brought the party crashing through.

'Hi, Tee, I thought I might find you here,' she said, as if Teresa were in the habit of skulking in the darkness.

'Elizabeth, he's here!'

'I know. Look . . . God, it's freezing out here! Come here.'

Teresa followed her into the bathroom. She felt safe when Elizabeth locked the door. The light was soft. Looking at herself in the mirror, she saw that her eyes were red and there were black smudges across her cheeks.

She sat on the chair beside the bath and Elizabeth bent over her with a flannel. Tipping back her head, she watched unflinching as her sister dabbed gently round her eyes. Strands of Elizabeth's blond hair fell forward prettily over her shoulders, framing the hot skin of her face, and her throat seemed long as she stretched towards Teresa. Her attractiveness was so blatant: Teresa couldn't imagine what she might be intending to say by way of comfort, but as soon as she thought this she felt ashamed because she felt the sympathy of her pliant touch. Elizabeth was impressed by the exceptional sight of her sister in tears, and her patience suggested that she too was surprised by Lucas's appearance.

'William must have asked him,' Teresa said.

Elizabeth sighed. She stepped back and reached into a bag on the chest-of-drawers by the basin for her mascara and eyeliner, then knelt down in front of Teresa to renew her make-up.

'Does he think I'll just smile and not mind?'

'I don't know what he's up to. Maybe he thinks he's done you a favour.'

'Is that what he thinks?'

'I haven't asked him.'

'What on earth has he come for?'

Elizabeth concentrated on applying eyeliner below Teresa's right eye. 'Maybe he was just sort of passing.'

'Huh!'

'You'll be all right.'

'You'll be telling me not to take any notice next.'

'Oh, Tee!'

'I know. I'll be all right.'

Elizabeth stood up to survey her work. 'Well –'

'Please don't tell me how I look!'

Elizabeth hovered by the door, waiting for her sister to stand up, but Teresa didn't feel like going downstairs quite yet so she told her that she would follow in a moment.

'Promise?'

Teresa nodded and, after a second of uncertainty, Elizabeth unlocked the door and left her.

Now Teresa stood up and went to look at herself in the mirror again. Her eyes were still puffy. Poking around in Elizabeth's make-up bag, she tried to find something else to disguise the redness.

Suddenly Lucy stepped into the room.

'What's the matter, Squeeze-Pops?'

'Panda eyes.'

'Let's have a look.'

Teresa faced her.

'Elizabeth told me you were up here.'

'Is that all?'

Lucy shook her head. 'Your eyes are fine. Leave them alone. It's that guy down there, isn't it? Lucas.'

When Teresa nodded, Lucy put her other arm round her and hugged her. 'Don't make me cry, I've only just cleared up the mess,' said Teresa.

Lucy let go and stepped back. Her moon face was unselfconscious, as if she would quietly just wait until Teresa had pulled herself together, even if it meant waiting there all night.

'Lucy, you're sweet.'

'Are you going to stand there and tell me I'm sweet, or are you going to tell me about Lucas?'

'Someone will want the bathroom. Come next door.'

On the other side of the passage is a spacious room with thick curtains and carpets and a four-poster. It was the spare room.

While Lucy sat on the bed, Teresa shut the door and walked over to the mantelpiece where she fiddled with a pair of tiny Victorian ornamental mugs. One bore an improving motto: *Happy the child whose tender years / Receive instruction well; / Who hates the sinner's path and fears / The road that leads to hell.* On the other, Little Boy Blue and Bo Peep, or some such, appeared to be playing skittles with a multicoloured beach ball.

'He's a friend of William's,' Teresa said at last. 'He came here for a weekend in the summer and I – I fell for him.'

Lucy prompted her: 'But he didn't fall for you?'

'It's worse than that. I wrote him a letter. I don't know why – it seemed all right at the time – but it was crazy, I know. Anyway, I wrote to him saying – you know –'

'Saying "Let's do it"?'

'I suppose so, yes.'

'Christ, you're brave!'

'It wasn't brave, it was stupid, because then he turned up here again. Although he hadn't answered my letter, I thought he must have – must have come because of me, after all. But he hadn't. He said thanks for the compliment but no thanks. If you see what I mean.'

'Tee, you poor poor thing!' Lucy said, and she got up from the bed and approached Teresa.

'You can't imagine how awful I felt. Such a fool and . . . And the worst of it was that I still wanted him.'

Lucy put her wrist against the mantelpiece and took Teresa's hand in hers. 'But he's come to your party, Tee, he can't not be interested.'

'But I didn't invite him! That's the whole point!'

'But then, you silly lemon, if he's gatecrashed, that must surely mean – have you spoken to him?'

'No! How could I face him?' Teresa cried, struggling to withhold a fresh current of tears. 'It's like he's come to laugh at me!'

Lucy produced a tissue from the sleeve of her blouse which Teresa touched to her eyes before continuing: 'William has asked him for some reason. Maybe he thought he could make it work but, from the way he said no before, there's no chance. I just don't understand why he's come, Lucy. I thought I was getting over it all, and now he only has to set foot here and I go all to pieces.'

'Tee, you're panicking, you're jumping to conclusions.'

'You mean he's changed his mind?'

'Maybe. He's come to your party.'

Teresa understood that Lucy's was the obvious explanation for Lucas's presence, but she did not believe it. 'I don't know what he's doing here,' she said, shaking her head, 'but I don't think it's for my benefit.'

'Oh, come on Tee! Don't be so gloomy! Even if he hasn't come because of you, it's not the end of the world! Ignore him! I mean, they're all your friends down there, you don't have to talk to him if you don't want to, and you don't want to just ignore all of them. You can't stay up here all night. If you're right, and he's come to gloat for some weird reason of his own, then don't let him see you're upset! Face him down!'

'I know, I know, Lucy, you're right. I must. It's just . . . difficult.'

'Now look, Squeeze-Pops, I've got a spare tissue here.' She reached into the pocket of her skirt. 'You don't really need it because you haven't blubbed again but –'

'But if it makes me feel better, I'm welcome?'

Teresa inspected her face in the mirror again. She sighed. 'If only I weren't so tired.' Then, turning towards the door, she stood up straight and said, 'Okay, let's go.'


'Even now, Jimmy,' she said – she was lying on the bench in the sunshine with her head on my knees; she held my left hand beneath hers against her stomach, while I stroked her black hair with the other – 'even now, as I recall coming downstairs and seeing Lucas, it makes me shivery inside all over again. It's all right, there's no need to be alarmed. After what I've said so far, I'm not about to get coy. I think everyone must have these moments in their lives, images which instantly remind them of what they were – what it felt like to be young. The lives they might have had if love had been returned or initiative taken.'

'Of course.'

How strange, this fathomless loss inside Teresa. Where does it come from? Is she conscious of it in me too? Are we born with it, like Original Sin? Is it the fluid and empty heavens? Or is it, as I feel, a specific loss – and would it then be easier to bear if heaven were safely occupied? Is she aware of the state of grief in which I exist? I am almost tempted to tell her about Iris.

'I suppose it was to prevent that weekend becoming such a focus of nostalgia that I took the initiative myself and wrote Lucas that silly letter, but I only succeeded in forcing up the pain quotient. Now, as I met Lucas again, I knew that this encounter would take its place as one of those talismanic events in my life. I was also aware of its absurd futility. And what made my awareness of it so acute, and makes the memory of it so painful, is the sweat of attraction he induced in me.'

Stillness seemed to surround him as he watched Teresa come down the stairs. Other people – William, certainly – were present, but as soon as she turned the dogleg, Teresa saw that he had spotted her. She could feel his gaze on her like feathers.

She avoided his eyes and looked instead at her feet, taking care to walk steadily. She knew that he was probably assessing her body in the way men do and, whatever else he saw, she wanted him to see that he didn't unsettle her. Determined to appear proud, she looked up, but still not at him. It almost hurt to look elsewhere, as if her eyes were floating loose in their sockets, disconnected, until at last they locked into place on him.

There was a tension in him, a suppressed agility, as if at any moment he might move forwards or back. She had the impression of a superb sense of physical balance. Although the lights were dim, she still saw – or imagines she saw – the blueness of his eyes from where she was standing. She read in them a confident indifference that accounted for the mess of his short black hair. Although his slim nose and delicate mouth were features most would covet, he himself didn't seem to care much about his looks. She had no idea what he was thinking as he watched her in her rose silk, but she knew it wasn't what she wanted him to think. Perhaps he was just registering the effect he was having on her. She couldn't even tell whether he was enjoying it or not. 'As for me,' she said, 'I felt powerless, like a stopped spinning-top needing his touch to liberate me into movement.'

His lips flickered. 'Teresa, hey, where the fuck have you been?'

The sense of déjà-vu was complete now, and she laughed, wondering if he spoke like that deliberately to echo his first words in August, when she had come down the stairs to meet him in the hall.

Conscious of Lucy at her side, she told him that she had been busy upstairs. Whoever was standing in front of him had moved aside, so that now she was facing him directly. She still didn't know what he intended, but she was expecting him at least to kiss her cheek in conventional greeting. She could feel herself staring at his dry-lipped mouth.

'I've got a present for you,' he said, stretching towards the chest and picking up a parcel in his long fingers. 'Happy birthday.' His throat was like a horse's neck to her.

It was obviously a book. For the moment she overlooked that he hadn't kissed her, or explained how he came to be there. Giving a book was such an intimate gesture. It was a hardback, which in itself was a rare treat. The paper came off easily, leaving the book face down in her hand. It had a wine-red cover, which for some reason made her think of Shelley, and her heart was ready to burst with the unmistakeable message in a gift of romantic poetry. Then she turned the book over and saw that it was *Seeds of Change: Five Plants That Transformed Mankind*.

I felt the ripple of her laugh under my hand. 'It's a great book. I read it eventually. But I thought at the time, it isn't even poetry!'

'It's a really fascinating book,' Lucas told her, and he smiled cheerfully so that she wanted to hit him. He didn't even realise what he'd done.

She looked down again at the book. Why had he given it to her? Why ever did he imagine it would interest her? Had he read it himself? 'Thank you,' she said, 'I'll look forward to this.' She did not kiss him. Then she added, viciously: 'Were the roads wet?'

'I'm sorry?'

'Nothing. Have you got a drink? If you'll excuse me, I must see to some of my guests.'

As she stepped round him, she caught William's eye. He recoiled. She was satisfied to see his embarrassment.

Graham and Dawn were standing just inside the passage-room door. He was trying to browbeat Hayley Simmonds: ' . . .in private you may think that, but out here in the real world . . .' But she wouldn't have it: 'Graham, what you don't seem to understand is that the real world is actually all about us, wherever we happen to be.' Meanwhile Hayley's brother John was talking to Dawn about farm machinery. 'Excuse me,' she said, and slipped past them. Graham pressed himself awkwardly against the door.

To her relief, Teresa saw that Lucy was following her. Negotiating the thick knot of people near the fire, she went through to the study, which was mercifully empty.

Lucy put some wood on the fire while, with her elbows tucked in at her ribs, Teresa leaned back against the cupboards. She tipped her head and heard rather than felt her hair on her silk jacket. If she pushed back a little further she could scratch the top of her head on the spines of books. She breathed in and out deeply.

'So,' said Lucy.

'So.'

Lucy poked at the fire. 'You think he's got it in for you, don't you?'

'Don't you?'

'Not necessarily.'

'Why else is he here?'

'I don't know,' said Lucy. 'You may be right. I'm not convinced, that's all.'

'He didn't even kiss me hello, Lucy. And what on earth is that book supposed to mean – a book on horticulture!'

'Maybe it's an interesting book though. Men are funny sometimes when it comes to presents.'

Teresa wondered what Lucy knew about men and presents. 'I bet he didn't even get it for me, but passed on something he was given and didn't want.'

As Lucy turned back to the fire, William entered. 'I thought you'd be pleased, Teresa.' When he saw Lucy, he stopped. His right hand forked into his hair, which was stiff with gel so that the hair stood up in a wonky coxcomb. Nervousness made his mouth twist up on the right side as he tried to smile.

'Well, at least you admit it,' Teresa replied.

'What's the matter? Why shouldn't I ask him?'

'Oh for God's sake, William!'

'What?'

'For a poet, you have the sensitivity of an ox!'

Teresa's jibe provoked William, as she had intended.

'I'd heard of William's temper before,' Teresa told me, 'but never seen it. It was bizarre, so *physical*. The skin on his face tightened so that his skull seemed to have edges and his neck was corded. His right arm was raised, with the hand spread in a spasm of energy and he was gulping air as if he desperately needed extra oxygen to fuel an engine within.'

Teresa's instinct was to pacify him. 'It's okay!' she said. 'Calm down!'

But a process had started in him which could not be so easily halted. He continued to gawp at her, trembling and speechless, as if a restraining leash in him had snapped. 'I'm sorry, it's none of my business,' Teresa babbled, 'It's your house, you can ask anyone you want . . .'

I pressed Teresa's fingers and said I found it hard to imagine her being so intimidated by William's anger. He did not sound like someone who was very good at asserting himself.

'I'd always thought of William as a gentle person,' she agreed, 'and he *was* basically gentle. But there was a vein of phosphorus in him that ignited when exposed to what, for others, would have been an innocuous puff of air. Then he seemed *dangerously* reactive, unstable; anything but gentle. Newspapers and feminist orthodoxy might give the impression that men are naturally raging psychotics whose behaviour towards women is typically violent, but I had never come across a violent man. In my experience men were controlled, even docile creatures, and violence was the domain of women. I mean Mrs Carew, not my mother, and it is somehow immaterial that her violence was more psychological than physical. But William's face was chalk-white, his lips were green, his face was ridged and his body rigid: he was possessed by something that very obviously wasn't within his control, which looked as if it might at any moment spill into manic, thrashing violence. It scared the shit out of me. The question of *why* he was so angry did not seem remotely relevant.'

'It's okay, William,' Lucy and Teresa repeated together.

His hand dropped to his side, then his neck relaxed and he passed a hand over his face. 'Shit.' He glanced at the girls, turned on his heel and left the room.

They watched him go, as if a ghost had stepped from the book-cases in front of their eyes. 'What was that all about?' said Lucy, and gave a low, nervous giggle.

'I haven't the faintest idea,' Teresa replied. 'But I think it means I have to face the music.'

From the deep arch of the doorway where she had paused, Teresa heard her mother urging people to supper. '. . . in the little dining-room, get yourselves some food and take it through . . . Yes, yes, the other side of the hall . . . *Allez*, you must be famished . . . Hello, Alix, what lovely earrings you're wearing . . .'

Then came William's voice, slightly raised: 'Come and get something to eat, Lucas, my friend!'

Lucy scrunched up her nose. Finding that their reaction was the same, she and Teresa laughed. Then, seeing that Lucas and William had gone, they went into the passage-room where they joined Josephine and Maurice. 'I'm feeling a bit peckish. Shall we go and tuck in?' Maurice said, and preceded the girls from the room in pursuit of food.

In the hall, Josephine was waylaid by Sam, who told her that Elizabeth was looking for her because the candles were dripping among her flowers on the dining-room table. Teresa wanted to see to the problem herself but the others insisted that she carry on, so she found herself having to join Maurice for supper.

As Teresa handed Maurice a thick white plate from the pile on the table by the door, its drabness made her glance ruefully towards the shelf in the left hand alcove, where stood the glass and china she had cleaned earlier in the day. She expected to see there the two surviving plates from the Carews' crested dinner service, but there was a gap. She turned to Phil, whose face split into a red grin, his little teeth showing like exposed bone in a wound.

'And what am I giving the birthday girl, then?' he asked.

He was standing over a table of meat. On one dish lay a slab of beef in a ruby pool; on another lay a savaged haunch of pork oozing with filaments of red blood. Beside them was the pallid hulk of a cold roast chicken. Steam rose from the beef into Phil's face, making him sweat. As he spoke, he opened his arms so that the carving-knife and fork flashed: it seemed as if he was presiding over some ghoulish sacrifice. Teresa forgot what she was going to say about the plates when her eye caught the picture of the hunting scene above the fireplace. Cheered on by a red-coated huntsman on his horse, four hounds with lolling tongues were about to corner a fox. Even the faded crimson silk on the walls suddenly seemed repulsive.

'Oh dear,' she said, 'I'm afraid I don't think I'm very hungry.'

'C'mon Teresa, y' must 'ave something, else y'll fade away.'

Unable to contend with the guilt of insulting Phil, she agreed to have a thin slice of roast beef. He cut through it like jelly. She watched with horror as he picked it up between the point of his knife and the long talons of the fork, for it seemed to quiver like a live thing. He placed it lovingly on the clean white plate, and the pink juices spread outwards. She was frightened because she didn't understand why, when normally she liked roast beef – it was she who wanted to offer it for dinner – the sight and the rich stink of it now made her want to gag. She couldn't watch Maurice filling his plate with food so she told him she was going through to the large dining-room.

It was a struggle to get across the crowded hall. Tom had taken over from Sam at the drinks table and he said something, but she didn't hear; she just smiled and carried on working her way through. Someone tried to talk to her and she said, pointing absurdly at her plate as if it were a ticket, 'I'm so sorry, I'll be right back, I must take this to someone next door.' She felt profoundly ill at ease, like the survivor of a road accident stumbling into a stranger's party looking for help.

Suddenly Elizabeth's hand was on her forearm. Her chin pointed towards the dining-room. 'I think it's love,' she said, and giggled; then she was gone. And when Teresa stood on the threshold of the dining-room, her sense of unease intensified.

At the end of the table, sideways-on to where she stood at the door, sat Lucas. His hands were clutching the tabletop and he was leaning forward, shaking with the effort of not laughing as he finished a story. Teresa had no idea what he was saying. Glen and Melanie sat on each side of him, helpless with laughter. Further down the table and around the room several other people had interrupted their conversations to listen. William had drawn up a chair a little to one side of Lucas, behind his shoulder, and he sat leaning slightly back, with his legs crossed over at the knee and his hands folded together on his thigh. His eyes shifted restlessly about the room. On the corner of the table in front were the two crested plates, roughly stacked with a fork and some food visible between them. His satisfied smile faded when he saw Teresa, but then he beamed stubbornly as if to say, for her particular benefit, 'Look! Isn't he the life and soul of the party?'

He seemed oblivious that Lucas was not paying him the least attention.

Teresa turned and left the room in disgust.

'Hey, Teresa, where are you going?'

She had forgotten about Maurice. His voice came as if from under water, sonorous and bloated. His plate was heaped high and a red paper napkin was tucked into the sleeve of his jacket. With his other hand he held his glass and cutlery. He prodded with his extended little finger at something on the plate to stop it falling off, then tried to wipe his finger without looking, but he missed the napkin and marked his jacket instead.

'There's no room in there,' Teresa said, pulling herself up to the air. 'Let's go into the drawing-room. There's a better fire there.'

★

Several couples and clusters of people were gathered in the drawing-room, but it is a large room and it did not feel crowded. As Teresa entered, still with Maurice in tow, she heard Ian Minton's measured, mildly teasing voice: 'Look, Elizabeth, when are we going to get to meet this fiancé of yours?'

'Yes, we want to have a proper look at 'im,' said his sister Cathy.

Elizabeth flushed. Teresa wondered if she was drunk, but then their eyes met and there was a childlike appeal in Elizabeth's that made Teresa think of a kitten stuck up a tree.

Alison Minton shifted her weight from one high heel to the other, smirked, and said, 'Don't worry if he only comes with his friend – what's his name?'

'Lucas,' Teresa said.

'I'll look after Lucas!' she vouched.

'Slow down, cow! Who says he's yours?' said Cathy, nudging her sister with her hip so that a couple of drops of Alison's drink splashed over her fingers.

'Who is this Lucas chap, anyway?' said Maurice.

'A friend of William's,' Teresa replied.

'Not of yours then?' Ian said.

'Well, yes. I mean no. He's a sort of friend but we don't really know him.'

'I bet you wouldn't half mind knowing him better though?' said Cathy.

'No!'

The Mintons laughed at Teresa's denial and she thought they would drop the matter, for while they enjoyed probing other people's – and especially one another's – relationships and puncturing their pieties, they were not actually cruel. But the sight of Teresa wriggling from this wild shaft like a pinned insect was too amusing for Ian to leave at once. 'No, you don't want him to be your friend? Or, no, you don't want him to be your *friend*?'

She wasn't listening properly; her only concern being to repudiate any association of her own with Lucas, she said hastily, 'I told you – he's William's friend!'

The Mintons laughed. 'Pity!' said Alison.

'Where does Elizabeth fit in, then?' Cathy asked.

Elizabeth smiled without understanding and Alison said, 'I think she's open-minded.'

'Open minds: open legs,' said Ian; and now it was Teresa who laughed as, with relief, she felt the focus move away from herself.

'Ian!' Cathy squealed. 'What do you mean by that?'

'I'm not sure. Can't I have it both ways too?'

'You'd be lucky to have it away at all if you speak like that!' said Alison.

'Gosh, I think we're getting into rather hot water here,' said Maurice.

'Some like it hot,' Cathy remarked.

'Ever done it in hot water, have you, Maurice?' Ian asked.

Teresa felt a rush of fondness for the Mintons. Although her secret was exposed, their triple-act defied anyone to take themselves too seriously: the speed with which they had switched to another target, and then another, diminished, in reflection, the importance Teresa attached to her own predicament.

Unnerved by any display of wit around her, sensing that the Mintons were making fun of her, Elizabeth looked hot and rather cross.

'It didn't enter my head that she might be worried on her own account,' Teresa told me. 'I thought she should encourage my own efforts by being a little less peevish. Show some enthusiasm.'

'I'm sorry, I don't see what she had to worry about.'

'Nothing – at least, I suppose we don't know for sure – but the point is that she suddenly felt everyone was laughing at her, or at William, making out that there was something more than met the eye between him and Lucas. It was just the sort of thing that

Ian Minton would imply for the fun of watching Elizabeth get into a tiz about it.'

Laura was standing with her shoulder against the mantelpiece, talking to Ahmed. When a chestnut popped loudly in the fire, she yelped and stepped back from the hearth. The two abrupt noises silenced the room. Overwhelmed by the theatricality of the hush, Teresa cried out, 'Aah! I'm hit!' She clasped her hands over an imaginary bullet-hole through her heart and crumpled slowly to the floor.

Surprised at herself, and taking care not to let her dying grimace slip into a grin as she caught the confusion and amusement on the others' faces, Teresa raised her eyes. To her dismay, she saw that no one was taking any notice of her feeble imitation of death. Their eyes were drawn beyond her, to the door. And with a certainty that sprang directly from humiliation at being found by him in this position, she knew that Lucas had just entered the room.

Still on her knees, she twisted round awkwardly at the waist and saw him watching. Conscious that everyone else was looking at him, he smiled, and said to William over his right shoulder, 'You'd better give her another drink!'

There was laughter; gratitude, perhaps, for the diversion from Teresa's antics. She rose, appalled by his remark. Did he really think she was drunk? His eyes had already moved away from her: he didn't care. He would amuse himself at her expense, regardless, and then pass on.

Cathy had separated herself from Teresa's group, stepping towards William with her head tilted slightly forward as she flicked the fringe away from her eyes. He was clutching a bottle in each hand and she held her glass out to him. 'Thank you,' she said, 'white please. What a good husband you'll make.'

'Two Bottles Bill. That's me.'

'Was that a joke?' Lucas asked laconically.

Cathy's mouth opened, ready to chide Lucas, but William didn't appear to have noticed the taunt: he was still smiling, as if Lucas had complimented him. With a little shrug, Lucas momentarily rolled his eyes, then looked away to see what else was going on in the room.

'Are you going to share that bottle round?' Elizabeth asked William.

His fatuous smile faded.

With her glass refilled, Alison drifted off to join Cathy and Lucas's splinter group. They laughed together. Teresa wanted to touch the white shirt creasing over Lucas's chest, and the hopelessness of her desire made her bones ache with despair.

'William, darling,' said Elizabeth, 'this is Ian Minton. He and his sisters are old friends. I've told you about them . . .'

'Hi,' William said, without looking up. He observed Ian's outstretched hand with puzzlement, as if he couldn't work out why it was being offered to him. Instead of shaking it, he turned without another word and rejoined Lucas.

'Something I said?' Ian asked.

Elizabeth swallowed. Her shoulders were tense. All expression on her face was suspended, like a trapeze artist at the top of her swing over an abyss. She licked her lips, pulling herself together as if preparing to dive. 'Perhaps he's jealous!' she said softly.

'Well, that's understandable,' Ian said with a smile. He must have sensed that trouble was in the air. But he was a habitual flirt and was provoked by William's insult.

Elizabeth ran her hand over her hip. Her fingertips rested on her thigh at the hem of her tight dress. 'The question is,' she said, batting her eyelids, 'has he got any reason to be jealous?'

Elizabeth's exhibition pained Teresa. Although she had her back to William, she knew that he could hear and probably see his fiancée's desperate gambit. She said her sister's name, intending to interrupt, but without conviction, for she didn't know how to utter a caution without it sounding like a prissy rebuke. Besides, her mind lurched with suspicion. Elizabeth had once had a fling with Ian: perhaps, despite her engagement to William, it had been revived? Perhaps William knew about it and his rudeness towards Ian was both deliberate and justified? Even while thinking this Teresa knew it was untrue, yet it subverted her understanding of what was occurring.

Already Ian was answering: 'If he hasn't, then perhaps we should give him something?'

'Is that a proposition?' said Elizabeth.

Teresa moved away to join Laura and Ahmed. She says she was in no doubt that Elizabeth and Ian's flirtation was a deliberate pose, 'and yet –' it still bothers my Teresa acutely: there is an added gravity to her voice when she speaks of it, a measure of her own sense of inadequacy in a situation that she could not control '– I could tell that on Elizabeth's part something terribly serious underlay it, as if she had suddenly, *suddenly* glimpsed a profound gulf between her and William. She was frightened. And her reaction, I suppose, was to tempt fate; to try proving to herself that the chasm did not exist by jumping into it.'

William's high, ostentatious laugh could be heard at something Lucas or one of the Minton twins had said. He wasn't properly involved in their conversation but he was determined to seem so. He had not responded to Ian and Elizabeth but he must have heard every word they said.

'Your place or mine?' said Ian.

'It might as well be here: William doesn't seem to mind.'

Suddenly we heard Debbie Harry's voice sweeping through the house: "*I'm in the phone booth it's the one across the hall!*" Jonah must have decided that supper was finished and it was time to get people dancing. For a couple of seconds it was at maximum volume, crackling with distortion and distracting everyone from what was happening in the room. Then, as the full sound plunged in, Jonah reduced it, confident of the response to his clarion call.

'Come on, Ian, come and dance,' said Cathy, stepping up to her brother and grasping his wrist.

Ian shrugged at Elizabeth. 'I always do what my sisters tell me,' he said, releasing himself from their act.

Alison moved towards the door.

'Possessive!' Lucas exclaimed.

William guffawed.

'You can come too, if you like,' said Alison.

'I think we're quite comfortable here,' said William. 'One has to digest.'

Lucas stared incredulously at William as he watched the Mintons leave the room. Then he looked over his shoulder towards Elizabeth, who was left alone, baffled and miserable in her sexy outfit. Teresa wanted to comfort her, but she didn't know how without drawing more attention to her.

Then Lucas stepped briskly past William. 'Come and dance with me, Elizabeth.'

And Elizabeth was so surprised and so grateful that she put her hand in his and allowed him to lead her away.

William's fleshy lips glistened as he stared after them. The shadow of the following day's stubble and a film of sweat made his face look unhealthily blue and red. Teresa said, 'You didn't expect that, did you? You've lost him now.' Then she turned to the group at the mantelpiece. 'Come on, Ahmed, come and have a dance.'

The cavernous marquee was studded with coloured bulbs. It throbbed with music. Elizabeth and Lucas were at the edge of the floor. Seeing Teresa, they smiled in welcome and edged back through the dancers. They behaved without self-consciousness, as if it were unremarkable that they should be together, so that Teresa wondered if in fact there was no occasion for surprise after all and her judgement was skewed by her own pitiful yearning.

It looked as if something in Lucas was freed by the music and Elizabeth too was neat and quick; she wasn't a show-off. Beside them, Teresa threw herself through a series of fast songs with Ahmed, but she remained conscious of Lucas's proximity. She felt driven by reckless urgency: for William would have to come and find Elizabeth soon, and Ahmed would go, and surely Lucas would then dance with her; and keep on dancing with her and nobody else.

Teresa was ashamed now of her spiteful remark to William. Everyone in the drawing-room must have felt that he had made a fool of himself, and it must be obvious to him too. It was cruel of her, she felt, and ungracious considering his generosity. While inviting Lucas behind her back was odd, perhaps it would turn out for the best after all. She glanced at Lucas now and her heart surged when he saw her watching. He waved to her in rhythm with the music. Elizabeth danced her appreciation of this little tribute to Teresa – with her arms stretched out level with her shoulders and the palms of her hands pushed outwards, she swung her hips from side to side with a confident BOM BOM BOM – and Lucas performed an exquisite bow, still in precise time to the music. Surely he was a good person, Teresa thought. She would apologise to William.

At the end of the next song, Elizabeth pressed her hand to the rucked fabric covering her breasts and signalled to Lucas that she was out of breath.

Lucas followed her.

As they passed between Ahmed and Teresa, she held her hand to her mouth and tipped back her head in a pantomime of needing a drink. And while Ahmed stayed dancing with Laura, who had just been deserted by Maurice, Teresa hurried after the others.

The dining-room was almost empty because the volume of the music in the marquee made conversation impossible. Lucas and Elizabeth walked straight through the empty room, making for the drinks table in the hall. People were still gathered nearby, for the hall was the fulcrum of the house. They were even sitting up the wide stairs. Paul and Angela were nested in the window-sill of the great arched window halfway up.

'Here, have some water,' said Lucas, and Teresa turned round quickly.

He put an empty glass in her hand and held out another to Elizabeth. As she took it in her left hand, she put her right index finger inside the low neck of her dress and pulled it away from her skin. 'Scuse me,' she said, tweaking it to and fro to make a tiny draught, 'it's hot in here.'

Lucas was leaning over the drinks table, reaching behind Josephine, who was sitting on the edge, for a bottle of water. Now he turned and filled the girls' glasses. Although he was flushed, he didn't appear sweaty. He wore a black jacket over his shirt and there was no trace of any dampness at all, whereas Maurice, who was standing nearby with a can of beer, had a sopping patch of perspiration spreading down the back of his shirt.

'Do you want some wine in there now?' Lucas asked.

'Yes please,' Teresa replied.

'Red or white?'

'White please.'

'I wonder where William is?' said Elizabeth, looking vaguely round the hall.

Lucas shrugged and swallowed a glass of water in what appeared to be one draught. Then he poured a splash of red wine into his glass and swirled it round; raised it, and drank.

Teresa tapped Josephine on the shoulder. 'Have you seen William?' she asked.

Josephine frowned and turned to David Mendoza, to whom she had been talking. They both shook their heads and she said, 'No.'

'Must be a while since this place has seen a good bop,' Lucas remarked.

Elizabeth laughed. A strand of her hair glistened against her neck and she fanned herself ineffectually with her hand. 'Probably never,' she said.

Leaving Lucas and Elizabeth, Teresa walked over to the passage-room door where Graham and Dawn appeared to have been stationed like sentinels all evening. 'Have you seen William?' she asked.

'William? No,' said Graham. He pressed himself against the open door to let her past.

She slipped behind a cluster of people round the sofa in the centre of the room and approached her mother near the fireplace. Marie was talking to John Simmonds and when Teresa asked if she had seen William, she shook her head. 'Everything all right?'

'Oh, yes.'

Teresa stood in the drawing-room doorway and looked around, but William wasn't in there either.

Lucas and Elizabeth were laughing together about something. When Elizabeth saw her sister return, she raised her eyebrows. Teresa shrugged. 'I can't see him,' she said, and Lucas uttered a curt chuckle.

Elizabeth rolled the wine round in her glass, as if testing the surface tension. Then she raised it to her lips, tilted her chin and drank. Perhaps she imagined she had hidden herself with this movement, but Teresa saw her eyes blaze with anxiety as she peered around the hall over the rim of her glass.

'I suppose he might be in the study,' Teresa said. 'I didn't look there.'

She hurried back across the hall, past Graham and Dawn again and into the passage-room, where she squeezed round by the windows, with feeble apologies to people as she nudged them, to the door of the study.

A small group was gathered in front of the fire. Teresa wasn't accustomed to seeing people sitting cosily in this room, and the serenity of the tableau was distracting. In the little sofa facing the fireplace sat Alix and Sam. Her father occupied the armchair beyond; his legs were loosely crossed and he held a thin cigar between the second and third fingers of his right hand, near the knuckles. Opposite him, on the other side of the fire, Lucy sat askew in a chair with her heels resting on the tarnished brass coal-scuttle. The only light, apart from that provided by the fire, came from a lamp on the desk behind her and two pairs of candles in wall-brackets. Flames danced in the grate, so that the book spines glinted and the angles of the heavy oak chair at the far end glimmered like polished brass.

'Hello, Teresa my dear,' Tom said. 'All right?'

'Yes. Why?'

'You look a bit fluttery.'

'Do I? I was looking for William.'

'William!' Sam called, as if his brother might be hiding somewhere in the room. 'No, he's not here.'

'It doesn't matter though.'

'Don't hang around the door, Teresa dear. It makes me feel nervous,' Tom said. 'Come in and join us.'

'Yes,' said Alix, pressing herself into the side of the sofa to make room.

'No, I want to . . . Maybe I'll come back,' she said.

Back in the hall, she was disconcerted not to find Elizabeth and Lucas where she had left them. Somehow it hadn't occurred to her that they might move. She felt caught out by their absence, confronted by her own anxiety. Until then she hadn't considered what she was doing, nor what Lucas and Elizabeth thought they were doing and why she was following them. Now she realised that she had been trailing them with pathetic desperation.

'They're dancing again,' said Maurice, who was still hanging about.

Was he mocking? Not knowing what to say, Teresa pretended indifference – 'Who? Oh' – whereupon he asked her to dance himself.

At first Teresa couldn't see Elizabeth and Lucas. But people shifted, and, as she slipped with Maurice into the mêlée, she saw them near the far wall. They seemed separate from everyone else. He was watching her: as she twisted and pranced, conscious of his eyes and avoiding them, she limited her gaze to his chest. Neither looked beyond the other, and Teresa was afraid to approach.

Not knowing what else to do, she danced mechanically with Maurice as her mind tore at the unfolding events. She recalled her jibe at William. Earlier, she had felt ashamed of it. Now she was upset less by the idea of his misunderstanding with Elizabeth than by Lucas's intimacy with her sister on the dance floor. It seemed that William, by his folly, was responsible for this fresh mauling of her heart. As if it weren't painful enough just endur- ing Lucas's presence after his rejection, now she had to watch while her sister, who had a perfectly good fiancé of her own . . .

While what?

What did she imagine was going to happen?

I would love to know what Teresa really thought, at this point, was going to happen. She could not have foreseen the upshot, but clearly she felt more than jealousy. Speaking of it, she suggests that everyone was aware that something was wrong, without knowing exactly what; which she, knowing the background even if she could not comprehend it, elevated to a sense of impending disas- ter. And I wonder too what Elizabeth thought she was doing – to which, I suppose, the answer is that she did not think. It is not her strong suit. It's a disparaging thing to say but I do not mean to be so, particularly. She is someone who responds. She might insist (if asked) that her actions proceed from thought, but it seems to me that it is the other way about with her: thoughts occur as justification or explanations of behaviour. This does not mean that she is not calculating: on the contrary, the behaviour of any animal unmediated by thought is, in a sense, pure calculation. There is charm in this too, or can be, especially in the young. And Elizabeth was young then, only twenty-two. It is hard not to feel sorry for someone so young who, in the face of sudden, overwhelming confusion, behaves naïvely, stupidly.

As for Lucas, perhaps it really was only misplaced gallantry that made him intervene; perhaps he only asked Elizabeth to dance to save her (and William) from a moment's embarrassment because William was too drunk, or mysteriously distracted, to ask her himself when he should have done. Even if Lucas were cynical enough to imagine seducing Elizabeth, what chance could he have when she was in love with William and engaged to be married to him?

Suddenly Maurice touched Teresa's forearm. She snatched it back, but when she looked up at him she saw that he was only directing her attention towards the marquee's entrance.

William stood there alone, round-shouldered and slack, staring through the scrum of dancers towards Lucas and Elizabeth, who still hadn't seen him. They were dancing as before, discreetly aware of each other, exclusive of other dancers. Her eyes were lowered and her lips were held in a smile that might have been demure, but was not.

William turned and went back into the house.

The song was ending and Maurice puffed out his cheeks. He was red and damp as if he had been running through drizzle. 'I need a drink!' he said.

Not knowing where to look if she were left by herself, Teresa followed Maurice into the hall, where her parents at once approached her.

'Teresa, dear, I think I'm going to take Mum home,' said her father.

'I'm afraid I'm *écrasée*,' Marie said, although she looked as fresh as she had all evening. But it was a rule of hers that one should leave a party while still enjoying it. They had already stayed longer than Teresa expected. 'We've had such fun, darling, what a wonderful party.' And she hugged her daughter.

When they had gone, Teresa decided to look in the old study again. Her father had seemed so settled there, and she was curious to know how the balance had changed.

The sofa and chairs which had been occupied so comfortably were now vacant. Nobody was standing by the fire, the room's natural focus. But as she peered into the shadows at the far end, she saw that William was sitting in the heavy oak chair, flanked by the old wooden filing cabinets and marquetry boxes which once contained the records of the Carew estates but now were empty, except for a few oddments which had survived more because nobody knew where to put them than because anyone had selected them for preservation.

He was clutching a bottle of wine which stuck up obscenely from between his thighs.

'Oh, you're here,' Teresa said.

'So are you.'

'Yes, I suppose I am.'

'I had to be somewhere.'

'I was looking for you. Are you all right?'

'Why shouldn't I be?'

'I don't know. I just . . .'

'Well, I'm fine. Having a bit of a sit-down.'

'Why don't you come and dance?'

He shook his head.

'Come on!'

'Maybe in a minute,' he said, but he was shaking his head again.

'I'm asking you to come and have fun, William, not to a funeral!'

His eyes closed. 'Go on.' He raised his chin towards the door. 'Maybe I'll join you in a minute.' He brought the bottle to his lips.

Instead of drinking from it, he suddenly lifted it higher. Closing his left eye, he looked at Teresa through his right eye over the bottle's rim, as if aiming a gun. 'What have I done, Teresa?' he said.

She watched him, trying to discover from his self-pity if he meant what she thought he meant, what she dreaded him meaning.

'What do you mean?'

'Has something happened?'

'If something has happened, maybe you should do something about it.'

He continued eyeing her, hiding in the gloom behind the neck of the bottle.

'For God's sake, what do you expect me to say?' she cried out at him, and hurried from the room.

She felt like slamming the door, but she didn't want people to see this so she walked on briskly through the passage-room without looking at anyone else, containing her exasperation. In the hall, she heard the Eurythmics song just starting with its poised, poignant beat. She saw Ian and said, 'Come on!' He gave a mock bow and together they went into the marquee.

Beyond checking that Lucas and Elizabeth were still there, Teresa hardly looked at them as she began dancing. She wanted the music to drain her pent-up anger with William. From the corner of her eye she saw that Lucas was singing along, *Love love love is a dangerous drug*. He was dancing without seeming to notice Elizabeth but, at the same time, he appeared to be directing himself wholly towards the space she occupied; and she held her position and kept pace with him. As the song was drawing to a close, the sound merged into Teresa's favourite Bronski Beat song. It didn't matter who she danced with, this track always caught her up in its own tide of jubilation. But as the momentum swelled into the repeated '*I'm in love*' sequence, she realised that the singer's manically energetic falsetto was being duplicated. Everyone was turning to see Lucas shrieking along to the music, either oblivious of the display he was putting on or revelling in it. Meanwhile Elizabeth was stirred by his energy into the jagged fervour of dancing that she loved so much, arms and legs like pistons.

Suddenly the volume was cut and an amplified voice was heard. 'This is Jonah in the womb of the whale, where the mood is rude and the music's loud. Something tells me that was one of our Birthday Girl's favourite numbers. Now here's a little something to let you get your breath back.'

Teresa was so surprised to be singled out like this that she didn't realise at once what was happening. One moment lots of people were looking at her: the next, she saw Elizabeth put her hands on Lucas's shoulders as he took her by the waist; and Teresa, matching her sister's movements like one in a trance, found herself locked in a slow dance with Ian.

Ian gave no sign of being astonished by Teresa's readiness to fall into his arms. She felt the confidence of his touch and it revolted her, yet she couldn't tear herself away because she was mesmerised by the spectacle of her sister and Lucas.

Held tight by Lucas's fingertips, Elizabeth's stomach was pressed against him. Her back was arched slightly so that she could look into his eyes. Their faces were inches apart and it looked as if they were about to kiss. Still Teresa couldn't believe that they would. Did her sister imagine that nobody would notice? Or that it wouldn't matter? Did she think people would laugh? Teresa did not know which was worse – the fact that this was happening in William's house, or the fact that Elizabeth was messing around with Lucas in front of *her*, when she was just a few yards away. What did they imagine she was thinking, let alone other people?

Moving her head to disguise her shudder under Ian's touch, she saw William at the marquee's entrance. He was standing still, as before, just watching, but other people had seen him this time. Only Lucas and Elizabeth appeared not to have seen him. They were moving gently, close together, looking into each other's eyes with little smiles on their lips, as if daring one another to initiate a kiss.

It seemed impossible for William to do nothing, but he suddenly turned around and left.

Even Ian sensed that something critical was occurring, for he lost interest in Teresa's flesh and said to her, 'What the hell are they up to?'

'Lord knows!'

Teresa broke away and hurried up to the disco. Leaning over the turntables, she shouted to Jonah above the music, 'Please – can you put on something fast?'

He nodded and the music changed as she turned back towards Ian. When she recognised it, her heart sank. '*Celebrate good times* . . .' A song she had always detested. But Lucas and Elizabeth removed their hands from each other and space opened up between them.

Teresa had no idea what to do. She longed for her parents but they had gone, nor were Sam or Josephine anywhere to be seen. She wasn't her sister's keeper, but she couldn't watch this happen without saying anything. Moving so that she was directly in front of her sister, she mouthed across the music, 'What are you doing?' Elizabeth chose not to understand her. Opening her eyes wide, she pouted. Stunned, Teresa stared at her in disbelief, then turned away.

Determined in their indifference, Elizabeth and Lucas formed a fluid but tight pocket of movement on the dance-floor. Everyone else orbited shakily about them, as if held at a fixed distance by rods on loose pivots.

As the song came to an end, a new one rose above it with adeptly managed continuity.

'I recall looking round as I recognised it,' Teresa says, 'wishing perhaps that my eyes would give the lie to my ears, or that someone would take control. Instead, I saw a click of alarm in Alix which confirmed that it wasn't all in my imagination: Jonah had put on "Sexual Healing".'

Suddenly a loud crack was heard above the music. People scattered from the marquee's entrance. Melanie staggered back with Glen crouching round her, his neck hunkered down into his shoulders, trying to protect her and himself. Teresa saw a snake dive in the air. The noise repeated, then William advanced through the parted dancers. In his right hand he brandished a whip, whose tongue now flashed out at Lucas. As Lucas hopped back William yelled at him, but Teresa could not hear his words above the music. He was clutching Lucas's leather jacket in his left hand and, as he approached the disco, he flailed with it at one of the turntables. The music slewed and scrunched and then ceased.

In the abrupt silence, the coloured lights still roamed and arced, plucking out tense, sweaty faces for scrutiny and then disposing of them in the darkness. The sound of the whip cracking again in their midst was like the splitting of a vault.

'William!' Elizabeth cried, edging back along the marquee wall beyond range of the whip.

'Shut up, you bitch!'

The whip lashed out once more, separating Lucas from the others. William stood braced in front of his friend with his arm raised to strike again. His swollen lips glistened and his face was clammy and ugly with furious humiliation.

'Out of here!' he screamed. 'Get out!' And he threw the jacket down at Lucas's feet.

'What the . . .!'

Someone had giggled and Lucas looked to see who it was, ready to laugh, but William cracked the whip again savagely, catching him on the legs.

'Someone stop him!' Mary shouted.

'William!' cried Elizabeth; then again, piercingly, 'William!'

'Shut up, bitch!'

'William, anyone here will tell you that Elizabeth and me have just been having a dance . . .'

'I know what you've been up to!'

'Is this what you call poetic justice?'

'Shut up! I'm telling you, don't make a joke of this, Lucas. All evening I've watched you making a spectacle of me.'

'*Me* making a spectacle of *you*? Look at yourself!'

'Get out! Get the *fuck* out of here!'

As Lucas bent down to retrieve his jacket, the whip sliced past his ear. Shying back, he stumbled and missed his footing. For the first time, he looked at William with direct antagonism. His lips were colourless and, as he got to his feet, the tendons in his neck strained. 'You stupid jerk!' he said, pulling on his jacket. Then he sauntered towards the entrance, ignoring William. Perhaps he knew that this controlled, deliberate departure would incense William. In any case, for an instant William hesitated, swaying drunkenly as the prospect of revenge slipped away, but then he lashed the whip again and tottered after him.

Lucas slipped through a gap in the side awning, heading off across the lawn to the outhouse through which he could pass to the front yard. William plunged after him, making the canvas shudder and ripple behind him. Everyone else followed in dread as the whip whirled and buckled. But despite the impression William gave of convulsive activity, like some frothing herald of apocalypse thrashing the air with his staff, he didn't hurry to catch up with Lucas.

243

Lucas was unlocking the box on his motorbike as Teresa arrived in the yard.

'That's right, get out of here!' cried William.

Pausing before putting on his crash helmet, Lucas said, 'Haven't you got a shotgun, William?'

William gripped his face with his left hand, as if Lucas had smashed it. He let out an eerie, etiolated yelp, a sobbed scream.

'Language deserted you, has it, Mr Poet?'

William lunged, and flicked the whip near Lucas's legs so that he capered ludicrously. He tried to get onto his bike but the leather thong caught him on the wrist and he leapt back.

'Who do you think you are, fucking Butch Cassidy?' he shouted.

'Get out! Get the fuck out!'

William relented for long enough to let Lucas get aboard, but as soon as the engine started he began attacking him again with his whip.

The bike shot off, sending back a jet of gravel at William.

For a moment William was transfixed by Lucas's disappearing bike. Then he reached into his pocket and swung sideways to where his own motorcycle was parked. Clamping the whip under one arm as he climbed aboard, he thrust the key into the ignition. The bike burst into life as he heaved it from its stand. He pulled sharply away, regardless of those who cried out for him to stop. The savage opening of the throttle split the night.

It was just a few seconds before they heard the smash and zoom and stillness of his end.

# Chapter Fourteen

KNOWING WHAT I now know, I look back on Lucas's visit five months ago – his first visit, I should say – with amazement. At what point did he realise where we were heading?

He said nothing when we came off the motorway, but it must surely have occurred to him that we were near the house he once knew. Only when we turned right into Sweynsend itself – which left him only a minute or so before we arrived – did he say something to the effect that he had been here previously; to which, I imagine, I said, 'You don't say!' and asked him, 'When?' 'Oh, years ago.'

As we pulled up outside the house, he said, 'Didn't you say your wife is called Teresa?'

And the unexpected urgency of his tone, as at last he made the connection to the Teresa Fairfax he remembered, made me guess there was some history between them.

It was too late to probe because Teresa approached from the lawn with a hedge-cutter, and her demeanour confirmed at once that I was right. Not that she didn't welcome him, but there was a moment's hesitation, a glance in my direction to see what I knew, as she put the hedge-cutter down and removed her gloves; an intake of breath perhaps, but above all a ferocious appraisal in her black eyes as she stepped forward – assessing the speed of the oncoming train – that steadied as she registered that he too was taken unawares. 'Lucas,' she said, 'this is a surprise!'

'For me, a nice one,' he replied.

The lack of any reciprocal 'Me too' from Teresa was conspicuous. From anyone else it would have amounted to rudeness, but she carries off such moments with an insouciance that sometimes initimidates people. Usually it is recognised that, if she doesn't engage in the full social banter, it is less from unfriendliness than a lack of interest in the form.

She smiled and offered her cheek for Lucas to kiss. He did so, accepting without question the implicit challenge in her manner.

Thanks to Teresa's subsequent debriefings I'm acquainted with what happened between them earlier, but it occurs to me that I still have very little handle on that April meeting. In view of all that she has told me since, I can see that it must have been very awkward for her, much more so than I realised at the time. When I came home that evening and found her in her dressing-room, I saw that she was upset but I had no idea of the predicament I had landed her in.

I gathered when I purchased Sweynsend that the place was on the market because of some family tragedy. I soon learned from Tom that the previous owner had been killed in a motorbike crash. I didn't like to pry beyond that, but at some stage Teresa told me the outlines of what occurred that night: that William was engaged to Elizabeth, that he had gone off on his bike, drunk, after freaking out because he'd got jealous when someone else started hitting on Elizabeth. But she dismissed it all with 'the tragedy was in being so young'. I took it for granted that Elizabeth had not encouraged the guy's advances; I didn't know about Teresa's passion for him; and there was no reason whatever to connect it all to Lucas.

It's not the first time I've brought a visitor to Sweynsend with very little notice. Teresa knew to expect a guest for lunch and tea.

Someone from Moscow, I guess I said, an Englishman. Probably she would find him agreeable. He would amuse and scare us with tales of life on the mean streets of Moscow and business with ex-Soviet men; he might show an interest in the house and garden. She seems to approve when I bring exotic birds to our quiet haven. She says they regard my taking them home and introducing them to her as a compliment, but I hope she also takes it as a compliment to her. She would not enjoy meeting all my colleagues, but I thought she would like Lucas.

'You didn't tell me you'd met my wife,' I said.

'I didn't know I had. Hello, Teresa.'

'Hello, Lucas.'

'I had no idea!'

'Why would you?'

But of course there are good reasons why Lucas might have known. I keep thinking, did I really never mention his name to her? Obviously I didn't. But surprising things happen all the time and we shouldn't be surprised, in a general way, that surprising things happen. I did not tell her: that's all there is to it. Come to that, it's surprising too that she didn't ask. Perhaps she's weary, after all, of these zigzagging, restless birds. (Why can't they fly direct? Is word getting round that there's something unmissably quaint about Jimmy's place? Or is it just the promise of a meal served on a plate instead of cellophane pouches on a plastic tray? Leg room? Or touching base with aspirations?)

Lucas's appearance has altered in the eight years since he left Sweynsend on his bike in the middle of the night. Teresa said – growing lyrical in the stillness of that coppery evening, as I held her in my arms; more lyrical, frankly, than I would expect about a casual friendship: but how confidences disarm! – she said that it wasn't just the effects of ageing: 'He hasn't lost his hair. He isn't grey and wrinkled, nor is he red-faced and jowly with a little tyre of flesh overlapping his collar. No, his looks will uphold his youth long after the rest of us are haggard and twisted, or pendulous with unwelcome swags of flesh. His skin has none of the blotches that creep into most complexions. His teeth are white and even, his eyebrows aren't straggly and his blue eyes haven't paled. You still notice them at once and, if anything, they seem more piercing. What has changed is his presentation of himself. His thick black hair is now brushed back instead of being left to fortune. He used to shave erratically, so that you noticed the stubble on his face instead of the fact that he had good skin, but now he's beautifully shaven and there's a whiff of aftershave instead of cigarettes. Previously I'd only ever seen him in jeans and an assortment of nondescript T-shirts and boots. Now he's impeccably turned out in grey chinos, expensive black shoes, a crisp cotton shirt with fancy cufflinks and a miraculously uncreased cream linen jacket. Quite the dandy. But what I noticed most of all was that, when he looked at me, I didn't feel humiliated by his indifference. For all their alertness, his eyes don't reveal so shamelessly what he feels: he has learnt to be canny. I can't say whether age has softened his arrogance or not, but it appears to have made him care what other people think.

'Poor Jimmy, you were shifting from one foot to the other and rubbing your hands together in spasms of agitation. Your face was folded into a smile of such largesse! You might have been rejoicing at the arrival of a long-lost brother instead of wondering if you had inadvertently produced an ex-lover. That must have been what you were thinking as you watched us control our embarrassment and inspect each other.'

'So you've been here before, to Sweynsend?' I said at last.

'Lucas was a friend of William Carew's,' Teresa explained.

'Right.' I nodded, as if everything was now clear. And because I knew the bones of the story, I added, 'Poor William.'

Lucas clamped his thumb and index finger on the bridge of his nose and squeezed his eyes shut. 'So you married Jimmy.'

'Yes. And you work with him,' Teresa observed with a dry laugh, reminding him that it was a surprise for her too.

'For his sins!' I said, trying to lighten things up because I suddenly thought, Christ! This is going to be one hell of a party! 'Come on in and have a drink. You two must have a lot to catch up on.'

Teresa asked us to excuse her for a moment while she went upstairs to change out of her gardening clothes.

She had often wondered how she would feel if she met Lucas again. Now, upstairs in our bedroom, she was pleased to find that her nerves were not a-jangle. There is always a fear that present happiness is a delusion, an expedient fiction maintained by an exhausted will to shield us from the sorrows of the past and the pain of sagging hopes. Well, how would I feel if Iris walked into my life unannounced like this? Teresa welcomed the discovery that she was pregnant but, in the wake of every granted wish, like wasps to honey, comes the thought, 'Is this really what I want or am I tricking myself?' And as she pulled tight the belt on her fresh pair of jeans and looked at the unused notches waiting for her further down the belt, acquaintances whom she was going to get to know better, I believe she probably thought of me – maybe putting my head against her tummy so that I could listen; or wondered perhaps what our baby's laugh would be like; the three of us together. And even though Lucas was in the house, I think she smiled.

Coming down the stairs, she recalled the previous two occasions when she had come down these stairs to find Lucas in the hall. Despite the span of years, the anguish she felt then flared at the memory, but it felt detached, like the spook of an imagined situation rather than her own experience. She heard me call out from the passage-room, 'In here, honey!' And my voice was a hand to support her as she stepped round the ghost of Lucas's younger self to join us.

249

'Lucas was just telling me about his flight,' I said. 'He was stuck beside some New Age nut from Milwaukee or somewhere.'

'I thought you were coming from Moscow,' she said.

'I was.'

'Oh.'

'There's nothing stopping New Age freaks from going to Moscow,' I said. 'Worse luck for the Muscovites.'

'They seem to like it,' said Lucas.

'But weren't you travelling First or Club Class or something?'

'The kind of New Age freak who goes to Russia in Economy is extinct,' I said. 'They all make so much money, it's a turn-up for the books having one on an ordinary plane instead of a private jet.'

'Why? What are they selling?'

'What aren't they selling? The same as everyone else – salvation.'

Lucas shook his head briskly. 'No, they're not. They're selling neuroses. Treatments for maladies people never knew they had. Ways to satisfy desires they didn't know they felt.'

'Isn't that just the same as everyone else?'

'They're not even selling objects, just mental states.'

'Advice. Like us.'

'No. They offer cures. We offer advice.'

We laughed and I said, 'Would you buy a used car from this man?'

'Miracle cures,' said Teresa. 'Perhaps we could market a cure for the guilt experienced by those who don't suffer from these neuroses?'

'Or for the guilt that *should* be experienced by those who don't suffer from the neuroses . . .'

'Those who claim not to suffer . . .'

I said I would leave them to fix Guilt while I went and fetched some drinks for us.

Lucas got to his feet and went over to the fireplace, where he stood with his hands in his pockets and his shoulder resting against the mantelpiece.

'What does Jimmy know?' he asked.

Teresa replied, 'Only what you've told him.'

'I haven't told him anything.'

'Well then.'

Although they hadn't seen each other since the night of William's death, it turns out that there was more between them than just the memory of the events themselves. I only learnt this afterwards, a few days ago; it was perhaps to provide a context for it that Teresa gave me all her lengthy explanations. For William's parents were not satisfied with the accounts they were given – who can blame them? Can there ever be a satisfactory reason for a son's death? – and in their grief they were unkind. They wanted revenge.

It is pointless for me to describe the desolation. However, Elizabeth was so enfeebled by distress and appalled by her own behaviour that she nearly allowed herself to be used by the Carews as the instrument of their revenge. 'Those of us who were there,' says Teresa, 'saw clearly that she was partially responsible for the argument that led to William's death, and she herself recognised this. This was hard for her to bear, especially when coupled with the apparent fact, pathetically exposed by the circumstances, that she didn't seem to love him quite as much as a girl might be supposed to love her fiancé. This was difficult to explain to Hal and Vivienne. Well, where would you begin? You can't just say to the people who were to have been your parents-in-law, 'I'm sorry, but your son was killed in an argument he had with someone I was flirting outrageously with.' Nobody likes to portray themselves as a monster, even if they are so sorry for what they have done that they would gladly change places with the wronged one. And I've never doubted for an instant that Elizabeth *was* sorry. Of course she was. She was so sorry that she would have done anything for William's parents. But she was afraid of them too.'

To start with, she must have said vaguely that William was upset because Lucas was dancing with her, or something of the sort. Really there was no reason for William to be upset about it, she had not thought that he would be . . . But then Lucas put his hands on her, which William saw, and this was what – quite naturally – had made him so angry . . . What did she mean by 'put his hands on her'? Didn't she object? Of course, but she didn't want to make a scene, she did not want to humiliate him and would have walked away at the end of the song . . .

Hal and Vivienne opined that letting herself be semi-raped in public, in front of her fiancé's eyes, in his house, was already 'making a scene'.

Elizabeth got scared. She sensed that they wanted a scalp for their son's death, and it was going to be hers. She didn't know what this would involve but her imagination conjured up a hazy courtroom with confusing words like 'Indictment' and 'Culpable' and 'Guilty' buzzing about her bowed head as she stood in the dock. Because she already *felt* guilty, she imagined that she must in some way *be* guilty even though she didn't exactly understand *how* she was guilty. But justice apparently required that *someone* be guilty and so, to help relieve her own guilt, she co-operated in identifying a culprit.

Elizabeth obligingly told them that Lucas had a go at her in the garden and they cooked up some charge of attempted rape against him.

Teresa was convinced from the start that Elizabeth had made it up. At least, if there had been any fumbling in the shrubbery, then she reckoned that her sister had her share of the action too. But having made the allegation out of fear, Elizabeth kept to it out of fear. She didn't seem to realise how serious it would be for Lucas if the charge was made to stick. She behaved as if it somehow didn't concern him. She wanted to believe that it would make things better for Hal and Vivienne, for herself and even for William: Lucas was mysteriously left out of the equation. Perhaps, in her desperation to justify the calamity (since it seemed to be regarded as a plausible justification), she even believed herself that he must have tried to rape her. It is hard to know what Elizabeth thought, and I fall back on Teresa's insistence that she was young: upset, frightened, and very confused, she was easily swayed.

When Teresa understood what was happening, she did her utmost to make her sister retract. She tried to enlist her parents but they were so stunned that they were ready to believe anything the Carews said, especially if it cast Elizabeth in a better light. It wasn't that Teresa thought Lucas was blameless: a part of her was quite happy to see him thrown to the wolves. Nevertheless, she thought it was wrong. However disgraceful his behaviour, he had not tried to rape Elizabeth and therefore he shouldn't be charged with it. Responsibility for William's death was a separate issue. The lie only made things worse. It would not bring William back.

'What else?' Lucas asked, turning and looking directly at Teresa.

She wondered if he meant her ancient passion for him but, not wishing to discuss that, she answered, 'Jimmy knows what happened to William and that it happened after an argument with someone over Elizabeth. But there's no reason why he should connect you with it.'

For all their smartness, Teresa found that Lucas's clothes looked sad. They were too new, as if there wasn't enough continuity in his life for a set of clothes to be suitable for more than one or two occasions. He looked as if he had dressed according to someone else's idea of how he should dress.

'What's become of Elizabeth?' he asked.

'She lives near Manchester.'

'And?'

'She's married. She has two children.'

Lucas nodded and then, it seemed for the first time, looked around. At the new furniture in place of the Carews' derelict old hulks; at the spaces made by the removal of drifts of ancient sowing boxes, photograph albums and board games whose rules nobody had known for two generations; the ceiling, which is now almost white instead of the murky brown from a century's tobacco and chimney smoke. Then he turned back to the mantelpiece, over which there hangs a picture.

'There used to be a virtually opaque mirror here,' he said.

'Yes.'

As if continuing a train of thought, he went on, 'So you married Jimmy. How did that happen?'

'When he bought Sweynsend from the Carews, he bought us too at the Manor. I mean he could have got us out, we would have gone, but it suited him to have us there.'

'The girl next door.'

'Don't.'

'I'm sorry.'

'What about you?'

'What a great picture!' he said suddenly, and came round behind Teresa's chair to look at my Maria Turner photograph. It shows an elegant, composed woman climbing out of a car on the edge of a cliff. She is adjusting her stockings as if she needs to be perfectly turned out, wherever she is going. But looking at her in that location, you can't help thinking that she's there because she intends to jump.

'And what about you?' she repeated.

She sensed him hesitate behind her, then he walked over to the window.

'Why don't you sit down?' she said.

'Thanks. I've nothing to report. I'm a salesman. Of advice which people think they want but shouldn't want. I rent a flat in

254

Moscow. I move about a lot, which suits me. I don't come to the UK much. I have no life.'

'No life here, you mean? In England?'

'No. No life.'

It was at this point that I joined them again, with a tray of drinks. 'No life?' I repeated, ignorant of the currents between them. 'What I hear, you have a life all right in Moscow!'

During lunch, Lucas made us laugh a lot and we swerved from one topic to another. But one subject to which we made no reference was his former association with Sweynsend. It was such an obvious thing for them to talk about that it became hard for me to introduce it myself once I'd noticed that neither of them was referring to it. It sat above us like a crow on a telegraph wire, waiting to be acknowledged.

As we were setting off for a walk in the garden after lunch, the phone rang.

'I'll catch you up,' I said, doubling back into the passage-room as they went out of the front door.

Lucas and Teresa walked a few paces – past the passage-room windows – in silence.

She was embarrassed at being suddenly left alone with him because the neglect of whatever they shared from the past already constituted a secret between them, as if they both understood that their own silence was a tacit admission of the other's significance. Had she popped a question about the ex-Soviet arsenal, or asked his views on the National Debt or Third World Poverty – some tittle-tattle – then she might have diverted him for long enough to fill my absence. It would have indicated clearly that she didn't want to engage in any talk which established a bond. For him then to take the initiative would have been a breach of some nebulous code of small-talk. Perhaps she felt that if she tried to head him away from what so palpably linked them then he would interpret this as proof, in her mind, of a genuine intimacy.

255

It is unclear to me exactly whether it was an intimacy she did not want. Inconvenient, yes; troubling, yes. But altogether undesired? I'm not so sure. Curiosity alone would have invited communication.

Although sunny, it was cold, and Teresa hugged her thick red woollen cardigan tight around herself. Passing the end of the house, Lucas said, 'I've often thought about Sweynsend. What I did, and William and Elizabeth.'

He paused, waiting for her to say something, but she said nothing. Nor did she look at him: she was looking at the blossom coming out on the crab-apple tree on the lawn.

'I behaved strangely,' he said. 'And I never thanked you for getting Elizabeth to drop those charges.'

Teresa noted that he admitted to behaving strangely but not badly. 'We all behaved stupidly,' she said. 'But none of us committed a crime.'

'You didn't behave stupidly.'

She wondered what he meant by this, but made no comment.

'I don't feel I can mention it in front of Jimmy,' he said.

Teresa told me later, 'I thought, "Damned cheek!" But it was true in a way. Before I had a chance to think of a suitable reply, I heard you calling us. I turned and waited for you to catch up.'

'Lucas tells me I've changed,' she said, wishing to demonstrate to him that any difficulty about his link with Sweynsend was in his own head.

She wanted to introduce the subject to me after all – to provide an opening for me to prove Lucas wrong, to undercut whatever his interpretation might be – yet she did so with a lie; a harmless one in itself (after all, no doubt she had changed even though he had not said so), but a lie nevertheless, which was recognisable to him as such, and therefore an act of collusion with him, a covert recognition of their bond.

'Well, I guess you probably have,' I answered. 'That was Pat

Bailey. He says he and Jilly would like to come for a drink before lunch tomorrow.' Addressing myself to Lucas, I continued cheerfully: 'They're a nice couple who moved in to what's known as the Home Farm last year. Funny thing about England is how history clings to places in names and the lie of the land. That name applies to when it belonged to this estate. You'd think that it would have been renamed "Bailey's Place" or whatever. Pat's a land surveyor, knows all about it, he's an interesting guy. Other places may have a longer history, like in the Middle East where they were talking astrophysics while you guys were still yodelling at the moon in your woad, but you have the continuity. Tamerlane didn't get here, or Napoleon, or Hitler. You don't rush around changing your street names . . . I'm sorry, I'm droning on.'

'Not at all,' said Lucas. 'But look what a mess we're in.'

'Oh, come on! You're not going to start telling me how awful this country is, are you?'

I guess Lucas's comment really was intended to be political, but it had a different resonance for Teresa which I did not get at the time. I had rebuffed her approach; deliberately, it must have seemed, avoided talk of earlier times at Sweynsend (though it was just plain native stupidity) – thereby, apparently, proving Lucas's point. And Teresa, by inventing a remark, had allowed Lucas to suspect her of the very uneasiness which she was anxious to persuade him that she did not feel.

After this, they didn't have another moment alone to talk about it before he left after tea.

When he was gone, I said that she seemed embarrassed as she said goodbye to him.

And then she produced this bizarre outburst: 'Why didn't you say anything, Jimmy? Are you so uninterested in my past? Do you think that everything related to me which is outside your experience is of no consequence? Or is it that you're just not interested in the past at all except where it can be valued as an item in a sale catalogue or identified as of Local Historical Interest? Did you really not wonder how Lucas knew me or Sweynsend, or were you afraid that asking would lead to an unwelcome revelation? When he told you that he'd been to Sweynsend before and met me, did you assume that it was a single brief occasion? Was it sheer egocentricity that stopped you…?'

Well, now she has told me all about it and I don't think she could charge me with lack of interest. It is rather the reverse. I have my own interest in her story, namely Iris. Teresa has volunteered what she thinks now about Lucas and she says there is no rekindling of her feelings towards him. Although that must be open to doubt, the candid way in which she told me about his second visit made him seem a bit pathetic. It sounded as if he was actually distasteful to her.

Not that I'm not very fond of Teresa – I love her, I suppose – but I can't help thinking about Iris. How would I feel if she came into my life again, as Lucas has come into Teresa's? How would it be for her? I have this image of her caught up with children, shopping, running a household – life – and now this messy business of Aaron's involvement with the Phantom of Liberty. I wonder how things might have been if she had come with me, years ago. But that is idle now beside the real question of how it will be when I see her again. For I am due to see her very soon. Just a couple of days. I have told Teresa that I'm going to meet a client in Paris. I suppose I could tell her that I'm going to look up an old friend, but it's better that she doesn't know. She'd only be envious of me hanging out on the Côte d'Azur.

It happened like this:

The day after we got back from St Petersburg, 'morning' sickness hit Teresa. At first I thought it was the effect of all that caviar, but she said it was not and soon I had to believe her. An idiot plumber had wrenched a boilerhouse-full of stopcocks back and forth inside her.

Neither of us was prepared for this. I had imagined morning sickness as a ladylike spit into a porcelain bowl during the morning toilette. Its violence took us both by surprise; its constancy drained poor Teresa. I had thought of this baby as something we were doing together. It would involve her in some physical inconvenience which I couldn't literally share, but I intended to participate fully in other ways – whatever those might be. It was a shock to discover how incontestably one-sided the burden is. Instead of finding myself in the domestic idyll I had fluffily imagined, where we admired her swelling belly together as she sipped cups of camomile tea, tenderly picked and lovingly brewed by my good self while she sat in a bower of cushions, smiling serenely – instead of this, she was desperately, irredeemably, alone.

I suppose all pregnant women feel a profound loneliness – at any rate, those who suffer from severe nausea. Others may try to soothe them but nobody can truly remove the physical discomfort. It is evident to everyone that the woman is on her own.

After a few days of this I called Iris, whose number in Sanary, thanks to Alec, had been burning a hole in my pocket for the last few weeks. I told her I was due to be in Nice and I knew she wasn't too far away from there . . . I cannot describe what it was like hearing her on the phone, it was – like a city full of church bells ringing out news of Easter. She asked if I could stop for a couple of days and I said, sure, I could manage that.

That was a month ago. Since then, things have eased with Teresa and she says I shouldn't worry about going away, she's quite used to my absences (her words, not mine). So I shall be reporting for duty at Gatwick South Terminal the day after tomorrow.

# Chapter Fifteen

IT HAS TAKEN me a while to piece it together, but the start – and the finish – are clear enough. However you look at it, things turned out differently.

I was at Gatwick on the little shuttle train that takes you to the South Terminal when I got Teresa's call. That train always makes me feel like I'm moving into a different zone, out of the usual world and into somewhere unimagined by the people I'm leaving behind on the ground, or in the North Terminal building. You half expect to be met at the other end by someone in a silver suit, Farrah Fawcett-Majors or a doomed extra from a James Bond film. It's to do with the doors in the wall, the soft glide of the vehicle and the view of the airport from the raised tracks.

Of course I saw that it was Teresa when I took the phone out of my pocket, and I knew immediately, with certainty, that I would not be going to Sanary to see Iris.

'Lucas is here,' she said.

I looked out at the tarmac terrain, the airplanes and all the paraphernalia of the airport, the flights of steps to nowhere, the busy little cars with their officious lights, a gigantic child's lay-out with working parts, a vast act of collaboration in the illusion of escape: in a few minutes I would see it all from the other direction and it would look just as convincing.

'I'm so sorry, I just had to speak to you, Jimmy. He's been so upsetting, making foolish declarations.'

'Is he still there?'

'Yes, in the garden. I told him I was going to the loo.'

'I'll come back,' I said.

'Oh, Jimmy, there's no need for that, you've got your meeting, I didn't mean you to come back, I just wanted to speak to you . . .'

'It's okay. I'll come back. I can easily cancel. I could probably deal with it on the phone anyway. I'll come back.'

'Jimmy that's ridiculous, I would never have rung if I'd thought . . .'

'I promise you it's okay, Teresa my darling.'

'But he'll be gone in a few minutes, I'm sure.'

'That doesn't matter. I'm coming back.'

I slipped the phone back into my pocket as the train drew in – 'docked' would perhaps have been the appropriate word, conjuring as it does an intergalactic journey, instant transmission to the fantastic, if I had subsequently boarded the plane. But I was feeling earthbound by now and looking for signs directing me back for the return journey. I paused at the North Terminal hub only long enough to call Iris. She was not there and I left a message on her answerphone saying due to unforeseen circumstances etc, such a shame, and I hoped to catch up with her another time.

Back to Victoria, Euston, Rugby, and a taxi home. It took me just under four hours to retrace my steps, and when I took Teresa in my arms I wanted to weep. Who knows for what. Let's just say I did not feel proud of myself.

But I did not weep. There was consoling to be done, and listening. To be honest, I was glad to listen because I didn't feel much like talking myself, and I was curious to know what had occurred during my absence.

Teresa was outside when I got home. Instead of the rather staged greeting back in April, when I found her up in her dressing-room with that music, she was weeding the round flowerbed in front of the monkeypuzzle. I saw her stand up as my taxi departed, and the curve of her when she smoothed the long shirt over her stomach was different. In her stride too was a suggestion of the heaviness that will come to her in the weeks ahead. It was a warm evening and her face was pink. Her hair was imperfectly tied back, so that she had to pull strands back from her face.

Her dark eyes still glistened; she was pale, and looked emptied out. I gave her a hug.

'Thank you for coming, Jimmy. It was kind of you. I'm sorry for messing you about.'

'I wouldn't have come if it wasn't possible.'

'Obviously.'

I laughed – unnecessarily: it was relief. 'You know what I mean.'

'I know. All the same, thank you.'

Holding her hand, I led her across the lawn, past a rug spread on the grass and a tray with two glasses and a half full jug, to the bench where we have taken to sitting this summer. She sat and told me what had happened.

At first Lucas asked to speak to me when he phoned but, when Teresa told him I was away, he said there was something he wished to talk to her about too. It so happened that he was driving up from Heathrow now; he was on his way between somewhere else and Moscow and had a few hours to kill, and had hired a car and set off on the offchance… he would be with her in twenty minutes.

Teresa felt breathless and angry. Instead of asking if it was convenient, or even pausing to ask how she was, he announced his intention with familiar arrogance. She acknowledged to herself that she could have tried to stop him, but she didn't try, nor did she refuse to see him when he arrived. He presumed: and he wasn't wrong. Thinking back to the conversation after she put the phone down, she realised that he had deliberately checked that I was not there before saying that he would come. Had I been home, would he have turned round and gone somewhere else in his hire car?

'I don't know what I was expecting,' she said to me, and sighed. 'Certainly not protestations of love, because I wouldn't have let him come in that case. Perhaps it has to do with feeling better. It makes me realise how inward-looking I've been the past few weeks. This morning at last I felt well enough to feel curious. I didn't feel guilty about his coming, as perhaps he imagined I would, just a bit cross at his manner. I suppose I was excited at the prospect of talking about the events leading to William's death. Having talked it all through with you, I saw no reason not to talk to Lucas about it. I had never done so, after all.'

It was a beautiful day. The garden was rich with warm grass and the scent of lavender in the corner by the terrace. Teresa had spread the rug on the lawn and lay down to wait with some cushions and a book. She could smell the honeysuckle on the garden wall. She felt drowsy in the sunshine and told herself she mustn't fall asleep, but then she thought, why not? He would know where to find her.

She woke because of a tickle at her nose. She sneezed and rose petals fluttered away from her face.

Lucas was standing over her with a shredded rose, smiling as he let the petals drop one by one through the still air.

'You look very beautiful, lying there asleep.'

Teresa shook herself and sat up. 'Hello, Lucas.'

'Hello. Better late than never.'

'What does that mean?'

'Once upon a time, you wanted me to come and find you. Now here I am.'

'If that's what you came here to say then you'd better go now.'

He dropped down onto the rug to sit facing her, cross-legged. He was wearing jeans and a T-shirt, like he used to.

A snatch from one of the Major's old songs rolled in Teresa's memory:

*His eyes were blue*
*When he looked at you*
*You thought this must be heaven*

And suddenly she was furious with his effrontery, the heedlessly damaging ways in which he seemed to feel entitled to behave. 'What do you mean by coming here and saying things like that? Now?'

'You mean Jimmy?'

'Of course I mean Jimmy! And I happen to be pregnant.'

'Congratulations.'

'Thanks, but spare me those.'

'Ah.'

'Is that all?'

'I just said was that you looked beautiful.'

'What was 'better late than never' all about then?'

'Maybe it was a joke, Teresa.'

'Please don't patronise me.'

'Jesus! Did I say the wrong thing, or what?' he asked of an imaginary jury to one side. 'Can we be friends? I mean, you didn't stop me coming, did you?'

'You didn't give me much chance. Maybe I should have.'

'But you didn't.'

She nodded and rearranged the cushions so that she could lean sideways on them, on her elbow, with her legs stretched out.

'Seriously though, congratulations. Do you mind if I smoke? Pregnant women always make me want to smoke.'

Teresa laughed and said, 'I'll stick with the fresh air but you're welcome to breathe whatever you like. Actually, yesterday was the first day I felt human in three months.'

'I'm sorry. I know it can be bad.'

'I'll say.'

Lucas lit a cigarette and drew deeply on it. 'It was a shock coming here the other day and seeing you again,' he said as he exhaled.

'It wasn't the other day for me,' she said. 'It was Before Nausea.'

He nodded. 'But it shook you too?'

'Yes.'

'I suppose you've clocked up a few hours thinking about it too, over the years?' He looked at her cautiously now, without arrogance. When she didn't deny that she thought about it too, he continued: 'I should never have gone to the party at all because it was unfair on you. But I did go, and I think the reason was really irresponsible curiosity.' He took another drag, checking her reactions through narrowed eyes.

'I kept quiet, Jimmy, waiting to see what he said. I'd been waiting to hear this speech for so long, imagining it so often. I wasn't tempted to interrupt.'

'I can believe it,' I said. 'It must have been a very strange moment.'

'It was.'

Lucas resumed, seeing that Teresa was prepared to hear him: 'William used to go on at me about Elizabeth, with these pseudo-poetic expressions, like he was bragging about an acquisition, or he wanted me to be jealous. When I came here I thought she was nice enough, and pretty of course, but I couldn't see why she would want to marry William. I wanted to take her aside and say, 'Find somebody normal, who'll take you to the pictures and make you happy. William's a head case.' But it was none of my business. I just hoped for both their sakes that she might be a bit of a head-case too. After all, you obviously were . . .' Lucas looked pointedly at some bits of grass with which Teresa was making patterns on the grass. She does this: plays with shredded flowers when sitting in the garden, and if there's a pack of cards by where she sits indoors, she'll soon be building a card house. She wondered if 'a head case' was all she had ever been to him.

'Then he called about this party he was giving for you,' Lucas continued, 'as if he was the Great Gatsby. I said I thought you might not appreciate me being there, but he said he was asking me himself and you wouldn't mind. It sounded sufficiently half-baked to be convincing. I mean, it sounded as if you had agreed it with him, at least. All that fuss, and I really wasn't very keen to come. I knew it was a hornets' nest which I would only stir up. But I wanted to see what happened. The image of William-mein-host parading about with his fiancée on his arm struck me as a bit ridiculous but I was intrigued and something made me want to see the charade. Also, believe it or not, I thought I might be helpful to him. Anyway, I said I would try to look in on my way down the motorway.'

'On your way down the motorway? So it was just an offchance thing? Never mind all your justifications – if you felt like a party when you were passing then you'd drop in.'

'Look at it like that if you want. As I said, I was curious. And I was right about something not being right between them.'

'How come you were always "passing by" on the motorway?' Teresa asked.

'I had a girlfriend in Birmingham.'

'I never knew that!'

'Well, why would you?'

'I don't know. Did William know?'

'No, I mean it wasn't a big deal –'

'But if I'd known then I never would have –'

'Why? It was a . . . a loose relationship. Friendly. Not exclusive . . .'

'A girl in every port? All the same, if I'd known . . .'

'If I'd known that x, y and z were the lottery numbers then . . . If I'd known – then I wouldn't have come to the party. Anyway, as soon as I arrived here something really creepy started happening. William started showing me off like a circus trick. I couldn't shake him off, and I couldn't just tell him to fuck off and leave me alone. I didn't quite have the nerve to tell him his business towards Elizabeth, because the sight of her being neglected by him in favour of me was just so embarrassing. I mean, who was he marrying – her or me?

'I don't know how many men you know who have – how shall I put it? – complex sexuality. I don't mean that William was gay, because he wasn't. I'm not saying that he was a repressed gay, because that tidies and simplifies what is essentially untidy and complicated. It's a cliché that a lot of heterosexually assertive men actually dislike women or are afraid of them, but it doesn't necessarily follow that they are repressed gays – although they might be . . .'

'What are you trying to tell me?'

'The thing is, he was funny with women. Although he had a couple of girlfriends before Elizabeth, he didn't really give the impression of liking them very much. He treated them more as trophies. But it wasn't just women he did this with.

'He always seemed to find it necessary to impress people. It was part of his charm: he seemed to care about people and make an effort to please them. Sometimes he latched on to someone as if people would think more of him if he was seen to be a friend of that person. I suppose he did this with me, in a way, but it didn't bother me much because he didn't follow where he wasn't comfortable. Anyway, I was fond of him. But it made him oddly fickle. He'd be hanging on to one person and then suddenly switch to someone else, as if that person would enhance him more in his own eyes. If you were the person he switched from, and if you cared, and if you didn't realise that he would just as soon switch back, then it would be difficult.

'As soon as I came in the door, he switched from Elizabeth,

who obviously didn't have any idea what was happening. She wanted him to be attentive to her all evening, and you can't blame her. She wanted to be shown off, wanted people to see that he was proud of her. When I failed to get him off my back, I led him to her. She was relieved, and immediately started trying to introduce him to her friends and – you remember – he cut her dead. This made me really angry. I mean, whatever his insecurity, I thought he must actually understand that Elizabeth wanted a little attention from him, what with being engaged to him. Then I thought about them getting married and I thought it was absurd. They – at least, he – wasn't a grown-up at all. It was a shambles. She was standing there looking so miserable, flirting pathetically with some creep to try and make him jealous. The only person with any power over him was me. I should have made up some excuse and left, but I felt so sorry for Elizabeth and it suddenly came to me that I should ask her to dance. It would be a relief for her and it would let me escape from him – even if only temporarily. And, more than anything, I thought it might shame William into some awareness of what he ought to be doing.

'As for seducing her, I have to say she needed no encouragement. I mean, she was all over me. She didn't exactly put my hand up her skirt, but if she thought anyone was looking then she gladly brushed my hand with her thigh, if you see what I mean. Not because she really wanted to but because she was confused and she wanted to make William jealous. But he still didn't do anything and the only thing for us to do was carry on. We were stuck with each other by then. It wasn't fun, it was awful. Ridiculous. I felt a bit hysterical. I mean, I didn't know what to do, the only thing was to carry on – and play up to it. It was obvious that something had to give. If it was their engagement then – better before the wedding than after.

'I should have known that when William acted it would be in

some mad way. Maybe I did know, and that was why I felt so out of control, because after a certain point it didn't matter what I did: whatever happened would have more to do with the inside of his head than with the circumstances.

'That stupid fucking whip. I thought, that's it, I'm going, he can deal with the mess he's made himself. It certainly didn't occur to me that he would try and follow. Poor sod.'

Lucas's gaze wandered vaguely round the garden. He seemed indifferent to the bloom and richness of it.

'Well, that's a version,' Teresa said.

'How do you mean?'

'Well, while you've been cooking that one up over the years, there's another one staring you in the face.'

'What's that?' he said.

'A cynical London friend of William's abuses his hospitality and makes mischief with his innocent fiancée. Naturally, William objects and, in the ensuing scuffle, he is accidentally, tragically killed.'

'I don't dispute "accidentally, tragically".'

'You're the cynical friend, by the way.'

'Thanks. You don't believe that, do you?'

'Sorry, did you expect me to congratulate you on your subtle analysis?'

He rubbed his knees, then unfolded his legs on the rug. He flexed his ankles.

'Not exactly,' he said, and there was an attractive hestitation in his tone suggesting that he really did not have a preconceived idea of how she might respond.

Suddenly he swayed towards her and his right hand darted out. Before she could move back, he picked a ladybird from a fold in her shirt. As quickly, he transferred it from his thumbnail to the back of her hand, which was lifted in futile defence. The deft, economic movement, startled her, like a pebble making ripples as it drops into a still pool, each one echoing in its motion the waves from a boulder's impact.

The insect was still for a moment, then it started on a long trudge up towards her knuckles. Watching it closely, she said, 'The last time you gave me a present, I was convinced you were just passing on something you didn't want. I was offended and didn't open it for ages. When eventually I started reading it, I found it fascinating.'

'*Seeds of Change*,' he said.

'I thought you would have forgotten what it was.'

'No.'

Although she did not look up, Teresa sensed that he was looking at the struggling ladybird too, and at her watching it. Neither of them seemed to know what to say, but the fixity of his regard made the air seem to quiver with possibilities which she didn't, at that instant, have the will or inclination to smother.

'That's not really why I came, though,' he said at last.

Teresa looked up as far as his hand. The wrist was still straight: only the pads of his curved fingers were resting on the rug between them. The thumb was raised too, so that she could see the bone leading to the wrist and what the Major used to call the 'snuff hollow', strangely accentuated, as if his hand were very tense. It looked as if he was about to reach out again and she recalled his knuckles glancing against her breast a moment ago. She imagined sliding two fingers under his arched palm and drawing his hand towards her. She replied, 'What isn't?'

'I didn't come just to tell you that it wasn't all my fault. You made up your mind about that long ago. If you did blame it all on me then you wouldn't have given me such a kind reception the other day. I would have been chased off the premises – again. I've always known I could trust you not to hate me. And when I came here, I could see that I was right. You haven't changed, but I have, and I see what I've known all along, how I was wrong . . .'

Teresa took my hand and pressed it against her stomach. 'A treacherous part of me wanted him to go on talking, to make a flood of words so that I didn't have to respond,' she said. 'The sensation of being swept up was soothing and buoyant. It relieved me of responsibility for the moment. Then I thought of you, Jimmy, and of our baby, and it felt as if you had intervened directly, wiping away the blue spray; the glitter of his eyes like the froth around rocks . . . I told him that I didn't know what he was trying to say, but I thought he should stop.'

Lucas replied, 'No, why shouldn't I admit it? For years, when I've thought about Sweynsend, I've thought that my crime wasn't what happened between Elizabeth and William. I was only the catalyst of that tragedy. What I did wrong was turning away from you, and I've had to live with that ever since.'

Teresa felt herself being pushed down into a torrent as he continued: 'I knew that this was true and I thought, I can't redeem William's death but I can at least reclaim Teresa –'

'Stop it! Stop it! I'm married!'

'And if I don't try then I'm doubly guilty!'

'Why should I believe any of this?' she cried.

'You know it's true. And I could see the complicity in your eyes the other day.'

'You're an arrogant shit!'

'What do you want me to do? I have to tell you. You have to believe me.'

'You're out of your mind! I don't have to do anything of the sort.'

'You said that you loved me once, Teresa, and I was a fool not to appreciate it then – but if you knew how much I've regretted it –'

'Then what?'

She said this without thinking but it struck Lucas like the recoil of a gun. He stared at her in wet-lipped amazement and she knew, beyond any doubt, that she had for once made him self-conscious.

Immediate consequences whirred through their minds like a runaway spool of film with impossible, ravishing glimpses of flesh and the sense of infinitely suspended time.

She shifted the cushions and resettled, displaying that she was still in possession of herself.

I wondered as she described this if she had been aroused. But I did not feel able to ask. Women's secrets are different from ours. How sometimes I envy that.

'I don't believe this is happening,' Teresa told Lucas.

'You're the one fixed point in my life. For years I've imagined that you were the only person I could love, and when I saw you the other day, I knew it was true.'

'Lucas, this is sheer fantasy. Do you expect me to feel flattered? What if I told you I am insulted?'

'I know, you don't owe me anything. I'm pleading –'

'I'm married, Lucas.'

'Stop saying that! I know –'

'I'm happily married.'

'Happily?' he repeated, as if this possibility had somehow not occurred to him.

'I love Jimmy. This is my home.'

'You say you love Jimmy but I don't believe you.'

'I beg your pardon?'

'There's no sense of any passion whatsoever between you,' he declared, his voice rising. 'You're a convenience to each other, you give each other respectability. It soothes something in Jimmy to have a nice wife tucked up in a nice home, while for you – he's made it possible for you to live here. How can you expect me to believe you love Jimmy when I've seen what you're like when you're in love?'

'The immense egotism, Jimmy. Is it just men? It is strange having it turned on you, as a woman I mean. It is repellent in a way, and yet there is something in it which takes your breath away and can be incredibly attractive. I told him to shut up and he just told me I loved him, I *must* love him. I asked why I must love him, why on earth should I just slip into his script and ruin my life now that he suddenly crooked his finger? And he answered:'

'I know, I know, but you have to take the chance, you know you have to take it!'

'No, I don't!'

'Admit it, you love *me*, not Jimmy!'

'That's your fantasy.'

'At least admit that it's not him you love, it's the place.'

'I don't deny that I love the place but –'

'Then you don't love him.'

'I didn't say that. I do.'

'No you don't.'

'Shut up, Lucas! How dare you – how dare you presume to know who or what I love? As if it's all so easy –'

I understood Teresa. Lucas might not, but I did. Even if she did not tell me in so many words, she was telling me that she loves Lucas, in a way, and wanted me to know it, while understanding too that whatever she feels for him does not exclude her love – if that is what it is – for me; and that it ought to be proof enough of the weight of her feelings that it is me she wants to stay with. She wants me, I think, to allow her this parallel or alternative love, while not feeling threatened by it. And why wouldn't I, thinking of Iris, as I do? It is easily said.

And I understand Lucas too. He was not wrong in thinking that Teresa still had feelings for him: had she not, then their conversation (if that is what it was) would never have reached this point. She would have terminated it long before, or he would have lost conviction. And of course I understand too that he has built all this on nothing, it is an idea that seeded itself years ago in his mind and lay embedded, an ember burning within him all that time, unknown to anyone else, which needed only a glimpse of her to burst into flame, at which point everything would suddenly come right, the icecaps would slide back and freeze like they should, we'd all have honey for tea on sunny lawns and angels would bless us as we slept. In her, he is cruelly confronted by his lost youth: how could he not be in love with her?

'So you won't?' said Lucas.

'Won't what? Leave Jimmy and come with you? No. Are you mad? I'm happy. I love my husband, I love my home, I'm pregnant. Why would I come with you?'

'Because I love you.'

'No, you don't. You love yourself. You love an idea of yourself.'

'Isn't that called self-respect?'

'It's sheer egotism, monstrous egotism. You love the idea of me giving everything up to come with you. You're a sadist.'

Lucas shook his head. 'So much for me.' He cupped his face in his hands and breathed out gently through his fingers.

'Did you really think you would persuade me, Lucas?' Teresa said after a moment.

He shrugged. 'I thought I would persuade you that I love you. As for what next, I don't know.'

'Well you have, in a way. But I can't love you now – you must see that?'

'What do you mean, "can't"? Either you do or you don't.'

'I don't think I really believe that.'

'How depressing.'

'I don't see it like that.'

'Its like saying you would love me in another life.'

'And what's wrong with that?'

'Because you don't get another life!'

'That's why I don't want to mess this one up.'

'So you're saying you would love me in another life?'

'I didn't say that. But maybe.'

'How sad.'

'Why?'

'Because you're deliberately limiting your life. It's a romantic failure, an abuse of life.'

'Not at all. If I'm limiting it, that's precisely because I value it. I learned the lesson in disillusion you taught me.'

'That's shit, and you know it.'

Teresa didn't answer. She felt exhausted and suddenly very hungry. 'Excuse me a moment,' she said, and stood up and went into the house. And that was when she phoned me.

'I think I'd better go,' Lucas said on her return.

His shoulders were rounded with fatigue while his head still craned obstinately forward, with its burden of frustration. There was a petulant swell to his lips and his eyes were defensive. It occurred to Teresa that his experience would not benefit him: he would become a man with a grievance against women. In refusing him, she seemed to be closing off not only his prospect of happiness with her but also condemning others, perhaps, to suffer the effects of her rejection. Such power made her feel ashamed of her faint-heartedness for an instant, but she maintains that she exercised it in order to preserve her chance of happiness with me.

Taking her silence as assent that he should leave, Lucas leaned over and kissed her, briefly, on the lips. It was like a breath of life warming the frozen possibilities of other worlds, a ripple through a field of wheat. Then he stood up and walked away. He turned and waved as he stepped from the sunlight into the deep shade cast by the end of the house. She could not make out his face any more, and his figure had lost definition; a shadow in another life. Then Teresa rolled from the rug onto the grass and wept among the gilded blades of her solitude.

Lucas, I know, is the most attractive man that my wife will ever know on this earth, and she sent him away.

★

I assume Lucas had the nerve to come up to Sweynsend behind my back because his work for me is finished. It would have been impossible to continue with him after that. I feel sorry for him in a way. Having declared himself to Teresa so resolutely that she had no choice but to reject him totally, it's hard to see that there is even any prospect of friendship with her: he is left with nothing. Whereas I still have Iris – in a manner of speaking, of course; I mean we are in contact, and I consider my recent visiting plan to be delayed rather than cancelled.

Teresa may have anticipated more jealousy from me. Hoped for it, for all I know: jealousy can be reassuring. But if she thinks I've been niggardly in this department then she must put it down, I think, to confidence. For she does not know of my own shadowy longings, nor the avid self-consciousness that listening to her has induced, and which is the real cause of my lack of jealousy. It is not creditable perhaps, but it is a lie that I will live with. Some secrets are necessary.

Five months have passed since I began writing after Lucas's first visit. I have learned a great deal, but what disturbs me most of all is not Teresa's distress, either in the past or now, because she will survive it now as she did then; nor the real story behind William's death, because it is after all only another pitiful tragedy of a poor little rich kid. No, I am left with the question whether Lucas really did love Teresa after all. There are three possibilities which encourage me to doubt it.

First, there is this. It seems that Lucas thought himself superior to William and, of course, in many respects he was. But William had something which Lucas didn't, namely the prospect of Sweynsend's security. He appeared to be on the point of consolidating it by marrying Elizabeth. Suppose Lucas felt threatened by this and, wishing to test it, struck at its heart: by seducing Elizabeth he undermined William's felicity and proved – or thought he proved – his edifice to be a sham. In so doing, he confirmed his own sense of superiority over William. He couldn't allow himself to be made to feel inferior by someone he felt to be beneath him. In just the same way, he tried to bust up our marriage. He thinks he's superior to us and it offends him to see us comfortably married at Sweynsend. Instinctively he tries to show that it's hollow, to prove to himself that he is the substantial one: if our apparent security couldn't stand up to his pressure, he would be satisfied that his own insecurity is no more pathetic than ours. I would love to know if he has done the same with others. One could argue, I think, that he has a pathological tendency to destroy other people's stable relationships; represent him as a 'case' and deviously, obligingly, absolve him of responsibility.

Now let's say this is false. Let's allow him, in all fairness, his *amour propre*, and say that it's just coincidence that his behaviour towards Elizabeth and his relationship with William seem to share features with his later behaviour towards Teresa and me. What troubles me next is slightly sinister. Lucas accused William of latching on to others and I would be a fool not to see the truth of this. A more elusive, but no less dangerous, obsession could emerge from a sensed void, possibility without form, which needs to be at once fuelled and filled. An attachment is made with a notional person, whose mantle is forced upon someone real who may be dramatically convenient but wholly unsuited to the role. This person will be the subject of intermittent fits of intense concentration which might be creative or destructive. Artists sometimes speak of a muse or a demon but the susceptibility needn't be confined to them. You could say that you perceive a genius in someone, which sounds good, or a genie, which sounds bad; both of these are attributes of the other person. Or you could turn it round and say that you are jinxed. For when a person occupies a place in our thoughts and dreams out of all proportion to their actual part in our own life, when they are a focus for our whims and madness and yet we do not properly love them, then we might say that we are jinxed. I think it's possible that Lucas was, as it were, jinxed by Sweynsend. For years he couldn't shake off what happened, and maybe he didn't even try. It lodged in the furnace of his imagination, repeatedly sending showers of sparks into his daily cycle of thoughts. It didn't matter that he didn't see Teresa or Elizabeth or Sweynsend, because the energy of the initial experience was sustained by the friction of his own nervous condition. In which case his love was a figure in a flame, not a thing of substance.

Now let's revoke this more nebulous fatalism too and make him whole again. Here is the third possibility. For years, what really bothered Lucas was neither William's misfortune, nor guilt about his own contribution to the tragedy, but the lack of a satisfactory end to the story. And suddenly, when he met Teresa again, there it was! There was an irresistible end to a story which had seemed fated to remain in a limbo without the conclusion that we want time to supply. And so it wasn't really love he was offering her but, like a tidy storyteller, an ending.

It wasn't the right end for Teresa because her responsibilities, in the end, are greater. For her, the end must be in the beginning of the baby we have made, whose feet she can feel kicking; who, very soon, all being well, will be with us.

As for me, my options are what they always were. Sustained by the conviction that my wife still harbours some feeling for that duplicitous monster, I need abandon nothing. In the small hours' frail reality, I will still live a little in a world where irises bloom.